'You would entry?'

Jane lifted her head and her eyes gleaming in her proud courageous challenge of his authority. 'Yes. I find your presence here in this house offensive, sir.'

'I see,' Edward's eyes narrowed and his smile was icy. He gave a barely perceptible nod of his head. 'Then tell me—is it the clothes I wear that offend you, or my person?'

'Both. The uniform you wear depicts the man. You are here against my will and no longer are you and I betrothed.'

Helen Dickson was born and still lives in South Yorkshire with her husband and two sons on a busy arable farm where she combines writing with keeping a chaotic farmhouse. An incurable romantic, she writes for pleasure, owing much of her inspiration to the beauty of the countryside. She enjoys reading and music; history has always captivated her, and she likes to travel and visiting ancient buildings.

Recent titles by the same author:

AN ILLUSTRIOUS LORD
LADY DECEIVER
THE RAINBOROUGH INHERITANCE
KATHERINE

AN UNPREDICTABLE
BRIDE

Helen Dickson

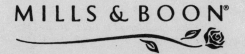

DID YOU PURCHASE THIS BOOK WITHOUT A COVER?
If you did, you should be aware it is **stolen property** as it was
reported *unsold and destroyed* by a retailer. Neither the Author
nor the publisher has received any payment for this book.

*All the characters in this book have no existence outside the imagina-
tion of the author, and have no relation whatsoever to anyone bearing
the same name or names. They are not even distantly inspired by any
individual known or unknown to the author, and all the incidents are
pure invention.*

*All Rights Reserved including the right of reproduction in whole or
in part in any form. This edition is published by arrangement with
Harlequin Enterprises II B.V. The text of this publication or any part
thereof may not be reproduced or transmitted in any form or by any
means, electronic or mechanical, including photocopying, recording,
storage in an information retrieval system, or otherwise, without the
written permission of the publisher.*

*This book is sold subject to the condition that it shall not, by way of
trade or otherwise, be lent, resold, hired out or otherwise circulated
without the prior consent of the publisher in any form of binding or
cover other than that in which it is published and without a similar
condition including this condition being imposed on the subsequent
purchaser.*

*MILLS & BOON and MILLS & BOON with the Rose Device
are registered trademarks of the publisher.*

*First published in Great Britain 1998
Harlequin Mills & Boon Limited,
Eton House, 18-24 Paradise Road, Richmond, Surrey TW9 1SR*

© Helen Dickson 1998

ISBN 0 263 80707 X

*Set in Times 11 on 12 pt. by
Rowland Phototypesetting Limited
Bury St Edmunds, Suffolk*

04-9803-68609

*Printed and bound in Great Britain
by Caledonian International Book Manufacturing Ltd, Glasgow*

Chapter One

1645

Mortar fire, which had been pounding at the walls of besieged Bowden Manor standing in the north-east of the county of Derbyshire, mercifully ceased for the first time in twenty-four hours, bringing with it a strange quiet of eerie expectancy that hung over the great house like a pall covering a tomb. With its massive surrounding wall the manor occupied a position on high ground, which favoured its defence. It also stood in an area susceptible to Royalist influence—until the King's defeat at Naseby had attracted the attentions of Parliament.

With a small Royalist garrison commanded by Captain Hamilton, and a combined assortment of loyal workers from her father's estate and a few female servants, Jane Marlow had courageously withstood the siege of her enemy—a troop of Roundhead soldiers encamped outside the walls—for two long months in the hope that rescue would come. But after an additional two hundred soldiers had arrived to join the enemy force, bringing with them more heavy artillery, the strength of the assault was too great for them to withstand, and hope, like the battered walls and turrets of Bowden Manor, was beginning to crumble.

Although of late the results of the siege were making themselves felt, an enemy far greater than the one beating against the massive walls had begun stalking the chambers and passageways of the house—starvation. The food which had been so painstakingly rationed had finally run out and, seeing how everyone was suffering, in moments of weakness Jane had almost surrendered to the enemy. Had they run out of water then their suffering would have been great indeed, but, because the manor was supplied by natural underground springs, fresh water had never been a problem.

From her vantage point in one of the four towers, each housing mounted guns—although they were of little use now their ammunition was spent—Jane's eyes focused on the enemy in the distance, beyond the trenches they had dug around the manor. The sun had gone down and their fires were lit, the soldiers looking like so many dark demons, fierce and impressive, their helmets and swords gleaming in the luminosity of the firelight. She knew that come the dawn they would launch a major attack, no longer prepared to wait until the defenders were forced to surrender. The parts of the wall already much weakened by cannon fire would be breached by the heavier artillery brought by the reinforcements, and it would not be long before the house was stormed by the Roundhead force commanded by Captain

Dugdale. She also knew that the people who had sought refuge within its walls could expect little in the way of clemency from him.

He was a surly, arrogant man, who had been amused, though somewhat surprised, to find a woman with courage above her sex so resolutely in command and refusing to surrender Bowden Manor in the absence of her father who was serving the King.

A begrimed and weary Tom Carter, her father's ageing, loyal steward, who had been a tower of strength to her during the two long months of the siege, came to stand by her side, looking at her with deep concern. After weeks of siege, of not having enough to eat, the bones of her face stood out sharply beneath her pale flesh, and her body was thin and screamed out for rest. He had watched closely as gradually her strength to go on was eroded, but she had courageously squared her shoulders, knowing she had to endure, for so many people depended on her. Throughout it all she had worn a brave face—a heavy responsibility, indeed, for a nineteen-year-old girl, when all around her her whole world was crumbling.

All the days were the same—full of discomfort and a constant struggle for survival, for the few remaining victuals provided inadequate nourishment and had to be divided equally among sixty people. Standing close by her, Tom could sense the alert tension of all her muscles. Her face was grave and sorrowing and the pain oppressing her heart was great indeed. She didn't turn, but acknowledged his presence with a sigh.

'It is almost over, Tom. We have nothing left with which to fight and they know it. Our guns have been silent these past five hours or more. Like our supplies of food, the powder and match, the bullets—all the essentials needed to sustain the siege—are gone. All we have left are our swords to protect us. What is to become of us?'

'As to that, when the time comes we will have to pray Captain Dugdale shows some mercy.'

'From what I remember of him I very much doubt it, Tom. And any hope I might have had of our situation being relieved by a troop of Royalist soldiers or by a miracle has faded long since. Little did I think all those weeks ago when I knew that such a thing as this could happen—when I began storing provisions and making all necessary preparations to withstand a siege—that it would come to this,' she said quietly.

Jane remembered that, when some of the menfolk of Bowden and the surrounding villages had left to fight for the King, how life in that part of Derbyshire—holding no strategic position for either side—had gone on uninterrupted. The arrival of the Parliament Army had come as an unwelcome disturbance to their otherwise peaceful lives. She well remembered the day when a troop of Parliamentary soldiers, all armed with pikes and muskets—a formidable, terrifying mass of soldiers—had surrounded the walls of Bowden Manor, and she remembered how her first terrified impulse had been to run and hide. But at the thought of Roundhead soldiers inhabiting and violating her beloved home, rage and rebellion had leaped in her breast, giving

her a strength of mind and body otherwise
unknown to her.

Abiding by the rules governing a siege, Captain
Dugdale had issued an official summons to Jane to
surrender her father's house without condition—and
her brother James, whom they knew to be sheltering
inside after fleeing north from the battlefield of
Naseby. James had indeed sought refuge after the
battle, but sadly, and unbeknown to Captain Dugdale,
he had also been suffering from smallpox and had
died a few days into the siege.

If she complied with the Captain's demands, then
everyone would be allowed to leave peacefully. If,
however, she refused to surrender, when Bowden
Manor was eventually taken by force no quarter
would be given to those who remained.

Knowing this and having no intention of surren-
dering, placing all her faith in the hope that relief
would come in the form of Royalist soldiers, Jane
had given all those who wished to leave the opportunity of doing so.

To protect her two young daughters, Susan and
Penelope, her stepmother Maria had already left
Bowden Manor to stay with Maria's sister at
Newington Hall, close to the town of Nottingham,
as soon as it became known that James was suffering
from smallpox.

Some of the women from the village of Bowden,
concerned for their children's safety, had also left,
even though they left their husbands behind and
exposed their own homes to destruction by Parliamentary soldiers. But many, both men and women,
emboldened by Jane's gallant determination to

stand firm, had remained to give their support.

But Jane recollected the moment when the massive doors in the gate-house had slammed shut, how those remaining behind the seven-foot-thick walls had fallen to their knees and entreated God to spare them from the enemy, trusting in him for both protection and deliverence.

'And had you known that it would come to this,' said Tom, 'would you have conducted things differently? Would you have surrendered everything to Captain Dugdale in the beginning and watched him establish a Parliamentary garrison here—in your father's house?'

Jane shook her head slowly. 'No. At the time it was unthinkable—but now. . .perhaps it would have been more prudent to have behaved in a more ladylike manner and with more humility. Maybe I should have stalled, played for time, instead of defying them outright. After all, how do I know my father will approve of what I have done?'

Having seen how she had worked daily, ceaselessly—how she had cast bullets from lead which had been stripped from the roof of the house until her fingers bled; how she had reloaded muskets for the men, often firing them herself with remarkable accuracy; how she had taken to sealing any breaches in the walls with sandbags and put out fires started by incendiary arrows fired over the walls—and at other times knowing she could be found tending the sick and wounded of which there were many, Tom thought any man would be proud to have sired such a daughter.

'Be assured he will be proud of you. You have

displayed a courage way beyond that expected of a woman.'

'These troubled times in which we live have left me and women like me with little choice, finding ourselves bereft of our men folk,' she said sadly, remembering her dear departed brother.

'Nevertheless, you have fulfilled all the expectations concerning your sex admirably, for it is the tenderness of the loyalty and love you feel for your family and home, and those dependent on you, that impelled you to take the bold step of implementing a siege over the aggressive might of the Roundheads.'

'Even though I have never possessed the stomach for fighting,' she sighed wearily. 'Oh, Tom, if only we knew what was happening—if my father is alive, even. Not since the Royalist defeat at Naseby in June have we heard anything. Before poor James died, he told me he had not seen Father—who, as you well know, was fighting under the command of Prince Rupert—but he heard how he fought bravely throughout the battle.'

'You would expect nothing less,' said Tom, shaking his head sorrowfully as he remembered his employer, Sir Ralph Marlow, a gentleman in every respect, a man he held in the highest regard. 'Your father is a good man. Indeed, I know none finer.'

Jane cast him a look of gratitude, her lips curving in a gentle smile. 'Thank you, Tom. Let us pray he is safe and well. I am only thankful that my step-mother and stepsisters managed to leave for Newington before the siege. You know how susceptible Penelope is to weakness. I doubt she would have withstood the hardships of these past two months. It's hard to believe that happiness once reigned within this house, that its walls rang with the laughter of children, when my head was filled with silly nonsense and girlish fancies and I could think of little else other than my father taking me to dance at the Court of King Charles and marrying a handsome lord.'

'You may not have succeeded in dancing at the King's Court—but you are betrothed to a handsome lord.'

Jane's face became grim and a hard gleam entered her amber eyes. 'No, Tom. It is true that before the war I was betrothed to Lord Talbot—but that was three years ago, before he took up arms against the King. I have to say the marriage contract is no longer binding for I have had no word or letter from him since and have no wish to.'

Jane had no mind to dwell on the man she might have married but for the intervention of the war, when each man had declared his true colours. When she had the chance to dream it was the image of a young man so very different who occupied her thoughts—a friend of her brother's, Sir Simon Butteridge, who had been to Bowden Manor on several occasions in the days before the war, and often since then between campaigns.

Her first encounter with him had been when she had been an impressionable sixteen-year-old girl and he had charmingly—and with all the practised arts of a philanderer—set out to steal her vulnerable heart and that of her good friend Anne Talbot, the sister of the man her father had intended her to marry. Simon was handsome, debonair—a young man who had danced attendance on her and then gallantly gone to fight for the King's cause with James.

She remembered how James had teased her mercilessly about him, leading her to believe he might have asked for her hand in marriage were she not betrothed to Lord Talbot. But he had warned her about Simon's character, telling her he was somewhat wild and a man of dubious reputation, which had made it all the more exciting and exhilarating for her to be in his company. What had become of him? she asked herself, not having seen him for almost two years. Was he still alive—or lying dead on a battlefield somewhere?

Tears sprang to her eyes at the recollection her thoughts conjured up of her childhood—for what was the use in thinking of all that now when defeat and possibly death was staring her in the face? Her eyes, shifting from the ghostly figures of the Roundhead soldiers where they huddled around their camp fires—exposed to all the rigours the weather imposed on them and the discomforts of being forced to sleep in the open—looked skyward, seeing heavy clouds beginning to settle over the surrounding hills. Feeling a cool August wind beginning to penetrate her clothes, she shivered, her stomach wringing with hunger.

'No matter what kind of day the morning gives birth to, Tom, at least we will sleep warm in our beds tonight. Goodnight.'

She bowed her head, which Tom saw as a palpable gesture of defeat, but as she turned and moved away from him she drew her shawl tightly about her with hands scorched by handling flaming grenades,

squaring her narrow shoulders courageously. It was
this gesture, after weeks of watching her conduct the
defence of Bowden Manor with a gallantry and val-
our equal to that of any man, that won his undying
admiration—but it was also a gesture which wrung
his heart the most.

Descending the stone steps to the courtyard below
she crossed to the house, stopping to speak to those
who huddled around fires heating iron pots to melt
the remaining pitch—which would be poured over
the walls should the enemy attempt to scale them
with their ladders. Others tried to settle down for a
brief period of respite before the dawn, and, unable
to offer them any words of reassurance, she went
directly to her chamber.

Her heart was empty and a sense of her own helplessness overwhelmed her. A sickening hunger
compounded with tiredness and exhaustion engulfed
her and her tired brain refused to think of what the
morrow would bring as she threw herself onto her
bed, longing to shed her clothes but too weary to do
so—and afraid lest she was wanted during the night.

As expected, the final Parliamentary assault came
with the dawn and Jane was woken from her brief
slumber by the sound of fresh bombardment. Stiff
and sore, she rose from the bed, knowing instinc-
tively that today it would be over. It was cold for
there was no fire in her room, and when she looked
out of the window it was to see a sky heavy with rain.

After swilling her face with cold water, she hurried
down to the courtyard, finding herself once again
caught up in the mayhem that prevailed. She was

filled with a deep sense of foreboding for by tonight things would be different—they might all be dead.

After a maelstrom of fire and noise, the heavy guns blasting without ceasing until one of the towers toppled and a wide breach was made in the wall, with the air filled with a choking black smoke, the Roundhead soldiers stormed the house, pouring through the breach and over the high walls from their scaling ladders like ants on a hill. Pandemonium broke out. The dozen or so soldiers of the defending garrison put up a brave fight but several were brutally slain. Others, too weak from hunger to do little other than cringe in fear, begged for mercy and, to everyone's amazement, it was given—for usually the victors slew anyone without respect, stripping and spoiling without regard for those who begged for quarter.

With a heavy heart Jane turned and went into the house, into the great vaulted hall to await her enemy, who would enter and take over this house, her home, contaminating this blessed building with his vile presence.

She heard Captain Dugdale approach before he entered the hall, his booted feet ringing out on the stone slabs in the antechamber outside. The sound was ominous and threatening, and she quailed, grappling with her fear and exhaustion, not knowing what to expect at the hands of the Parliamentary Captain. But some instinct deep within her drove out fear and gave her a determination to defy him.

Without ceremony, Captain Dugdale crossed to where she stood watching him with authority and dignity. He removed his three-barred helmet to reveal his short-cropped and greying hair. He was of medium height with a full, florid face and the neck and shoulders of a bull. After suffering the humiliation of being bested by a woman, he savoured his victory over Jane Marlow with relish, but he was tired. In the beginning, not for one moment had he thought that taking Bowden Manor would be a problem, but the two months it had taken to break the siege seemed more like two long miserable years which could have been better employed elsewhere.

He was in an ill humour, for shortly before they had stormed the walls as victors, fully expecting to plunder the house—which, it was believed, held sufficient treasures to make the two months of siege well worth it—a messenger had arrived with orders from a higher authority, instructing him that the surrender of Bowden Manor must be secured with little or no bloodshed and that the house must not be sacked of any of its possessions. Which was a pity, Captain Dugdale thought salaciously, feeling a stirring of carnality in his loins and experiencing a sharp pang of disappointment when he took in the full measure of Mistress Marlow's beauty, of her thick coil of pale blonde hair which had come loose of its pins and snaked its way down to her waist. Thin, she might be, and begrimed too after the days storming of the house, but she was certainly a beauty.

He had been hard put to persuade his soldiers not to avenge themselves on the defenders of Bowden Manor—usually they would have been put to the sword at once. The slaying of the defending Royalist soldiers had been unavoidable.

'Well, Mistress Marlow—what have you to say to me now? Still defiant, are you? Still foolishly determined to hold on to Bowden Manor?'

Jane ignored his question. 'Forgive me if I do not welcome you into my home, Captain Dugdale—although I have to say I did not expect such leniency from you.'

Captain Dugdale glared at her, her contemptuous expression and the manner in which she held herself erect and with pride after all she had endured angering him further. His small, glittering eyes narrowed and his face became ugly.

'It is not I you have to thank for that. If I'd had my way, you would have been given no quarter. You would all have perished under the sword. To my mind you sealed your own fate the day you refused to surrender Bowden Manor to me.'

'Then to whom am I indebted?'

He shrugged his massive shoulders, moving away from her, leaving her question unanswered and looking around the great hall with greedy admiration, assessing the fine quality of the contents and fixing each individual item with a price; coming from humble origins, what he saw eclipsed anything he could possibly hope to gain in his lifetime with honour.

'As you are aware, Mistress Marlow, I have been ordered to install a garrison here at Bowden Manor.'

'I fail to see why Parliament feels the need to hold my home as a garrison,' Jane argued. 'Situated where it is, it can hardly be of strategic value.'

'None the less, it must be secured for Parliament. Now we have taken possession, you will all move out. Is that understood? Unless, of course, you wish to remain and keep me company, Mistress Marlow,' he remarked, his eyes sweeping over her with bold insolence, the underlying implication of his words causing Jane to shudder with disgust.

'I would rather die than continue living here under your conditions, Captain Dugdale.'

Again he shrugged. 'That can easily be arranged. Accidents happen. It could be explained and your name would be filed away on a report as just one more casualty of the war.'

Seeming totally unconcerned by the noise coming from outside the house, he continued to walk calmly around the hall, continuing to assess its contents before speaking at length, his question taking Jane completely unawares.

'Where is your brother, Mistress Marlow?'

She stared at him, momentarily at a loss for words. 'My—my brother?' she asked hesitantly.

'Yes—your brother. You do have a brother?'

'Of course. What gives you reason to suppose he is here?'

Suspecting she was going to prove difficult in divulging her brother's whereabouts, Captain Dugdale came to stand in front of her, hoping she would feel intimidated by his nearness.

'Come, now, tell me the truth. A warrant is out for his arrest. He was last seen heading this way after the battle at Naseby. Questioning some of the villagers employed here in the house—who wisely chose not to get caught up in the siege—I was informed that he did indeed come here but was not seen to leave.' He thrust his angry face close to

Jane's, forcing her to step back. 'Your brother is hiding here in the house. Is that not so, Mistress Marlow? Come—admit it.'

Thinking of James's unburied body lying hidden deep in the cellars of the house, awaiting the time when it could be taken to Bowden Church and interred within the Marlow family vault, she answered with venom, 'I admit nothing.'

'Deny it all you like, but I do not believe you,' he hissed.

'You may believe what you like. I care nothing for your bullying.'

'This is not a game I play, Mistress Marlow.'

'Game!' she scorned. 'Games are for children, Captain. I do not care for games.'

'Nor I, Mistress Marlow. Nor I,' a voice rang out sharply from across the hall.

Jane spun round to see who had spoken and her heart lurched in her breast, beginning to pound in fear and disbelief. The tall stranger crossing towards her had a commanding presence, forbidding and intimidating, and she felt the full force of his ruthless vitality. With a menacing-looking sword swinging at his side, he bore himself with military distinction. He was dressed in the uniform of a Parliamentarian, his buff leather coat tied around with an orange sash, and high boots spattered with mud, which told her he had ridden hard. His head was bare, his thick, short dark hair rough and tangled.

His presence stirred her memory, taking her back to the days before the war. His mouth had acquired a bitter line, but his clearly defined features she recognised—although she did not remember him as being so tall or so handsome.

She stared aghast into the imperious dark eyes that bored down into her own, for the man was none other than her betrothed, Lord Talbot, neighbour and once good friend of her family—now traitor and commander of a regiment of horse in the Parliament Army.

Chapter Two

Edward turned his eyes on Captain Dugdale who, for the first time since he had found his way into the great hall, was at a loss for words at being confronted by the illustrious Lord Talbot, a man thought highly of by both Cromwell and General Sir Thomas Fairfax.

Lord Talbot was already an able and experienced soldier, having acquired his training in military arts in the Netherlands prior to the Civil War and, the speed with which he took decisions and acted in the field had elevated him to a cavalry leader of undeniable skill and courage. He was fearless in danger and inspired the respect and loyalty of his troops, but he would not tolerate incompetence or was not one with whom to cross swords.

Edward did not care for Captain Dugdale, who was renowned throughout the ranks for his butchery. Alarmed upon hearing of the siege at Bowden Manor and that Jane would be at his mercy once it was broken, and knowing she could expect no clemency

from Dugdale, he had hastened to prevent any
bloodshed.

'I am relieved to find you obeyed my orders,
Captain. Now leave us,' he commanded, his voice
harsh and deep. 'I wish to speak with Mistress
Marlow alone. See to it that the dead are buried and
the living fed before you find you have to bury them
also. I'm sure you have provisions enough to
see to it.'

No longer inflated by his own importance, Captain
Dugdale made a hasty departure to do his bidding,
and once again Jane became the object of Edward's
scrutiny. Her expression was remote and unreadable,
and there was nothing about it that told him she was
pleased to see him.

He could see she was much changed—but it could
not entirely be put down to the siege. All signs of
her habitual childishness had gone and he suspected
it was some time past since her feet had skipped
and run in the meadows around Bowden, when her
delighted laughter had filled the air like music and
her eyes had sparkled with mischief and merriment.

Her wonderful wealth of blonde hair, liberally
streaked with silver, coiled down her back, and there
were smudges of dirt on her face. She was as slender
as a wand and as fragile as lace. If he were to lift her
up, he was sure she would be as light as swansdown,
giving the impression that a puff of wind would blow
her away.

Her head lifted. Now that the shock of that first
awkward moment had disappeared, she was studying
him unreservedly and with a measure of unsmiling
resentment, with eyes the colour of amber flecked

with green huge in her pale face, which gave her a wraith-like, saintly appearance. Yet, despite the ravages she had endured over the past months, she was still lovely to look at—achingly so, with a full, passionate mouth.

He had known her from the day she was born, watching her grow. She had been small and elfin-like, extremely pretty with huge, inquisitive eyes; until this moment he had never thought of her as anything other than an innocent child, but she now exhibited a self possession he had not thought her capable of.

Their families were hereditary friends, acting as guardians, godfathers, executors and trustees to each other. Edward remembered when he had come home from serving with the army in the Netherlands, when he had intended settling down at Deighton and their betrothal had been celebrated by both families, and how, in a twilight haze, he had been content to let everyone arrange it—for it had seemed a good match and neither party had raised any objection.

But studying Jane now, Edward, eight years her senior, looked at her as if for the first time, seeing her as a woman and not a child. He was happy to see that in her robust, patriotic endeavour to stand so heroically against Parliament she had lost none of her femininity. He was astonished—how could he have neglected to think of her for so long? There had been times when she had ceased to exist for him as he became embroiled in affairs troubling the country in those turbulent pre-war days.

'You remember me, I think, Jane?'

Jane had watched him, feeling sick inside and

cold with nervous apprehension, but she faced him bravely, meeting his gaze directly, the heat of rebellion which had spurred her on through those early weeks of the siege beginning to stir again inside her breast.

'I have not laid eyes on you for three years—but I am hardly likely to forget the man to whom I was once betrothed, sir.'

His dark eyes narrowed and his arrogant lips curled across his even white teeth. 'Was? Why—what is this? Nothing is changed.'

Jane's eyes narrowed angrily. 'How can you say that? You disappear out of my life and then turn up—quite out of the blue—and say nothing is changed between us. Why—your impudence astounds me.'

Edward's dark eyebrows arched and his eyes gleamed hard. 'Impudence is not something I am often accused of. However—I repeat—nothing is changed.'

'Only your allegiance.'

'My allegiance to you is as it always was. As to my allegiance to my country—to right and the preservation of our laws and liberties—that has not changed either. Whether I fight on the right or the wrong side, only time will tell—and if it happens to be the wrong side then that is something I shall have to live with. I would have come to Bowden Manor before, but it is only in recent days that the unfortunate events taking place here were brought to my attention.'

'I see. So you came directly. I am flattered to discover I rate so highly on your list of priorities,' she said with a heavy trace of irony. 'However, had you arrived before Captain Dugdale's final assault, then you would have been a long time knocking on my door.'

'What? You would have refused me entry?'

Jane lifted her head and squared her shoulders, her eyes gleaming in her proud courageous challenge of his authority. 'Yes. I find your presence here in this house offensive, sir.'

'I see.' Edward's eyes narrowed and his smile was icy. He gave a barely perceptible nod of his head. Then tell me—is it the clothes I wear that offend you, or my person?'

'Both. The uniform you wear depicts the man. You are here against my will and no longer are you and I betrothed.'

'No? Then can you tell me what has changed?' he asked, one dark brow arched, his eyes gleaming derisively,

She tossed her head defiantly and the stubborn set to her chin told him how she had hardened her heart and her attitude towards him. Her look dared him to attempt control of her.

'A little matter of the war and our opposing sides.' Her eyes snapped and her lips clamped wilfully.

Edward shrugged, as though he considered the matter to be of little importance, but his eyes glowed dangerous and dark. 'My own mother remains loyal to the King, but our relationship remains civilised.'

'Civilised! You call war civilised?'

'No,' he answered sharply, his jaw tightening. 'War is never civilised. You did realise, when you closed your doors on Captain Dugdale, that under the terms of a siege you would be given no quarter?'

'I knew that and expected none.'

'Then it is fortunate for all of you that I chanced to hear of it and was able to prevent any bloodshed. After having fought in the battle at Naseby, there was much to be done in the aftermath and I had not returned to London. In my opinion, I find it an unbecoming and unnatural occupation for a woman to conduct a siege. Where is your stepmother?'

'Fortunately she left for Newington with my sisters before the siege.' She cast him a challenging look. 'So—you reproach me for defending my home—even though I was left with little choice?'

'You risked your life.'

'And where would you have had me go, pray?'

'My mother would have happily accommodated you.'

'I have great affection and respect for Lady Blanche, as you know. When my own mother died she was of great comfort to me. But my duty, as I saw it at the time, was to defend my home. Besides— as far as I was concerned all connections between us were severed when I learned of your intention to take up arms against the King.'

'I understand that you were compelled by circumstances to act as you did, but now the siege is over I expect you to surrender with grace.'

'And turn myself over to your subjection, no doubt.'

Edward sighed and his expression softened, for he remembered that by nature Jane—who had been a bright, precocious child—was a gentle creature and quite submissive, which was why he had been all the more shocked when he heard how she was standing

against the Parliament Army alone, and surprised at
the pain he had felt when he thought of her distress.
He came to stand close to her, looking deep into her
hostile eyes.

'Clearly the past two months have changed you.
I remember a gentle, harmless, iridescent young creature with never a thought in her head for warfare.'

'If I appear changed to you, then any gentleness
and weakness I may have possessed has been sorely
challenged by the aggressive nature of your contem-
poraries.'

'Then I am sorry to hear it. Women should not be
associated with battle.'

'Nevertheless, through man's doing that is where
they are often to be found.'

He nodded slowly. 'Yes—you are right. However,
I did not come here to argue with you.' He frowned,
seeming curious suddenly, looking at her closely. 'I
overheard Captain Dugdale questioning you about
James. Is he here within the house? Because if so,
you must tell me. Is he the reason why you did not
accompany your stepmother to Newington?'

Swallowing hard, Jane looked at him, her back
poker straight and her gaze unwavering, but Edward
saw at a glance that she was close to tears, that her
lower lip trembled and it was with great difficulty
that she answered his question.

'Yes. James came here after fleeing from Naseby.
Sadly he contracted smallpox and died shortly after
the siege began.'

The immense shock registering in Edward's eyes
showed how he was deeply affected by her words,
for James and he had been close friends throughout

their lives, all through the years of their education which had been spent at Oxford—and not even their divided allegiance in the King's favour had come between them.

'James is dead?'

She nodded, swallowing down the hard lump that had risen in her throat, for whenever she thought of her handsome brother's cold and lifeless body lying deep in the cellars of Bowden Manor, she was overwhelmed with a deep sense of sorrow.

Edward turned away as he tried to come to terms with this unhappy news. When he again looked at her, his face was taut with an emotion which astonished her, for it gave her a brief insight into a softer side to his nature—one she was beginning to believe he had lost on the field of battle.

'Then what can I say? I am grieved and so sorry. I loved him as you did—you know that—and shall miss him sorely. But where is he buried?' he asked, his voice low with compassion.

'His body lies in a coffin hidden in the cellars awaiting the time when it can be taken to Bowden Church for interment.'

Edward was touched by Jane's frail and tragic appearance. Even in the depths of his own sadness he felt her despair, and a wave of almost unbearable pity and tenderness swept over him as he fought the impulse to take her in his arms and hold her close, knowing there had been an absence of family to offer her comfort in her misery. How much harder it was for him to tell her of the other matter that had brought him to Bowden Manor today. He sighed, knowing it could not be put off.

'Jane—I have another reason for being here today—one which, I know, will cause you some distress—doubly so—because of James.'

Observing puzzlement and fear in her eyes, he took her hand and led her towards a settle beside the great stone hearth, the fire unlit in its iron grate. She sat watching him, like a marble statuette, waiting for him to speak, a feeling of impending doom invading her body, her instinct telling her she was going to need all her strength for what he was about to disclose.

'It concerns your father, Jane. It grieves me sorely to have to tell you that he too is dead.'

Jane was stunned and grief-stricken by this latest tragedy. It came as a devastating, crushing blow, causing pain to tear through her heart. She stared at Edward piteously, like a lost child, shaking her head slowly in disbelief, unable to comprehend his words at first, then not wanting to, refusing to absorb the awful truth that she had lost both her father and brother in the space of two months.

'My father is dead? But how? When?'

'He was wounded at Naseby and taken prisoner. Sadly, he never recovered from his wound.'

At last the impact of the tragedy burst upon Jane and an awful cry of grief broke from her. Her body dissolved into tears, tears of anguish and absolute distress, piercing Edward to his very heart. Unresisting, she allowed him to draw her tenderly into his arms, to cradle her head against his chest and hold her as she cried, her tears unstoppable.

Smoothing her hair away from her face, he placed his lips against her brow and murmured, 'Weep,

Jane. Weep for them both—for they are worthy of your tears.'

She wept until she could weep no more, and when her sobbing ceased she slowly disentangled herself from his arms and rose, her legs trembling.

'Please excuse me. I—I think I'll go to my room for a while.'

Overcome by a tide of dizziness she swayed, the solid walls of the hall seeming to sway around her. Reaching out her hand, she groped for the edge of the settle to prevent herself from falling. But it was useless for, on the verge of collapse, darkness was falling like a curtain over her eyes. With a little sigh she gave in to it, but before she hit the floor she felt herself being scooped up into two strong arms and carried across the hall towards the stairs.

When next Jane opened her eyes it was to find darkness had fallen outside and that a fire had been lit and had burned to a red glow. Finding herself alone she gave way to a few silent tears of grief. Her father was dead. No more would she feel the protection of his love wrapped around her.

One of the few remaining serving maids at Bowden Manor came in carrying a bowl of steaming broth—the first proper meal Jane had seen in weeks. After being without food for so long, her stomach revolted at the thick broth, but she forced it down and immediately began to feel a little better.

She refused to give in to her sorrow further, to lie in bed when there was so much to be done. She must see what was happening—and Tom had to be told of her father's death. After washing herself free of the grime that still clung to her skin, caused by the smoke of the Parliamentary guns during their final assault, she donned a clean dress—but her heart was too heavy to appreciate the caress of the soft scented material against her skin. She brushed her hair and proceeded to go swiftly and with purpose down to the courtyard, a deadly calm and a coldness stealing over her that were to see her through that day and the next—until the time came when she could dwell on her loss without the agonising pain that seared and ripped her heart in two.

Stepping out into the cool night air made her shiver, even though it was still late August and the days were sunny and warm. She paused for a moment, taking in the unfamiliar and unwelcome scene before her. Smoke still hung heavy in the air and the ravages of the siege were everywhere, but clearly some attempts were being made to have them removed.

Many of the people who had shared the horrendous hardships of the past two months had been allowed to return unmolested to their cottages—or what was left of them, for Bowden village had not remained immune from the soldiers' plundering. Farms had also been robbed of corn, sheep and cattle, and anything else that could be carried away to sustain the besieging soldiers, callous individuals who cared not which side they fought on, caring little for either cause provided they got pay and plunder.

It made Jane's blood boil to see impudent and coarse Roundhead soldiers loafing against the walls, men who had been intent on destruction and now behaved as though they belonged at Bowden Manor.

She thought of her father and the manner of his death, of him being wounded at Naseby and never recovering from that wound. A murderous rage burned within her as she looked at these intruders in an agony of grief and anger—and frustration at not being able to order them out of her home, for it was men such as these who had caused his death.

She looked to where a group of them stood laughing and jeering as they mercilessly tormented an elderly man she knew to be one who had shared the months of siege, showering him with odious and obscene insults. He was clearly distressed at being so set upon and humiliated by these coarse ruffians who sheltered under the guise of soldiers, and fell to the ground when he was purposely tripped up by one of them. When he tried to rise he was brutally shoved back down to the ground by a soldier's boot.

Quickly Jane went to the poor man's aid, ignoring the soldiers and helping him get shakily to his feet. The ordeal having temporarily caused him to lose command of his tongue, he stumbled away. Throwing the soldiers a blazing glance of absolute contempt she turned away, hearing them laugh derisively at her retreating back.

'My, my—what a pretty sight,' one of the soldiers mocked.

'Not so haughty now, is she?' another sneered, spitting into the dust beside him as she swept by.

Jane saw Edward striding towards her across the courtyard; he had seen what was taking place. After speaking harshly to the soldiers, who immediately sidled away—although it was clear they were unmoved by his harsh reprimand—he turned his attention to Jane, his firmly marked eyebrows drawn together.

'How are you?' he asked with concern.

'As well as I can be,' she replied tersely, wishing she could treat him with detachment, with indifference—but she was powerless to prevent him slipping through her guard, to force her into an awareness of him when all she wanted was to avoid and forget him. 'I apologise for my weakness earlier. I am not in the habit of giving way to outbursts of such emotion. It can only be put down to hunger. I am better now that I've eaten—for which I have you to thank, I believe.'

'After all you have endured—and after receiving the tragic news of your father—it is hardly surprising you gave vent to your emotions.'

'As you will have seen from the sick—and others who died during the siege, from both wounds sustained in attacks and sickness, and have yet to be buried—we could not hold out much longer. Fortunately, the smallpox James contracted was contained with just one other casualty.'

'And did it not concern you that you were in danger of contracting the disease yourself?'

She looked at him directly. 'At the time I cannot say that it did. I had no choice, you see. Someone had to take care of James—and there was no one else. Besides, I did not think I would become infected. My mother firmly believed—and it has shown—that the disease might be prevented by placing children in contact with a person suffering from it. This is what she did with me as a child when a smallpox epidemic swept through Bowden and the surrounding villages.'

'And did you not become infected?'

'I suffered just a mild attack and on recovery had none of the disfiguring scars which frequently occur with the disease.'

'So I see. Your complexion is quite unblemished.' Edward smiled crookedly, beginning to realise there was so much about her he didn't know that would never cease to amaze him.

Confronted by Jane in her clean dress, and with her hair brushed like a halo framing her lovely face, he looked at her appreciatively, this beautiful girl with her finely chiselled features, and was happy to see a little colour had been restored to her cheeks. Whether from the food she had eaten or the cool wind blowing from the north, he knew not which, but he thought it most becoming.

But he could feel her nerves stretched tight. She had weathered the storm of the siege admirably, although he would have preferred her to have surrendered to Captain Dugdale in the beginning. However, he understood her reasons for not doing so and admired her strength and courage. Few women would have withstood what she had over the past weeks. Noticing how she was attracting the leering glances of the men around them, he took her arm and steered her towards the house.

'Your dress is inadequate to keep out the cool wind. Have you no cloak with which to cover yourself?'

'I am warm enough. It is unnecessary for you to express concern for my well-being.'

'Nevertheless, please go inside if you wish to avoid insults from the soldiers.'

'And if I wish to take a walk to the village?'

'I would not advise it,' he answered drily. 'Especially not in the dark.'

'Would you try to prevent me?'

'Yes.'

'And why, pray? Oh—do forgive me,' she said with haughty sarcasm. 'How soon I forget. You are my gaoler, are you not?'

'You are not my prisoner—and nor am I your enemy, Jane. It is simply that I cannot vouch for the conduct of the soldiers,' he said, unmoved by her fit of temper. Having made him aware that her Parliamentary prejudices were very strong, and after enduring weeks of having her home besieged, Jane seemed to find that his presence gave her something tangible on which to vent all her bitterness. 'If you must go to the village, then I shall arrange an escort for you tomorrow. But tonight I have to talk to you. There are urgent matters concerning us both which must be discussed. If you feel up to it, that is.'

'As far as I am concerned, we have nothing to discuss.'

'Yes, we have,' he said, refusing to let her taunting attitude cause him to lose his hold on his precarious temper. 'Come inside where we can be alone.'

They went into the house to a small room off from the hall, which Jane's father had used as his study.

'Come and warm yourself,' Edward said, crossing towards the hearth where a welcome fire had been lit. 'The night has come in cold.'

In silence Jane moved forward, glad to feel the

warmth, letting the heat seep into her body. They stood together, silently looking down into the flames before Edward turned to look at her, his expression silent and thoughtful, studying her delicate profile, watching as the light played on her hair. One minute it appeared pale and tawny and the next it was the colour of golden honey, folding softly about her shoulders and down her back.

She really was lovely—a harmonious combination of her hair and warm amber eyes. For a moment it was as though a window had been flung open, and the sunlight had rushed in. Why had he never truly seen or looked at her beauty before? Why had he never noticed?

Since reaching Bowden, he had been made aware by Captain Dugdale of a matter that would be of interest to her, which he was reluctant to impart, for he sensed it would cause her further anxiety. It concerned Sir Simon Butteridge—a man he did not know well but whose reputation had done little to credit him in his eyes. Knowing of the close friendship that had existed between Sir Simon and James, that he had visited Bowden Manor often in the past, he had intended telling her of a fierce skirmish that had occurred several miles to the east of Bowden.

It would seem that Sir Simon Butteridge, who was accompanying the King—who had over two thousand men and had intended marching to Scotland, but had been forced to turn back at Doncaster on being warned of a large enemy force approaching, and was constrained to move south-east instead—was with a foraging party when they came upon a local troop of Roundheads.

The attack by the Royalists led by Sir Simon, and the defence by the Roundheads, had been savage and bloody. It had been reported to him that Sir Simon—easily recognised by his flowing blond locks—and one other, were the only Royalist survivors, that both had been wounded but managed to escape under cover of darkness.

It was suspected that they were still in the region and were being sought, although with the countryside being almost bereft of Parliamentary troops—for the New Model Army was still campaigning in the West Country—there was little chance of them being captured. However, because of Jane's weakened state and deep sadness, he thought it best to keep this from her. Nothing could be achieved by telling her except further sorrow.

'What is this matter of such importance you wish to discuss with me?' Jane asked, her eyes, wide and questioning, coming to rest on his.

'First of all, I think you might like to know that I have arranged for your father's body to be brought back to Bowden,' he said gently.

Disarmed by the mention of her father, Jane had to force down the tears which threatened to flow once more. She lowered her eyes. 'Thank you. Father and James can be interred together in the church.'

'I have also obtained a protection for Bowden Manor from Parliament. You can rest assured that it will remain intact.'

'And the garrison?'

'Is to remain here for the time being.' Observing how her expression hardened to one of resentment, he sighed. 'Perhaps it will help if I tell you that there will only be a small contingent of soldiers—a dozen at the most and well disciplined—and that Captain Dugdale is to be relieved of his command.'

'Why should it?' she replied coldly. 'One Round-head commander is as much like another to my eyes. And how long do I have to share my home with the garrison imposed on me?'

'A few days, that is all. As soon as the funeral of your father and James has taken place, it is my intention to take you to my home—Deighton Hall.'

Jane stared at him in stunned disbelief. 'You mean that I am to abandon my home to the Round-heads?'

'You will not be abandoning anything?'

'That is not how I see it. When they leave doubt-less I shall find it plundered and spoiled beyond all recovery. No,' she said finally. 'I will not leave. I refuse.'

Edward gave her an impatient look. 'Yes, you will. I cannot remain here indefinitely—and from what I have seen of your household there are few to take care of you. Your housekeeper and remaining maidservants have fled to their homes in the village. You will go to Deighton and stay with my mother and sister for the time being. My mother, I know, has been most anxious about you over the past months—and with good reason.'

'I am sorry to be the cause of any anxiety Lady Blanche might feel—but by what right do you appoint yourself my keeper?'

'Since your father appointed me as such.'

Jane stared at him aghast. 'My father?'

'Yes. As you know, he strongly disapproved of

me taking up arms against the King—but it made little difference as far as our remaining friends was concerned. I will say no more on the subject until you have read his letter.'

'Letter?' she asked in bewilderment.

'Yes,' he said, taking a letter from inside his coat and holding it in his hand. 'The savage nature of this war prompted him to write it just before he died. In the event of his own death—which he knew would be soon—and should your brother not live to see the end of the war, it was important to him that you, your stepmother and sisters, and Bowden Manor, would be taken care of. No doubt you will question what he has written, but I sincerely hope you decide to abide by his wishes.'

Jane stared at the letter in his hand. How heavy the silence hung between them. She said nothing as she continued to stare at it, feeling reluctant to read what her father had written. Her expression was fixed, her eyes betraying neither surprise at the production of the letter nor grief, but tears started to her eyes, rolling down her cheeks and piercing Edward's heart. Reaching out her hand, she took the letter from him.

'I shall leave you for a while. I'm sure you would rather be alone.'

She nodded dumbly, unable to speak as she continued to stare down at the letter addressed to her in her father's hand. When she was alone she brushed away her tears and slowly opened it, staring at the familiar writing on the parchment. Feeling her legs begin to tremble, she seated herself in front of the fire and began to read, unable to shake off the hurden of doom that descended on her the more she read of her father's letter.

Chapter Three

The letter was long and contained many legal matters which Jane could not fully understand just then, but one thing was clear to her: should James not survive the war, then Edward Talbot was to take over her guardianship. It was also her father's dearest wish that she would abide by her betrothal and become his wife.

He explained that of the many battles fought since the beginning of the Rebellion, more were lost than gained of late, with the impenetrable strength of Cromwell's Ironsides being left in charge of the battlefields. He had come to lose heart, and after the bitter and brutal defeat of the Royalists at Naseby he strongly suspected that the King's cause was doomed.

Suffering greatly from a sword wound in his side, his thoughts had turned to his loved ones, to Bowden Manor and what would become of them all—and if James were to perish also, then his wife and daughters would be truly alone in a hostile world. Haunted by these thoughts as he lay in his prison in Coventry, he had enquired of his captors as to Lord Talbot's whereabouts. Being in the area—for he had also fought at Naseby—and made aware of Sir Ralph Marlow's tragic plight, Edward had gone immediately to be by his side.

Jane stared down at the letter, her mind in such a turmoil she felt faint. She was unable to fully comprehend what she had read, what it was her father asked of her—which was all the more terrible because she could not contradict him now he was dead.

When Edward returned, he found her standing deep in thought, the letter open on the table beside her.

'I can see that what you have read has surprised and shocked you. I knew you would receive it badly. What have you to say?'

'What can I say? How can he ask this of me?' she said fiercely. 'Am I to have no say in the matter? Do I have to answer to my father even though he is dead?'

'You wish to challenge it?'

She shook her head in defeat. 'No I did not challenge him in life—I cannot do so in death.'

'So you agree to honour your troth—to become my wife?'

Jane turned from him, staring down into the flames once more, trying to whip up her anger, to not forget who he was or what he stood for—for by marrying him it would seem that she had turned against everything she had been fighting for, even against the King himself.

'You have no obligation to me of any sort,'

Edward said quietly, sensing the struggle going on inside her. 'Feel free to change your mind. I shall not force you. Remember, a betrothal can always be broken—whereas marriage is a great step and for life. But I ask you to think back to the day of our betrothal, and, if you can, recollect the words your father said—for I shall never forget them. He said, "Nothing will make me happier than to see our two families united by marriage—to tie a knot between you so blessed by both our houses that nothing can divide."'

The almost-forgotten words brought tears to Jane's eyes. How strange, she thought, that after all this time Edward should remember them. 'Yes, I too remember what he said. But how fragile a knot can be when there is such discord between the two people concerned.'

'Then we must put whatever discord there is behind us. Come, Jane, what is your answer to be?'

Bowed down by a force stronger than her own she sighed, lowering her head in decorous acceptance, knowing where her duty lay. 'I have an obligation to honour the promise I made—one which I know my father would expect me to fulfil,' she said, feeling physically, mentally and emotionally exhausted, having no wish to go on fighting. 'But understand that I do so out of duty and for the future security of my family and Bowden Manor and for no other reason. It is my father's wish and I shall honour that.'

Edward subjected her to a long, cool stare, his lips taking on an ironic twist. 'Thank you.' he said drily. 'Although I have to say I would have preferred a more favourable response to my proposal. I admire your loyalty to your family and how staunchly you defend your home and I can hardly blame you for being angry with me or for the way everything has turned out. But I am relieved you see the sense and wisdom of your father's letter.'

'Why are *you* willing to accede to my father's wishes?' she asked, suddenly curious as to what his own feelings were on the matter. 'Surely a marriage between us cannot be favourable to you, either.'

'This is not about what is happening to the country but to us, Jane. We must not allow outside influences to interfere in something that is of a highly personal nature. Your father and I remained staunch friends to the end. He understood that I did my duty as I conceived it and followed the dictates of my conscience and fought for the principles I believed in. In the face of the threat posed by the King's policies to our liberties, property and religion, I felt the need to oppose him by every legal means. I am only sorry that many, sharing my own views, were willing to carry their opposition to the extreme of arms. Your father understood that my grievances were towards the King and his advisors—and his unwillingness to accept the constitutional reforms put forward by Parliament—but that I bore him no personal animosity.'

'His letter states that you saw him in prison.'

'Yes. It may be of some comfort to you to know I was with him when he died.'

'Yes—yes, it is. Did—did he support the King to the end?'

'Yes. I well remember, when Parliament was called in sixteen forty, that almost the entire members of the two houses were critical of the King's policies and administration. Your father was among those who insisted legislation should be forced through to prevent the King from exploiting his prerogative rights to increase taxes. But when the time came to take sides, he never forgot his duty lay with the King. He never lost faith in himself or the cause. I always held him in the highest regard—and I believe you know that.'

'Of course. But it is not my father you will be marrying. Clearly you were not enamoured of me on our betrothal—for when the King raised his standard at Nottingham and you chose to fight against him, I received no word, no letter from you. What was I to think?'

'Yes—that was inconsiderate of me. I do apologise.'

'Clearly you spared me not a moment's thought. Come, admit it. Spare me and yourself any embarrassment. I think we know each other too well.'

He moved close to her. looking down, his eyes penetrating and searching her own.

'Do we? I beg to differ. Yes, I admit we have known each other almost all our lives, but does that mean we know each other—*really* know each other as well as two people should who are to marry, to spend the rest of their lives together? Think of it, Jane—and you will realise we are almost strangers to one another.'

His lips curved in a smile, his teeth flashing from between his parted lips, and his eyes came to rest on her mouth, soft and full-fleshed. 'It should be interesting getting to know one another, don't you think, within the confines of marriage?'

His voice was as smooth as the finest silk and his dark eyes, almost black in the dim light, danced as though he found the confusion which engulfed her vastly entertaining. She took a step back from him, her aversion to him heavy in her breast. And yet what was it about him that filled her with bewilderment, that made her feel so very vulnerable and want to question her reasons for disliking him?

She trembled with a strange kind of emotion—revulsion mixed with fascination, cringing and yet drawn towards him when she remembered their past relationship—yet, if she could swing from anger and rebellion to doubt and to question her own better judgement with the same man, then how could she ever trust her emotions? All the years from childhood through to womanhood she had known him, and yet her life under her father's strict rule had been sheltered and guarded, which had prevented any kind of intimacy between them.

But what he said was right. They were acquainted yet strangers. But the kind of intimacy he spoke of that came only with marriage perplexed and embarrassed her, for she had never given much thought to what would happen past her wedding day. And yet, recollecting the strength of his arms when he had held her earlier as she had sobbed against his chest and he had comforted her—how gentle he had been and how soft his lips had felt on her brow—then she realised that any social barriers that had existed between them were beginning to crumble and no longer did he see her as a child.

Hot-faced, she looked away in an attempt to hide

her confusion. 'So—I—I am to live at Deighton.'

'Yes.'

'And Bowden?'

'Belongs to me.'

What he said seared into Jane's heart. A wave of sickness swept over her and she stepped back. She must be going mad to think that Bowden Manor no longer belonged to her family—that it had been passed on to this Parliamentarian, who was so cool, so self-assured. After all she had been through, it was like having the final nail hammered into her coffin. Her throat constricted painfully and suddenly she wanted to cry, but she forced herself to remain calm.

'But if James were still alive then, now Bowden Manor has fallen into the hands of Parliament, am I right in thinking a sequestration order would have been passed? That all my family's goods and property would be confiscated?'

'Yes—that would be the case.'

'Then allow me to congratulate you,' she said tartly. Having composed her feeling, she was able once more to meet his gaze directly. 'It would seem that the misfortunes which have befallen my family have turned out in your favour.'

Edward's eyes narrowed with anger. 'I did not acquire your father's house and lands by any dubious means. When I agreed to the terms of his will—which he has explained to you fully in your letter—I did not anticipate James's untimely death. The last thing I wanted was to profit by it.'

And my stepmother and stepsisters? What will become of them?'

'Financially they will benefit very little from your father's estate. A succession of bad harvests and his generosity in helping fill the King's coffers to finance the Royalist cause virtually ruined him. But you may set your mind at rest that they will not starve and will continue to live here as always.'

'And if my stepmother should remarry?'

'Then the manor will be disposed of at my will. It may be passed on to either Susan or Penelope on their marriage—or to any offspring we might have.'

'I see. It would appear that everything has been taken care of.' Sighing, she turned from him. 'I must write to my stepmother immediately. She will be quite devastated to learn of my father's death and will want to return to Bowden at once. Can we delay the funeral until then, do you think?'

'I don't see why not. If you write her a letter, I will see that it is sent to her at Newington without delay.'

'Thank you. A-and you still insist that I leave with you for Deighton after the funeral?'

'Yes,' he replied firmly, with a note of finality, completely assured in his masculinity that he would have his own way in this, however painful she might find it, with utter disregard for her feelings.

'And—and our marriage?' she asked hesitantly, feeling herself flushing, unable to look at him. 'When. . .?'

He smiled crookedly when she left her question unfinished, but was able to provide her with an answer. 'I am not so insensitive to all you have been through. Normally I would be prepared to wait until you feel you are ready before we marry, but unfortunately these are not normal times. I do realise that because you are in mourning we should wait for a respectful period, but since I cannot remain at Deighton long, it is best for the ceremony to take place before I leave.'

Jane turned and looked with fresh eyes at the man who was to be her husband—whose name she was to bear—the man her father had signed his property and his daughter over to in the hope that he would be their salvation. He was handsome enough, that was plain, being tall and lean but with a well-muscled frame, and he carried himself with a languid, aristocratic grace. His eyes and hair were dark, his features firm and his chin strong, and there was an arrogant curl to his lips.

There was also a hardness about him, an inflexibility of mind and will, and a toughness imbued by his military life. There was also something about him that made her feel uneasy, something about the way he was looking at her now that was unnervingly intent.

She turned away in confusion to avoid his penetrating gaze but, feeling like a trapped bird, as if he compelled her, she turned again to face her captor, standing stiffly, every nerve in her body tense, her eyes wary as she watched him.

'What is it?' Edward asked softly, finding the atmosphere within the room more relaxed. She was a seductive vision of loveliness, bathed in the orange glow of firelight. Her saintly fragility had a power beyond beauty. He crossed to where she stood. 'Don't you find marriage to me palatable? You don't love me, is that it?' When she didn't reply he smiled, reaching out and taking her hands in his. 'I know of few well-bred young ladies who married for love— but in many cases it comes with marriage. I have to say that when I first saw you earlier I hardly recognised you.'

'To my advantage, I hope,' she said, disconcerted by the feel of her hands in his. 'I—I have had three years in which to grow up.'

'To become a very beautiful and desirable young woman.'

Jane flushed, unused to such compliments. 'I must cut a sorry figure in your eyes.'

'No. Quite the opposite, in fact,' he said, turning her hands palm upwards, showing no surprise on seeing the startling evidence of the part she had played in helping to maintain the siege. They were red and sore; a half-healed ugly blister staring up at him.

Jane grimaced. 'They are hardly the hands of a well-bred young lady.'

'They are beautiful hands—hands to be proud of,' he murmured, bending his head and kissing them softly, taking her completely by surprise. 'I doubt you will find it so very terrible being my wife.'

Jane stared up at him mutely, like a moth mesmerised by a flame, riveted by the darkness of his eyes, seeing something in their depths she was too innocent and inexperienced to understand, but it made her heart beat wildly at the same time as a softness seemed to enter it. His strength, his masculinity, unnerved her, and all at once his hands were on her shoulders. He seemed so large as he towered over her, his powerful body emanating heat and strength.

She wanted to turn, to leave the room and this threat he posed to her sensibilities. Taking her chin gently between his fingers, his touch gentle yet strong, he tilted her face up to his, lowering his head to hers, his lips brushing hers in the gentlest of caresses, kissing her slowly, kindling a flame inside her, causing her heart to beat as though it would burst. She quivered under his touch, confused by his tender assault of her lips, but she did not draw back.

But she also experienced a feeling of power in those lips, a power that had the ability to cast her down into the realms of damnation if she married him—and yet his lips, so soft, so warm, made her feel that damnation could be sweet.

Only when he raised his head and released his hold on her shoulders did she step back, her cheeks flushed in bewilderment so that she did not know what to think. He had awoken in her a need otherwise unknown to her, one she did not understand. She had struggled and fought the Roundheads for two long months, enduring without complaint all the indignities, sufferings and hardships a siege imposed,— but it had taken just one kiss from Edward Talbot to break down every barrier of her carefully held reserve.

Edward smiled slowly, watching her go, knowing as she did so that his kiss had stirred an unknown passion in her innocent heart. She was like a fragile flower, fragrant and sweet, and as yet ignorant of just how tantalising and sensual she was—he had no doubt that she would delight in their marriage bed.

* * *

With a gradual lightening of fear and some sem-
blance of normality being restored to Bowden Manor
following the siege, Sir Ralph Marlow's body was
transported back to his home, causing a heavy sorrow
to descend upon the whole community. His distraught wife, Maria, also arrived from Newington
with their two small daughters, Susan and Penelope.

Jane's forthcoming marriage to Lord Talbot was
received by Maria with understanding and she gave
her blessing, having a high regard for Lord Talbot,
despite his decision to take up arms against the
King—a decision, she knew, he had not made
lightly. But in all conscience, feeling as he did, he
could not have done otherwise. She also understood
why it had been her husband's wish that Lord
Talbot's marriage to Jane should still take place—
that both Bowden and his family would be well taken
care of in the event of both his and his son James's
deaths.

Sadly, the close-knit community of Bowden did
not share Maria's understanding. As Jane had feared,
most of them believed that, coming from a staunchly
Royalist family, she had gone over to the enemy and
betrayed both her father and the King, and the honour
of them all, and that she was about to destroy the
solid front they had shown to the besieging Parlia-
mentarians.

When her father's body was brought from
Coventry, where he had been imprisoned before his
death, most offered polite words of sympathy, for he
had been held in the highest esteem by the whole
community of Bowden and the surrounding villages,
but only Tom Carter, her father's loyal steward,

understood and approved of what she was doing, knowing it was Sir Ralph's express wish that she marry Lord Talbot and that he would not have advocated this had he not had good reason for doing so. Better to have Bowden Manor in the capable hands of Lord Talbot, despite the fact that he was a Parliamentarian, than have the manor and the estate sequestered to some unknown.

Because of Tom's undimmed loyalty to the Marlow family, Edward saw no reason why he should not retain his position at the manor and continue with his duties as before.

The melancholy proceedings of the funeral service in the church were attended by few mourners, for half the male population of Bowden had accompanied Sir Ralph Marlow to the war and many had not returned. Some had shared the same fate and others were either prisoners of the Roundheads or fugitives.

After Sir Ralph and his son had been sealed for eternity with their ancestors in the dark crypt of Bowden church, the mourners returned to their cottages immediately, leaving Jane deeply hurt by their reaction to her forthcoming marriage. All through the ceremony, standing beside the tall, stiff figure of Edward, she had felt their staring, accusing eyes burning holes into her back, which had added to her sorrow but, sadly, it was as she had expected and, in all fairness, she could not blame them.

After the funeral service, when they returned to the manor and Jane was alone with Maria, she expressed her anxiety to her stepmother of her remaining alone at Bowden.

Of excellent birth, Maria was quite tall, a delicate-looking woman, her skin translucent—Jane's senior by some fifteen years. Her features were too thin to be described as beautiful, but her grey eyes were full of kindness and intelligence and her bearing did not lack the nobility she had acquired at birth. She had married Sir Ralph Marlow three years after the death of his first wife, when Jane was eight years old, providing him with two daughters whom Jane adored.

Jane had mourned her mother's passing but had welcomed her father's new wife warmly, their relationship over the years having developed into a deep friendship.

Maria was heartbroken by her husband's death and deeply saddened to learn that James had also died, but she had borne up well, conducting herself with dignity and grace ever since she had returned to Bowden. There was a grim, knowing smile on her face as she tried to put Jane's mind at rest, determined to remain in her husband's home but saddened that Jane was to leave for Deighton. Yet, aware of the deep feeling of hostility directed against Jane over her forthcoming marriage to Lord Talbot, she thought perhaps it was for the best. Besides, the perpetual peace and tranquillity of Deighton Hall might help heal the scars exacted on her by the siege.

'Don't worry about me, Jane,' said Maria, smiling kindly. Putting out a slender white hand, she drew her stepdaughter down beside her on the sofa, still as disturbed by her appearance as when she first saw Jane on her return to Bowden—she was so thin, with pain-filled eyes and despair in her heart. 'I have the comfort of Bowden and your sisters to sustain me. And I do still have Tom. I shall miss you, of course, but Deighton is only ten miles away—and what is ten miles to a stout carriage and pair?'

Jane smiled at her, knowing she was trying to make her leaving easier, and she loved her for it and was grateful. 'And you will visit me often?'

'Of course I shall. I know you are anxious about your forthcoming marriage to Lord Talbot, but I am sure you worry needlessly. He is the same man you became betrothed to—a good man, with your best interests at heart. He will take care of you. You have been through a great deal, my dear. Putting the welfare of others before your own needs has quite worn you out. You are too pale—too thin. Deighton and Lady Blanche's ministerings will be beneficial to you.'

'Yes,' she acceded with a deep sigh. 'I'm sure you're right, Maria. But I have missed you and my sisters so much these past weeks—I hate having to leave so soon. I cannot see why I have to go to Deighton—why I cannot be married from here, my home, which would be in the order of things?'

'Feelings against your marriage are running high in Bowden, so it is not a bad thing for Lord Talbot to take you away at this time to be married from Deighton. Try not to worry too much about what people are saying. It will pass when the war ends— and when one hears of the sorry state of the Royalists after their defeat at Naseby, then I suspect it cannot be long.'

'But I do mind what people are saying, Maria, and that's the problem. It hurts so much. Most of the

people who live in and around Bowden I have known
all my life. They are the people who stood by my
side during the siege—who faced hunger and death
in their loyalty to defend Bowden. I know exactly
how my marrying Lord Talbot must seem to them—
that I have changed—betrayed them—but I am still
the same. Edward knows my feelings—and that
come what may I remain loyal to the Royalist cause.
Oh, why did my father have to place me in such an
impossible situation?'

Maria was aware that over the days following the
end of the siege Jane had put on a brave face—not
once had she seen her cry or heard her complain,
but she knew that inside Jane was extremely unhappy
and hurting desperately, having to come to terms
with the double tragedy of losing her beloved father
and brother, and also her home. She also knew she
stood in awe of Lord Talbot and that her heart was
filled with doubt and fear for the future.

'Let us not talk of it, my dear. Clearly it distresses
you. But I shudder to think what might have happened to you had Lord Talbot not learned of the
siege and come immediately. I believe you do like
him, don't you—more than you care to admit,
perhaps?'

'Like him! If I am to marry him, Maria, I should
more than like him. However,' she sighed, 'I have
to say that where Lord Talbot is concerned my feelings are all confusion, so that I know not what
to think.'

Tired as she was following a long and sorrowful day,
Jane could not sleep that night—the last she was to

spend at Bowden until she knew not when. She rose before daybreak, feeling stifled inside the house and in need of some fresh air. Wrapping herself in a heavy cloak, she slipped silently out of the still-sleeping house into the clear morning air.

The soldier of the garrison on guard duty at the gate house, although curious as to where she could be going at such an early hour, let her pass unhindered. Until the siege, the war had had little impact on the village of Bowden, but now, outside the walls of the manor, brutal evidence of it lay all about her: the beautiful, undulating countryside ravaged with ugly earthworks for the batteries still remaining— until April, when spring green and meadow grass would cloak the scars. Thankfully the soldiers had moved on.

Absently she took the rutted lane down the hill to the village, listening to the mournful sighing of the wind as it blew through the branches of the trees on either side of her, their boughs meeting overhead like fingers laced together. In summer time the lane was always sweet smelling and cool. Feeling the need to be close to her father and brother, her feet took her towards the church standing a little apart from the village, its square, squat shape looming darkly ahead of her. To be alone in the church with her thoughts and prayer might ease some of the sorrow that hung heavy in her heart.

Passing silently through the lych gate, she walked up the narrow path to the porch, reaching out and gingerly pushing the heavy wooden door open on its hinges and stepping inside. It closed behind her with a muffled thud. The interior was dim, with just a

thin grey light beginning to penetrate through the
windows. Moving slowly down the nave, she looked
towards the chancel, her eyes fastening on the golden
crucifix glowing dully on the altar.

The church smelt dank and musty and the air was
cold, but the atmosphere was one of peace. Drawing
her cloak about her, she slipped into one of the pews
and sank to her knees, placing her head on her folded
hands and beginning to pray, finding the nearness of
her father and brother where they lay at peace with
her mother comforting.

Her thoughts began to wander from her prayers
and to dwell on other things—the most prominent
being her marriage to Edward. In spite of her father's
wish that they should marry, and the fact that Edward
had done everything within his power to restore her
home to some form of normality following the siege,
still her mind was not easy and she was in no hurry
for the wedding to take place, or to enter into any
form of bondage that was hateful to her. Her tormented heart cried out to be set free, to be allowed
to remain at Bowden and choose her own destiny.

But, since the war, nothing was the same. She
must not look back—it was too painful for her to
remember how things had been. But in the mists of
her mind she saw a young girl with flowers in her
hair, laughing and warm, dancing with a fair young
man in the great hall of Bowden Manor, of sunlight
rippling through the windows like white silk and
setting alight the flowing blond locks of this handsome visitor to her home, Simon Butteridge, who
had merry twinkling blue eyes and was clad in the
finest clothes.

Oft were the times when he would arrive with James and, with a nonchalant air, charm the young Jane into rapturous awe. How very different her marriage to the arrogant and assured Edward Talbot would be. She sighed sadly. Was she being selfish? Was it so very wrong of her to dream of love and passion—to want to be close to the man she was to marry?

There had been no gentle courtship between her and Edward, no shared and cherished glances, no touching of hands or gentle caressess—no exchanging of hearts. How could they be close—become husband and wife in the true sense when they weren't even friends—when his stance against the King set her solidly against him?

And yet she found herself thinking back to the trauma of the previous day, which had passed in a haze of grief. Few words had been exchanged between them, but he had remained close by her throughout. In some strange way she had derived comfort from his nearness and his strength, feeling a closeness between them she had never felt before.

She also remembered how disturbed she had been when he had kissed her on his arrival at Bowden after the siege—feeling an unaccustomed warmth steal through her when she remembered the feel of his lips on hers, the sardonic tilt of his dark eyebrows and the awareness of her body coming alive beneath the caressing boldness of his hands—and she realised she had not wanted to face up to the fact that his kiss had given her pleasure, had made her aware of her own body's weakness and its readiness to betray everything she fought against.

There were times in his presence when she would find her eyes drawn to him, remembering his kiss, his embrace. Sensing her watching him, he would meet her gaze boldly, seeming to possess a keen ability to know the reason for the confusion which would swamp her at times like these and cause her to blush like a young girl and avert her gaze. He would smile knowingly, amused by it, and it would infuriate her.

So lost was she in her thoughts that the noise when it came—a low moan and a faint rustling from the back of the church—made her eyes open wide in fear. She knelt, silent and frozen, too afraid to turn, but knowing she must. Slowly she rose, turning and staring into the murky light at the back of the church, seeing the fleeting glimpse of a shadow which seemed to retreat and shrink towards the gloom.

'Who's there?' she cried, her voice echoing inside the hollow emptiness of the church.

Gathering all her wits about her, she looked to where she had seen the shadow, her eyes huge and transfixed. She listened, straining her ears, beginning to move to the back of the church, the silence so profound she could almost hear the old building's foundations creaking, and the collective breathing of all those sleeping in the vaults below.

Chapter Four

'Who is it? Who is there?' Jane asked again, her voice trembling.

In answer to her question there was a gentle rustling and her heart almost ceased to beat when two shapes emerged out of the gloom—one, the taller of the two, stepping forward and speaking quietly, while the other seemed to lean against one of the stone pillars for support.

'Jane? Jane—is that you?'

The figure who spoke her name with such familiarity stepped into the grey light that was beginning to lighten the church. Jane stood frozen to the spot, unable to move, staring at the man who emerged with fear and disbelief—as if he had stepped out from her dream—for it was none other than Simon Butteridge, the man who had occupied her thoughts just a moment ago. He stopped before her, his eyes fixed on hers. He was wearing simple peasant clothes, dirty and torn, his boots old and worn, with a tall, battered hat held in his hands which he threw down carelessly on to one of the pews.

Jane had a sudden vision of how she had last seen him, in his wide-brimmed hat entwined with blue-and-white plumes dancing merrily as he had ridden away from Bowden with James, with a song on his lips and his cloak flapping behind him like the wings of some gigantic bird. Surely this person who resembled a vagrant could not be the same. But then he smiled, the same charming, irresistible, beguiling smile she remembered so well lighting up his eyes. Reaching out, he took her hands in his own; despite his ragged appearance, he adopted his habitual good-humoured expression.

'So it is you, Jane. Little did I know you would come to me. I thought I would have to be the one to seek you out at the manor,' he laughed softly, speaking in his familiar, incredulous drawl.

Jane stared at him with undisguised amazement. 'But—but—what are you doing here in Bowden—in the church—and in such sorry attire?'

'I could ask the same question of you. What errand brings you here at this ungodly hour—for I do not remember you being so dedicated to your devotions?'

Jane sighed deeply. 'None the less, that is my reason for being here. This is one time I feel the need for solitude and prayer.'

Simon looked at her with some concern, his smile fading. If he thought her changed in appearance he did not mention it.

'I sense all is not well with you. What news have you of James? What has happened since last we met?'

That was the moment when Jane realised that

Simon did not know of James's death—or her father's. Quickly and haltingly she gave him an account of what had transpired, watching his face drain of colour and his expression become tense as she spoke, his eyes filling with pain and disbelief, for he was unprepared for what she was telling him.

'Dear Lord,' he breathed softly when she had fallen silent. 'I knew none of this. James—is *dead*?'

Jane nodded. 'Yes. And my father.'

Simon shook his head, stricken by what she had told him. 'But—how? What caused James's death?' he asked quietly. 'I was with him at Naseby. We became separated—but I do not recall him being wounded.'

'No. It—it was smallpox. He died here at Bowden. Unfortunately, we were besieged by Parliament soldiers at the time—it lasted two months. James died a few days into the siege but could not be buried until yesterday—with Father, who was wounded at Naseby and died recently as a prisoner in Coventry. Lord Talbot saw to it that his body was brought back to Bowden.'

Simon's eyes were full of pity when he looked at Jane, evidence of the terrible strain she had been under and the deep sorrow her father's and brother's deaths had caused her staring out at him from her huge eyes.

'I am so sorry, Jane. How you must have suffered. I shall miss James sorely—as you know, he was my closest friend. But—Lord Talbot?' he said, his expression becoming grim and curious. 'Is he not your betrothed?'

'Yes.'

'Then—forgive me—but does he not command a cavalry regiment in the Parliament Army?' he asked, expressing some bewilderment.

'Yes.'

'And you are still to marry him?'

'Yes,' she answered, a faint, cynical smile touching her lips. 'My hand was promised to him long ago. Nothing has changed. We leave for Deighton Hall, his home ten miles or so to the west of here this very day.'

'I do not believe it,' Simon said incredulously, unable to hide the resentment and bitterness he felt for the man who had secured the hand of James's sister before the war, a position he had once coveted himself. Although there had also been a time when he had aspired to the idea of a match between himself and the charming Anne, the pretty young sister of the aforesaid gentleman, who had succeeded in making a deep and lasting impression on his fickle heart. 'I do not believe you could marry a traitor, Jane. You cannot love him?'

This was true, but Jane did not care to admit it. 'No matter what my feelings are concerning Lord Talbot, Simon, we are to marry,' she said resignedly.

'Then what can I say but to wish you joy on your forthcoming nuptials. But tell me about his charming sister, Anne. How fare's she?'

Jane felt an unaccustomed pang of resentment when he mentioned Anne, for she saw in his eyes a warm glow and a soft smile curved his handsome lips.

'Anne is well, I believe. We have seen very little of each other since the outbreak of war. However, I am very much looking forward to seeing her later today.'

'And what of your stepmother and stepsisters? Are they in good health, also?'

'Apart from their obvious grief—yes, they are very well. However, Bowden Manor now belongs to Lord Talbot. My father bequeathed the house and manor to him on the event of his own and James's death, knowing Parliament would confiscate them and give them to some unknown otherwise.'

'Better the devil you know, eh,' retorted Simon, his tone heavy with irony.

Jane gave him a trembling little smile. 'Perhaps. But whatever my father's reasons, Simon, he was always a good judge of character and was extremely fond of Edward,' she said softly. 'However, it is not a matter I feel inclined to discuss just now. Tell me what you are doing here? You were at Naseby, you said?'

He nodded grimly. 'Yes—and like the cause, which is full of dissension and chaos, I have been bedevilled by ill luck ever since. With what remained of the cavalry after the battle—which can only be described as a military disaster for the King—I marched with him to Hereford and on to Wales, where he hoped to recruit fresh infantry to replace those who had surrendered at Naseby, but there was little support to be got from Wales.

'There are many Royalists, myself among them, who, disheartened by their defeat at Naseby, share the opinion of the King's nephew, Prince Rupert. He believes there is no other way the King can preserve his kingdom and posterity but by a treaty. Better to retain something than to lose all is what Prince Rupert is reported as saying—and I agree with him wholeheartedly. But the King refused to consider this and marched north, determined to go to Scotland in the hope that an alliance might be made with the Scottish Covenanters.'

'And you went with him?'

'Yes. However, after reaching Doncaster and hearing of huge enemy forces gathering to the north and others approaching from the west, we were again forced south. Captain Digby and I were in a foraging party a few miles to the east of Bowden,' he said, indicating his companion, who had sunk on to one of the pews, his head having fallen forward as if in prayer or sleep. 'We became separated from the main body of the army and came upon a local Roundhead troop. Unable to do other than stand and fight, we led the attack, but soon realised our mistake. Under cover of darkness we failed to notice the Roundheads had superiority in numbers.

'All those in the foraging party—apart from myself and Captain Digby—were killed in the skirmish. We were forced to abandon our horses, but managed to escape. Unfortunately, Digby here was wounded. I was recognised and an attempt was made at pursuit. We have been forced into hiding many times—and to take on the guise of peasants, as you see,' he said with wry humour, drawing Jane's attention once again to his poor attire. 'The journey here has been hazardous—and I believe we are still being sought, but I came in the hope that should James or your father be at Bowden then we could beg the use of fresh horses.'

'I understand,' Jane said pityingly. 'But, as you see, it would be impossible for me to attempt to shield you at the manor. Lord Talbot has installed a garrison there. On the whole, this part of Derbyshire remains loyal to the King, but since Bowden fell to Parliament it is not safe for you to remain in the area. However,' she said, observing his tiredness, thinking how changed he was, that he was much more serious than the man she remembered and that war had done that to him, 'you are weary, I can see, and in need of refreshment. I shall do what I can.'

Because of the close friendship that had existed between Simon and her brother, Jane saw she had no choice but to do all in her power to help him and his friend. Calmly she accepted her decision—but in doing so she also accepted the possibility of her own destruction, for the penalty for aiding fugitives was severe indeed.

Refusing to think of the seriousness of what she was about to do—or the anger it would arouse in Edward should he discover his betrothed was involving herself in something that would cause him acute embarrassment should it become known—she thought of Tom's cottage standing close by on the edge of the village. It was no secret to her that he had played an active part before the siege in aiding fugitives—and there had been many after the battle at Marston Moor, finding their way south.

'I shall see to it that food is brought to you and direction to a safe house is recommended—although obtaining horses may be another matter. Since the siege the stables at Bowden Manor are depleted— all the horses have been requisitioned by the army. How badly is your friend wounded?'

'It's just a flesh wound—but he has lost a lot of blood and is very weak. He needs rest, that is all.'

'And what of you?' she asked with some concern, noticing how he seemed to wince slightly, as if with sudden pain, as he took a step back. 'Are you hurt, also?'

'Only slightly in the leg—which is not serious enough to worry about, I assure you,' he grinned.

'I see,' said Jane, not entirely convinced, suspecting he spoke lightly of his wound to prevent her from worrying. 'My father's steward lives close by and is most trustworthy. Stay here inside the church—it will be safe enough for the time being—and I will send him to you.'

'Thank you, but you must take care not to endanger yourself on our account.'

'I will be careful, I promise.'

After saying a hasty, fond farewell to Simon, who promised her they would meet again, she slipped quietly away. After alerting Tom to the fugitives hiding inside the church—he promised to see them fed and directed to a place of safety until Captain Digby was recovered enough to travel—Jane hurried up the lane back to the manor. She felt a lightness of heart on meeting Simon again and frantically invoked the protection of every prayer and saint she knew to keep him and his friend safe from harm.

Jane was about to enter the house at the exact moment the door opened and a glowering Edward stood there. So lost was she in her thoughts that it took her a moment to comprehend that he was there.

She started violently when she became aware of him, which forced her to take a step back and bright colour to flood her cheeks. A scowl of deep displeasure marred his darkly handsome features. Clearly he was angry on finding she had been up and about before dawn outside the protective boundary of the manor.

'Looking out of the window, I thought it was you I saw coming through the gatehouse. Would you mind telling me where you have been to at this hour?'

Jane clenched her fists in the folds of her dress to keep herself from trembling. 'I—I couldn't sleep. I felt the need of some fresh air and went for a walk,' she said as he stepped aside, allowing her to sweep past him into the hall, but he continued to frown, noticing how she averted her gaze, the slight tremble to her voice robbing it of its conviction.

'Really! I would prefer it if you did not go roaming about the countryside at such an unearthly hour.'

'And why not, pray?' she retorted, facing him mutinously. 'Now the soldiers have gone I feel it is safe to do so.'

'Nevertheless, you will do as I say. All manner of undesirables are wandering about at this time.'

'I find your overprotection and high-handed manner irksome, my lord. I told you—I have merely been out walking—and I am quite capable of doing so without having to ask your permission for my every move. You seem to forget I have spent the past two months protecting myself.'

Coming to stand over her, Edward looked down at her with a faintly quizzical expression, for her behaviour he found strange, giving rise to suspicion.

'Come—join me for breakfast and tell me where

it is you've been walking to that is so stimulating, that causes you to return with such bright colour to your cheeks and your eyes to sparkle like they used to when you were guilty of some misdemeanour. Is it merely the sharpness of the morning—or something else which has brought about this change?'

He sounded amiable enough, but there was an underlying harshness to his voice. He was studying her intently, one of his strongly marked eyebrows raised, his gaze altogether too penetrating—beneath which Jane was beginning to feel decidedly uncomfortable and quite perplexed. She stood mutely, feeling herself flushing and unable to meet his eyes, at a loss to know what to say. This was unusual for her, for she was usually in command of herself— although deception was something which did not come easy to her, for she was not adept in concealing her thoughts and emotions.

'S-something else? Why—I—I'm sure I don't know what you mean. What else could there be?'

Edward continued to eye her curiously, making her conscious of a sudden feeling of embarrassment and also of guilt, which was quite ridiculous, for how could he possibly know she had met and talked with Simon in the church?

'I don't know. I was hoping you would tell me. There *is* something, I know, for your lack of composure gives you away.'

Jane's eyes slid away from his and she shrugged nervously, turning away from him. 'I really do not know what you're talking about. There is nothing to tell,' she replied, removing her cloak and beginning to move away from him. 'I thank you for inviting me to join you at breakfast—but I have no taste for food. However—I—I have a favour to ask of you,' she said hesitantly, turning to look at him once more. 'One which I hope you will grant.'

Edward's black brows drew together, for his suspicion—his soldier's instinct that something was amiss—was something he could not shake off. 'Then you only have to ask,' he said, speaking in a carefully lowered voice. 'What is it?'

'After the events of yesterday I—I feel rather tired and not much like travelling. Must I leave with you today? Can I not remain here a while and travel to Deighton in a week or so? And besides—I would like to spend a little more time with Susan and Penelope. I've seen so little of them of late and have missed them dreadfully.'

Edward looked at her sharply. 'Maria is at liberty to take them to Deighton at any time. My mother is always more than happy to see them—you know that. I know yesterday was a terrible ordeal for you, and I am sorry if you feel tired, but you will have plenty of time to rest when we reach my home. It is only a short distance and the carriage I've had sent over from Deighton will be comfortable enough.'

Fearing for Simon's safety and not wanting to leave Bowden until Tom could reassure her he was quite safe, there was an expression of desperation in her eyes when she looked at Edward.

'Please, Edward—just a few more days,' she implored.

'No. We leave together,' he said firmly, in a voice that implied there was nothing more to be said on the subject, a voice which gave Jane an insight into the iron control he normally employed with his troops, one which told her he was used to obedience from those about him. 'It is all arranged. My mother is expecting you.'

'I am sure Lady Blanche would understand— besides, normally a bride would leave for the church on her wedding day from her father's house,' she persisted defiantly.

'Normally, yes—but as I remember saying to you before, these are not normal times. Hostility towards an alliance between us is running high hereabouts, and to have our union sanctified in Bowden Church would not be received with favour. Indeed, it might even result in outright rebellion—a situation I know we both wish to avoid.'

Jane looked at him indignantly. 'Am I to have no say in the matter at all?'

'No,' he answered harshly, his mouth tightening slightly and his expression becoming one of exasperation. 'It would seem that you have a propensity to flout my wishes and argue at every turn. I care not for this new Jane Marlow. I would have you as you were before the war.'

'Ha!' she exclaimed. 'A foolish simpleton of a girl, you mean? Let me tell you, Edward, that I am not like that any more. Like everyone else the war has changed me—if not for the better, then that is no fault of mine. Whether you approve or not matters little to me. If you marry me, you will have no alternative but to put up with it.'

Unusually for Edward, he was not dressed in his buff coat or flaunting his orange sash, which was always so offensive to Jane's eyes—like a badge never letting her forget that he was her enemy. Dressed in his white shirt open at the neck to reveal the strong muscles of his neck, and leather waistcoat, he seemed younger somehow, although his features as he stared at her were as if made of stone. But then a faint smile lightened his sombre countenance and his eyes gleamed appreciatively at the sight of her lovely face turned towards him. Without taking his eyes from hers, slowly he strode towards her.

'Despite the harshness of your tongue and your hostility towards me, Jane, I have seen that in your eyes and felt the response in your lips when I kissed you that gives me hope for a better understanding in our future relationship.'

'Hope!' she snapped, the amusement in his tone making her blood boil, finding it impossible to conceal her feelings. 'I fear, my lord, that you are mistaken. Your kiss I found offensive—contrary to what you may think.'

He nodded slowly, continuing to smile. 'We shall see. Perhaps when I begin to repeat the offence often—when we are wed and you are maid no longer and it is time for me to leave Deighton—then I will have you at my mercy and begging me to return with haste.'

Jane's cheeks stung with heat and her eyes blazed with anger and defiance. 'How dare you speak to me in this—this cavalier fashion?' she fumed.

Edward's smile broadened, his dark eyes alight with laughter, but when he looked at her, seeing her slender body moulded beneath her dress, how her angular cheek bones were flushed with anger and her amber eyes shone almost yellow as they sparked with fire, he found himself wanting her.

'Cavalier! An odd choice of word to apply to a soldier in the Parliament Army, don't you think? However,' he said, his eyes fastening on her soft lips, 'I have a mind to repeat the offence this very minute if you continue to glare at me in that belligerent manner.'

Jane took a step back in alarm, afraid he would do just that. But she was not unmoved by his close proximity, and the memory of his kiss, his touch—and how he had succeeded in stirring up deep, hidden pleasures inside her—roused her to fresh paroxysms of anger.

'Don't touch me,' she said angrily, 'and you delude yourself if you think you will have me at your mercy. When we are man and wife I shall do my duty and that is all.'

Edward shrugged casually, continuing to smile infuriatingly, his face set in an expression of smiling challenge. 'Duties you will not find so offensive, I promise you. In no time at all you will learn what pleasures can be had and enjoyed under the cloak of marriage, and to look on them as pleasant and perform them willingly and happily.'

'Never. If you think I will love you and swear eternal devotion to you, then you are under a false illusion. I do not care for you in the slightest.'

Edward's black eyebrows rose, his eyes travelling from her face to the gentle swell of her breasts beneath the bodice of her dress before fixing themselves again on her eyes.

'Hate! Love! What's the difference? Both inspire passion—which I believe you possess in abundance, my dear. A passion I intend savouring to the full in the not-too-distant future.'

The soft flush that mantled Jane's cheeks deepened to bright crimson and she gasped, appalled that he should speak to her in this unseemly manner. 'Why—why—how dare you?' and without further ado, unwilling to prolong a conversation which was only succeeding in putting her at a disadvantage, furiously she stormed off across the hall as though she'd been violated, hearing Edward chuckling infuriatingly behind her.

Edward's smile was replaced by a worried frown as he watched Jane cross to the stairs and disappear into the darkness above. Arriving back at the manor, she had seemed more than a little startled at seeing him in the doorway. In fact, he thought she resembled a young animal which had become trapped in the sudden glare of a bright light, and before she'd had time to defend herself with her feminine instinct from his sharp eyes, he had seen there was a look of enchantment in her eyes, that she glowed with the fragile beauty of a young girl recently awoken to love. There was a softness to her features and a lightness to her step which, did he not know better, would have told him she was returning from a secret tryst with a lover.

But no, this he would not believe. There had never been any suggestion of this. She was virtuous, of this he was certain, but she was also young, of an impressionable age, whose head could easily be turned by a handsome youth. It was the thought of just such a youth that brought Sir Simon Butteridge to mind, bringing him a sudden feeling of unease. Why he should think of him now he knew not— once again, maybe it was his soldier's instinct that made him think that Simon, wounded, would seek the aid of people he knew in the region, people like the Marlows,

Was it possible that he had made contact with Jane—that he had sought her out and that she had seen and talked with him? That Simon Butteridge was a Royalist and a fugitive mattered not to him. There were thousands like him all over England, but it was not his task to hunt them out. What did matter and concern him deeply was how Jane felt towards him.

He recalled the deep impression Simon had made on his sister Anne when she had met him on occasion during her visits to Bowden Manor to see Jane. In fact, she had even imagined herself to be in love with him, which he thought was quite ridiculous. But, more importantly, what impression had he made on Jane's young and vulnerable heart? Had she also fallen under his spell—fallen for his winning ways and easy charm?

Whatever the truth behind her absence from the house before daybreak, the first seeds of suspicion had been sown, making him determined to be more vigilant—and even more determined to take her with him when he left for Deighton.

Besides, he had no mind to be parted from her in a hurry. He was beginning to feel her magnetism the more he was with her, making him realise the full measure of her beauty, which had begun to disturb him greatly. The siege had taught her to think for herself; her will to succeed, to survive, had given her a self-possession he understood. But he also saw the change it had made in her. Her amber eyes shone with bitter pain and memory of endurance, and her pallor and weight loss gave her a soft, fawn-like, fragile vulnerability—an ethereal look, one he found did not detract from her beauty in the slightest, and one which gave him a strong impulse to protect her.

Her deportment since the ending of the siege had been dignified and admirable, and she appeared to be coping with her grief well—although he knew exactly how she suffered. But however much she wanted to remain at Bowden, he would not allow it. Their relationship was one of unease and there would never be harmony between them if he granted her her wish and let her remain. Because they had been apart for so long, it was important that they spend as much time together as possible if they were to be married.

But as he turned away to go outside to find the captain of the garrison, he wondered at the true reason for her wanting to remain at Bowden, for he did not believe it had anything to do with her weariness or wanting to remain with her sisters a little longer.

Very soon he would have to leave Derbyshire. His regiment, much weakened by desertions and loss of life after Naseby, had been disbanded and the remaining soldiers were being integrated into a newly formed regiment of the New Model Army which trained at Windsor. He was expecting to be summoned to take up a new command at any time and it was his wish for the wedding to take place before his departure, for as Jane was proving unwilling though complaisant about her marriage to him, in making her his wife he would be sure she would be waiting for him on his return.

He fully intended being at Deighton for the winter months, when it was not unusual for many soldiers and officers to be given extended furloughs to go home to be with their families, to concentrate on the management of their estates and spend the cold season in more comfortable quarters.

On the point of leaving Bowden Manor, Jane stood by the window in her room looking out over the glowing heights of the hills to the west, towards Deighton, letting her eyes drink their fill of the distant moors clothed in the full flush of purple heather, which would soon turn to the deepest russet brown and copper fire, before giving in to the subdued drabness of grey and black for the long months of winter, when cold wet gusts of wind would sweep down from the lofty gritstone peaks to the valleys below, heralding the whiteness of snow.

She had looked upon this prospect many times, which brought to mind the memory of herself as a girl who had inhabited this house since she was born, had slept every night under its roof, and who was now to leave its protective shell at last. The sadness that this caused her, combined with the deep sorrow she felt over losing her father and brother, was heavy to bear, but seeing Simon again, and knowing of his sorry plight, had placed an added burden on her heart and was making it more difficult for her to leave Bowden.

She remembered how her body had exploded with joy when she had recognised him in the church earlier, how glad she had been to see him again, although how she wished circumstances had been different and he wasn't in danger of being captured by Roundheads.

Absently she found herself comparing him with Edward, thinking how, apart from them both being the sons of lords, they were different in every aspect. Having perfect breeding and manners, with an air of indolence and easy wit and charm, Simon was the male epitome every young woman dreamed about. He was appealing in every sense—and a memory of James's gentle warning that he was often in the habit of compromising ladies' reputations only added excitement to his attraction, whereas Edward, with his dark, forbidding looks, essentially masculine, and strong, well-muscled body, was of a more serious nature. There was a hard, cruel force inside him, an indomitable will that drove him on.

How could she endure it? How could she endure being married to a man she did not love, to live in his house, magnificent though it was, which had no part of her, to make it her own as Bowden had been? The only consolation she would have would be the moors—the heather-clad moors would still be there for her to look upon.

Chapter Five

Maria entered Jane's room to have a quiet word with her before she left for Deighton, saddened by the unhappiness she saw in her eyes when she turned, noticing how the weight of her sorrow caused her shoulders to droop. Knowing how difficult Jane was finding it to leave Bowden, quickly Maria moved across to where she stood.

'Don't fret so, Jane. Deighton is not far from Bowden. We will see each other quite often. Look on your leaving here and your marriage as a new beginning. Lord Talbot is a fine man. He will make a good husband.'

'How do we know that? How can we know that?' she cried tearfully, with all her pent-up misery. 'I don't love him, Maria. How can I love a man I don't even like?'

Maria sighed. 'Love is not always present when two people marry, Jane. It is only one side of the relationship. That will come later—I'm sure.'

'No. I know exactly what it is I feel for Edward and it certainly isn't love—or friendship, even. But you loved my father, didn't you, Maria?'

'Yes. I was fortunate. I could not fail to love such a good man. We loved each other deeply—as he did your mother before me.'

'Then why can't it be like that for me? Why does it have to like this? Why—oh, why do I have to leave Bowden?' she asked, her voice rising with something in it of a frustrated, frightened child.

Maria hated seeing her so distraught and for an instant was tempted to reach out and place her arm about her shoulders in a gesture of affection. But she hesitated, for in trying to check Jane's emotions she was every bit in danger of weakening her own.

'Because you must, my dear,' she answered.

'But I don't want to,' cried Jane, tears of rage and misery spilling over her lashes, which she angrily dashed away with the back of her hand.

Hearing the violence in her voice Maria was suddenly alarmed and cast her a harsh, suspicious look.

'What is this?' she asked quietly. 'What has happened to shatter your composure? Until last night you were resigned to leaving Bowden.' She looked at Jane sharply. 'Could your reluctance to wed Edward be that you have a preference for some other? Is that it, Jane? Is there someone else who has found his way into your affections?'

Jane looked away from Maria as though she could not bear to see her, knowing it was her meeting with Simon that had brought about this doubt, this change in her. Oh, why did images and memories of childhood have to rise up and haunt her now? Were they to do so her whole life through? Maria looked at her, her expression one of bewilderment.

'Jane—what is it?' she asked, her voice almost a whisper, dreading what her stepdaughter would tell her.

When Jane stubbornly continued to avert her eyes Maria reached out and gripped her upper arms, forcing her to look at her, sensing she was in the grip of some powerful emotion and able to feel the resistance pouring out of her. Her face was flushed with a combination of anger and fear that she was faced with little choice but to obey Edward and leave Bowden.

'What is it?' she repeated insistently. 'What has happened?'

Jane swallowed nervously, eyeing Maria warily, unsure as to how she would react to what she had to tell her. 'It's Simon, Maria. I've seen Simon,' she said quietly.

Maria stared at her, trying to comprehend what she was saying—what her words implied. 'Simon? You—you mean Simon Butteridge?'

Jane nodded.

'But—but where? How can you have seen him? To my knowledge he hasn't been to Bowden in at least eighteen months or more.'

Maria listened in an appalled silence as quickly Jane recounted her meeting with Simon in the church, of the unfortunate events which had brought him there, and how she had enlisted Tom's help and was waiting for him to come to the manor to assure her of his safety before she left for Deighton.

It was no surprise to Maria that Jane had turned to Tom for help. There was a network of people all over the country loyal to the King's cause who hid eminent fugitives in their homes and either saw that they reached their regiments or left the country. They had played an active part themselves on occasion, especially after the battle of Marston Moor a year ago, which had seen the defeat of the Royalists and lost the King the north.

'You speak as if there is something between the two of you—but—if my memory serves me correctly, he was James's friend and nothing more. Tell me I am not wrong, Jane?'

'No, you are not wrong. But Simon is part of everything I hold dear—James, Father—the happy times before the war. Oh—I could love him, Maria,' she said, her voice quivering with passion. 'I know I could.'

Maria saw a vibrancy shining in Jane's eyes she had not seen in a long time—but how she wished it had been put there by excitement over her marriage to Edward. She remembered Simon Butteridge as being a young man with delicate, almost effeminate good looks, with a deceptively mild manner, who flattered every young woman he came into contact with, convincing them they were the most beautiful creatures alive.

But Jane had not been the only young lady at Bowden to succumb to his charms, for she well remembered how willingly Anne Talbot, on her visits to Jane, had fallen under his spell, how she had been unable to resist the lure of his flattery which had sent her into paroxysms of delight, convincing her she would never love another as she did Simon Butteridge. On his visits to Bowden Manor with James in the past Maria had liked him well enough and he had always showed Jane the most perfect courtesy—but it was clear he had made an impression on her innocent, tender young heart.

'Oh, Jane,' she whispered, 'I never expected this. Has he made any advances towards you?'

'No.'

'Then how do you know it is the same with him?'

'I just do. I know it is only my betrothal to Edward that prevents him from speaking out.'

'Oh, dear Lord. Should Edward find out about any of this, then I shudder to think what his reaction will be. I know of his violent temper—his rage will be terrible indeed. You would do well not to aggravate him—not to provoke him to anger,' Maria said in a warning voice.

'Edward! I care nothing for him,' Jane said fiercely, dismissing her betrothed with scorn, trying not to think how he had stirred her emotions with his embrace, his kiss, weakening her so that she did not know herself.

'Nevertheless, he is still the man you are to marry.'

'He is a tyrant, Maria—and has been so unreasonable on insisting that I leave Bowden at this time.'

'In the light of what you have just revealed to me, then I have to say I am thankful,' Maria said harshly. But she sighed sympathetically when Jane cast her a look of utter despair. 'Oh Jane, you must forget Simon—put him out of your thoughts. I remember him as being gracious and charming—a man of the world and an expert in breaking the hearts of many young ladies. He is not for you and it is no use dreaming of what might have been. Besides—if he is a fugitive, then it is imperative that he leaves the district before he is caught. If he can find his way back to his regiment, all well and good—but either way you have to accept that you may never see him again.'

Blinded by scalding tears that sprung once more to her eyes and trembling with the force of her emotions, Jane uttered a painful cry and turned away. 'I must—I will see him again, Maria. I have to.'

Saddened by this unfortunate turn of events and unable to encourage or approve of the kind of relationship Jane wanted to exist between herself and Simon, believing that, in her misery, Jane saw him as a means of holding on to the past rather than as a serious romantic attachment, gently Maria put a comforting hand on her arm.

'What we want we don't always get, my dear, and you must recognise and accept that. Look to the future and receive your new life with courage. Promise me you will try and make it work. Remember it was your father's dearest wish that you should marry Edward—for our two families to be united in marriage.'

Dry-eyed, Jane stared at Maria, suddenly remembering what Edward had said to her when she had read her father's letter and he had asked her if she intended honouring her troth. 'To tie a knot between us so blessed by both houses that nothing can divide,' she whispered, almost to herself.

'Yes,' murmured Maria, almost overcome with emotion, for she too remembered her dear husband had spoken those words on the day Jane had become betrothed to Edward. 'I am so sorry, my poor dear Jane. I know exactly what you are feeling and how painful all this is for you, but what do you expect me to say to you? Even if you were not to marry Edward, he is still your guardian, and I cannot urge you to resist his will. Will you promise me that you will put all this behind you—that you will try to forget Simon Butteridge?'

Jane bowed her head in dejection, knowing there was little else she could do and, knowing there was no other excuse she could present to Edward which would persuade him to relent and allow her to remain at Bowden, she nodded. 'I will try to put it behind me, Maria—I do promise. But please don't ask me to forget Simon. That I cannot do.

Relieved, Maria smiled and placed a kiss on her wet cheek. 'Then no more tears. Come, you must say goodbye to Susan and Penelope. They are quite distraught that you are to leave them so soon after their return from Newington.'

When Jane entered the room where her sisters were waiting to say goodbye to her, she looked to where Edward was standing by the fireplace, his hands clasped behind his back, calmly watching her. She met his dark eyes but did not speak to him, going instead to where Susan and Penelope were sitting on the sofa, unable to understand why she had to leave at all.

They had been downcast ever since returning to Bowden and learning of their father's death, but to be told that their beloved elder sister was to leave them to live on the other side of Derbyshire—which to two girls of such tender years was like the other side of the world—was almost too much for them.

Jane sat between the two little girls with her arms about them, looking down into their earnest, attentive faces upturned to hers. Susan was a robust, forthright girl, whereas Penelope was of a more gentle nature and more susceptible to illness, which was a constant worry for Maria.

'Why do you have to go?' asked Susan, looking at her in dismay, at seven years old two years older than the tearful Penelope. 'Mama has told us you are to be married. May we not be there to see you?'

'Of course you shall. You shall both come to Deighton for the wedding. Come dry your eyes, Penelope,' she said gently. 'You know what happens when you cry—you make your face go all blotchy.'

'But what if you don't like living at Deighton? Will you come back?' Penelope asked hopefully, having stopped crying, but her lips still quivered and tears hung on her lashes like huge dew drops.

Jane was aware of Edward's watchful eyes, but she didn't look at him. 'Yes—of course—but I'm sure I shall like living there very well indeed,' she said, speaking with a conviction she was far from feeling. She lifted her eyes and glanced across the room at her betrothed, catching him unawares, and what she saw puzzled her.

There was a softness in his expression and his eyes were warm as he watched her, quite enchanted and bewitched by the delightful picture she presented sitting between the two little girls, doing her best to reassure them that all would be well. She was so very feminine, soft, womanly and beautiful, as pure and graceful as the swans that swam on the lake in the grounds of Deighton Hall, his to possess in a short time.

But she was still young and so very vulnerable, which meant he would have to be gentle with her, not to subdue the sweet wild essence of her nature which was so essentially her. Drawn compulsively towards her, he crossed the room, pausing and looking down into her eyes.

'Susan and Penelope may come to Deighton whenever they wish, is that not so, Edward?'

'Yes, of course'. He smiled. 'Any time Maria cares to bring them over they will be welcome. And now, if you don't mind, Jane, I think we should be on our way while there is still plenty of daylight left.'

Jane nodded. 'Yes, but first I must say goodbye to Tom. Please excuse me. I will not be long.'

Ignoring Edward's expression of impatience, she went in search of Tom, finding him bent at his desk. He rose when she walked in, knowing she had come to bid him farewell, but also to ask after the young man.

'Did Simon and his friend manage to get away, Tom?' she asked with a note of urgency, fearful that someone would walk in on them before he was able to tell her what it was she wanted to know.

He nodded. 'They ate and rested awhile in the church until the man I employed to act as their guide arrived to take them to their destination. They should be well away by now. Much better to get them out of the district altogether after their attempt to lead an attack on a Roundhead troop failed. It is known who they are and information has it that they are still being sought.'

Jane's heart lurched fearfully at the thought of Simon being hunted down. 'Where did they go, Tom?'

He shook his head, looking grim. 'It's best you don't know that.'

'But. . .why?' she asked, puzzled. 'Please—I must know. I have to know.'

'I cannot tell you.'

'Why? Because I am to marry Lord Talbot? Tom—do you really believe I would betray Simon's whereabouts, to see him fall into rebel hands? He was my brother's dearest friend. After losing both James and my father, I could not bear it if anything should happen to Simon also.'

Tom looked at her steadily, and it was then that Jane knew he had been talking to Maria—that she had told him not to disclose Simon's whereabouts, believing it was best that she tried to put him from her mind completely. She felt a rush of bitterness enter her heart, annoyed that Maria should have inter-fered in a matter that was entirely personal, but it soon dispersed, for she knew that Maria only had her best interests at heart, and in all truth she could not blame her.

'I see,' she said, understanding his reluctance. 'Then I can only assume that Maria has asked you to keep it from me.'

'Forgive me—but that is the reason,' Tom said, knowing her well enough after their many weeks of being confined together during the sige—and a lifetime before that—to know she would try to make contact with him, which would bring Lord Talbot's wrath down on them all should it be found out, and have them arrested and imprisoned for aiding and abetting.

'Your stepmother desires only your happiness. When you marry Lord Talbot you must give up many things from the past—however painful that may be. Ever since I taught you to ride as a child I have always been your most affectionate friend and faithful servant. But in this I must keep my silence—and I beg you to allow me to have that privilege.'

For a long moment Jane looked into the grey eyes beneath the white gristly brows which stared unflinching into hers. 'I see,' she said at length. 'Then I shall respect your silence. We have travelled a long road together, you and I, have we not? I also have enjoyed a happiness in our friendship and will do nothing to jeopardise that. I shall value and treasure it always. Goodbye, Tom.'

She turned from him, about to leave, but he halted her one last time.

'You may rest assured that your friend will be safe. There is not a man or woman loyal to the cause who would betray him or Captain Digby. They will stay in hiding until Captain Digby is recovered from his wound and is strong enough to return to the army.'

With that Jane had to be content, but if she had seen the worried expression on Tom's face as she left him, caused by his concern over Sir Simon's health—for he strongly suspected that the sudden fever which had arisen was a result of the wound in his leg having become infected—then her anxiety over his well-being would have been great indeed.

One hour later, with a crack of the driver's whip

over the backs of the four snorting black horses
Edward had had sent over from Deighton, the coach
carrying Jane and her betrothed left Bowden.

They were alone travelling in the coach, a large
leather vehicle with a domed roof. The only view to
be had of the passing countryside was to be seen out
of the door, which had a leather curtain suspended
from an iron bar, raised for the time being. Jane was
quietly, sitting across from Edward her face like a
marble mask, her eyes shuttered, her gaze never
straying from the passing scenery. It was as though
she had forgotten the still figure of Edward across
from her, only speaking when spoken to, but she was
finding the journey excessively trying to her already
overwrought nerves on being in such close proximity
with him for so long.

Although they sat apart she could feel his strength,
his warmth, the complete masculinity of him. She
was immersed in a sea of loneliness, having accepted
the imminence of her fate without further protest,
but she was gripped with a nervous, frantic feeling
which she later realised was fear of what the future
held in store for her.

Looking at Jane's stiffly upright figure, her polite-
ness was beginning to irk Edward. He was
determined to make her relax and unbend a little
before they reached Deighton—even if it meant sitting beside her and repeating the kiss he had given
her on his arrival at Bowden Manor after the siege,
the kiss he had given her to remember and which he
knew, by the softness and glowing in her eyes when

she thought he was not watching her, that she had not forgotten.

She looked enchanting with her costume of pale green spread about her, the full skirt caught back to show an embroidered petticoat underneath, the tight-fitting jacket emphasising her slender figure. Her face was like a pale cameo, her eyes hollow, the contours of her face all soft shadows and light. Nineteen she might be, a child still in some respect, yet he believed that behind her childlike exterior beat the heart of a sensual and passionate woman. He wondered what went on behind her cool expression, behind her shuttered gaze.

'Are you comfortable?' he asked.

She turned her head and looked to where he lounged indolently across from her, his dark brown eyes looking at her penetratingly from beneath heavily fringed thick black lashes. His words scarcely penetrated the mists that clouded her mind. She stared at him, knowing he had spoken but not comprehending what it was he had said.

'I asked you if you are comfortable?' he repeated.

'Yes. Perfectly, thank you,' she answered. 'I am a little tired, but pray do not concern yourself on my account.' She immediately returned her gaze to the passing scenery.

'Nevertheless, your welfare is my greatest concern. When we arrive at Deighton you will be able to rest.'

'Which I could have done equally as well at Bowden,' she retorted frostily.

Edward scowled with annoyance at her continued coldness towards him, and it was only out of consideration for her sensitivity at this time and her exhausted state that he controlled his precariously held temper.

'Come, Jane,' he said, sounding harsher than he intended. 'I will not have you addressing me like some barely acquainted stranger all the time. Seeing that you hold such a low opinion of me, I think it would not go amiss to use the time we are alone to clear the air a little between us before we arrive at Deighton.'

Jane regarded him in silence, the air tense between them, her eyes trapped by his compelling gaze.

'Well?'

'If we must. Although you can hardly blame me for being just a little apprehensive when I am about to enter the enemy camp—in a manner of speaking,' she plied sharply.

'Of course. But do not forget that my mother shares your sympathies for the King's cause—or what is left of it.'

'Then it will make living at Deighton easier for me to bear.'

'I hope so. The bond of kinship between other members of my family and myself survives the divisions that war has induced. From the very beginning we were determined that the dispute would not create a quarrel between us. Knowing we would have many to fight with, we would not fight among ourselves. Our affections for one another are unchanged. Can you not feel the same?'

'You must forgive me. It is difficult to think that way when my father was killed by Roundheads.'

'Do not forget that my own father lost his life at Edgehill.'

'I don't. But do not forget that he too was fighting on the side of the King—against the cause you so righteously uphold.'

Edward's eyes narrowed and his tone became icy. 'Of that I do not need to be reminded. It was his allegiance to the King that plunged my family into serious debt and took him into the war.' His expression was one of gravity as he leaned forward a little, resting his arms on his knees and looking at her closely. 'I admire you, Jane. Few women would have defended their home as courageously as you have done. But you must learn to be more lenient towards me. All men are sinners, are they not? Wherever my allegiance lies, do not take it upon yourself to judge me.'

'I was not aware that I did.'

'You are resentful towards me because of my support for Parliament—I understand that—and you are angry with me because I did not write. But I confess I am no hand at letter writting, so let your anger be punishment enough. But you did not write to me either,' he said quietly, his voice holding a trace of accusation.

'Forgive me—but when you took up arms against the King, I felt unable to do so. I—I believed our betrothal to be no longer binding. The war has set father against son and brother against brother— dividing almost every family in the land, I know that.'

'That may be—but let me make it perfectly clear

that there will be no division between us, Jane. Not when we are wed.'

Jane raised her chin in defiance. 'I am not your wife yet, Edward—and when we are married I shall have control over my own mind. I have no intention of becoming your obedient servant.'

Edward sat back, his expression one of faint amusement as he looked at her from beneath his half-lowered lids. 'Far be it from me to ask the impossible of you,' he laughed softly. 'But you will not always be so headstrong or so troublesome. I have my own form of persuasion that will subdue your tendency to argue.'

'By that do you mean to use force on me, my lord?'

His dark brows rose and his voice was low and seductive. 'Force? No. Far from it. I've never had to resort to force on a woman in my life. The kind of persuasion I speak of will be of the gentlest form—one you will enjoy, I promise you—and one which I am urged to show you this very minute.'

His eyes sought out and lingered on Jane's lips and she felt herself flushing as they travelled to the gentle swell of her breasts outlined beneath her jacket.

'Then I would beg you to restrain your urge, my lord. Your conduct is quite unseemly,' she retorted heatedly, taking refuge in anger as she tried to shake off the effect he was having on her emotions.

'Are you afraid of me, Jane? I have told you I am not your enemy.'

'No. I am not afraid of you, but how can I rate you in any way other than as my enemy?' she asked, realising as she said this that she was not so very much afraid of him but of herself and how she would respond if he were to cross the small divide that was between them in the carriage. 'Your own brother followed your father's lead and fights for the King, I believe,' she said, making a concerted attempt to divert his attention to other matters. 'How will you feel should you meet in battle?'

'That is unlikely. William is in Ireland at this time. Besides, after Naseby, with Parliament in possession of the Royal Standard and every infantry regiment on the field, the King's cause is in peril. There are those on both sides who hope for a settlement, but the King seems set against it.'

'Having been cut off from any news because of the siege at my home, I fear I am out of touch as to what has been happening in the country. Where is the King now?'

'After Naseby he marched into Wales. With his only field army wiped out he was—and still is—desperate to recover his losses by obtaining fresh recruits. When support failed to materialise in Wales he marched north through Derbyshire and into York-shire. But he was driven back south by Parliamentary forces gathering in the north and west. I believe he is again moving towards Wales.'

Jane already knew the King had marched into Yorkshire, for was this not the reason for Simon being in the north? If the King was marching towards the West Country again, then he would be hard pressed to join him.

'After the battle, along with the King's train of artillery, his baggage train was taken. Letters from his wife in France, and also copies of his letters to her, were seized, revealing plans to bring in outside assistance in the form of French troops—and, more damning that that, Confederate Catholic troops from Ireland—promising them favours if they agreed to fight on his side.'

'And when one considers the reaction this ever-emotive nation has on the English population at large, then it is a damaging weapon indeed for his enemies to use against him,' Jane said with a trace of bitterness, for she was deeply disappointed to learn that the King had betrayed the trust of those who supported him.

To bring over Catholic troops from Ireland to fight his own people would not be tolerated. Undoubtedly, the violent uprising in Ireland in 1641—when the atrocities committed by Catholics against the Protestants in that country had shocked the English nation into disbelief—had fuelled the hatred of Catholics and the fear of popery amongst the English.

'True. It has resulted in his loss of popularity and prestige. Scattered pockets of Royalists are giving up—many compounding with Parliament.'

'Then it grieves me to hear it,' Jane said frankly and with sadness. 'But, whatever he is guilty of, I shall never forget he is the King and that his majesty is sacrosanct. My loyalties to the Crown will always remain steadfast and worthy of sacrifice. But do you not think it shameful to have his private letters from his exiled queen opened in such a manner—for the prying eyes of strangers to read that which is entirely personal?'

'Maybe—and I too regret that, but it was necessary all the same. When those letters were opened, revealing his plans to bring outside military assist- ance on to English soil, many who had been sympathetic have turned their backs on him. His duplicity has shown him to be a man who cannot be trusted.'

Jane glanced across at him sharply as a thought suddenly occurred to her. 'You are not a Puritan, are you, Edward?'

Her suggestion caused him some amusement. His lips widened in a broad smile to reveal his strong white teeth, and his eyes danced with merriment. 'Lord, no. Neither virtues nor vices of my upbringing harmonise with the Puritan ideal. Unlike a great many of my compatriots, I am not motivated by religious zeal—although I have no liking for popery either. No doubt you will be relieved to know I still adhere to the true Protestant religion.'

'Then if the King's cause is in such peril as you say it is, it would seem that choosing to support Parliament ensures the survival of the Talbots, that your house and lands will remain intact.'

Sighing deeply, she became silent and again looked at the passing scenery unfolding outside the window, the rocking and swaying of the coach lulling her into a state of semi-inertia. 'When one looks at the beauty of Derbyshire—of the moors—it is hard to believe there is so much discord and dissension in England, that it is split by Civil War,' she murmured softly, almost to herself.

Edward smiled crookedly his eyes glowing seductively from between his half-lowered lids. 'There are many who would disagree with you. In court circles before war broke out, Derbyshire was talked of as being an inhospitable, desolate wilderness, and was acquiring the reputation of being the place to send troublesome and rebellious wives.'

Jane cast him a cold look. 'Then if that be the case, my lord, when we are man and wife you will be saved the trouble of having to send me anywhere.'

Edward grinned roguishly, the sort of grin that must have charmed half the ladies from Derbyshire to London. 'Why—does this mean you are to continue to vex me by being as difficult as you have been so far?'

'I shall continue being as difficult as I please.'

He smiled at her reply, not in the least discouraged. In fact, despite her hostility, on observing the heightened colour of her cheeks and the glow in her amber eyes, he was encouraged and well pleased with the way the journey to Deighton was progressing.

'It is clear you have been allowed to have your own way too often, Jane. When we are married, I shall continue to let you have your way in many things, but in the privacy of our bedchamber I shall have my way.'

His voice was soft and deep as he conveyed his message to Jane, whose cheeks burned bright crimson. Feeling all the power and provocation of his gaze, she looked away, quite perplexed. In fact, never had she known a man so perplexing. She felt an unexpected quiver pass through her body beneath her clothes, and also an urgent desire for him to sit beside her and hold her in the warmth of his embrace—but she knew that if he were to lay one finger on her at that moment she would be beyond all help.

Shocked by the force of her feelings, she leaned her head against the soft upholstery of the coach and closed her eyes in an attempt to banish his face from her mind, but she could not banish the essence of his warm animal magnetism that filled the inside of the coach.

She felt bemused, utterly and completely bewildered by her feelings, by her emotions, which made her so unsure of herself. What was the matter with her that she should desire the embrace of a man she was so very much against—even though that man was her betrothed?

She was not as strong as she thought she was; having once felt his arms about her, tasted the warmth of his lips on hers, and having experienced the excitement this had given her, was it so very unusual for her body to want to savour it all again? Whenever they were together he troubled her, but was that so very bad when he was to be her husband in such a short space of time?

Chapter Six

The hills around Deighton were of a wild, fierce aspect, a region oozing with antiquity where legends were many and varied. The landscape was of undulating limestone hills scored by the beautifully wooded Derwent Valley and the River Dove, of high peaks and plateaux with their crags and gritstone edges and black peat hags, of peculiar shaped stones and the dark holes of open-mouthed caves.

Along with sheep paths and rough cart tracks disappearing over the directionless moor to some remote farm, they were possessed of a complete system of trade routes, the 'packways': the long-distance tracks used by trains of packhorses for the transport of lead, wool, timber and charcoal for the smelters.

The moors were possessed of a timeless nature, in late summer through to autumn they were clad in purple heather with gently swaying cotton grass, but the burdens of winter could be relentless—this was the time when isolation reigned supreme and it became an inhospitable region, a bleak and bitter lonely wilderness.

Surrounded by a high ring of hills, magnificent Deighton Hall was built of golden yellow stone and enriched by splendid carving, which made it an impressive building. It was surrounded by walled courtyards and gardens and situated in a valley full of light and grandeur against a rich backcloth of woods and a patchwork of open fields; the grounds, spacious and green, were threaded through with a natural lake—a perfect habitat for a large colony of swans—fed by water from the crystal-clear springs high up on the moors.

The vast estate at Deighton had come into the hands of the Talbots in the fifteenth century. Since that time, they had been accumulating wealth largely through lead mining and sheep rearing, with rents from several scattered tenements. This had raised the family to a secure place and brought them virtual right to a peerage.

Lady Blanche, Edward's mother, was a woman small in stature but great in character. She was regarded with great respect and reverence and was known throughout Derbyshire for her thoughtfulness for other people. The poor and the beggars who roamed the moors were the objects of her generosity and charitable good works. She was waiting on the steps to welcome Jane to Deighton Hall.

After assisting her down from the carriage, Edward took her arm and led her towards his mother who was coming forward to greet them. It was no more than a touch but, oddly, Jane was strengthened by it as she stepped forward, about to embark on her new life at Deighton Hall.

After welcoming and embracing her eldest son affectionately, Lady Blanche drew Jane into her arms, greeting her warmly.

'My dear, dear Jane. How very good it is to see you,' she said, stepping back and looking closely at her future daughter-in-law, shocked by her appearance, thinking she looked quite unwell. 'It's been so long since last we saw you that—why—I hardly recognise you. How are you really, my dear?'

'I am well, thank you, considering the terrible events of the past weeks, Lady Blanche,' Jane replied, smiling softly at her, for there was no mistaking the genuine warmth in her voice and her eyes.

Lady Blanche was a handsome woman with dark hair, which had become liberally streaked with grey over the three years since Jane had last seen her. Her face was much older than Jane remembered; she quite rightly thought it had been brought about by the death of Lady Blanche's husband at Edgehill, which had been a terrible blow to her. To these cares was added the burden of Edward's dissension over politics, for his decision to take up arms against the King had come as a bitter disappointment to the family as a whole.

'Oh, how we have worried about you all at Bowden, when the siege and how you were courageously standing firm against the Parliament Army was brought to our notice. I wrote to Edward immediately, informing him of what was happening, for him to come at once and secure your safe release. Thank goodness he reached you in time.'

Jane stared at Edward in surprise, for until that moment she had not known how he had come to learn about the siege.

'Edward sent a letter on ahead informing us of when to expect you—and he also told us of James's death. I was deeply grieved to learn of the death of your father—but James too! Oh, my dear—I was so shocked. I have been told they fought bravely at Naseby—and that your father was wounded, which resulted in his death. He was as good and noble a friend as any I have known. May God comfort you in your great loss, my dear.'

Tucking Jane's arm affectionately into her own, she led her into the house followed closely by Edward, content to let his mother take over for the time being. Jane had not set foot in Deighton Hall for over three years, but it was just as she remembered. Swans were everywhere in the decoration, for the swan was the Talbot crest. The rooms were rich in tapestries and plasterwork, and decorated in alabaster and black Derbyshire marble from the Talbots' own quarries, carved by local craftsmen.

'This terrible war has been a great trial,' Lady Blanche went on. 'Let us pray it will be over soon. But come—I have had refreshments made ready. Ever since we received Edward's letter informing us of your arrival, Anne has been in a state of excitement. Indeed, she has talked of little else. We also have an added guest. . . Ah—here they are now.'

On entering the hall, they looked up to see a smiling Anne hurrying down the long stone stairs. With her was another young woman whom Jane recognised at once, causing her heart to plummet like a stone. A feeling of suffocation came over her, for was it not enough that she'd had to leave Bowden, without having to endure the insufferable companionship of Isabel Marchington, Edward's cousin, at Deighton Hall?

The daughter of Lady Blanche's brother—an only child who had been spoilt and indulged shamelessly by both her parents—she had frequently stayed at Deighton in the past, always during the summer months, and often accompanying Anne to Bowden, which Jane had always found extremely irritating. She had little liking for Isabel, who was envious because Jane was to marry Edward. However, there was little love lost, for Isabel had no liking for her either.

Whenever Isabel was in Edward's presence, the way she had of always following him around like a lovesick calf would annoy Jane immensely. Indeed, Jane often thought that Edward would have done her a favour had he succumbed to his cousin's charms and chosen to marry her instead.

With Anne by her side, Isabel swept towards them. Enveloped in swirling folds of blue gown, the bodice off the shoulder and cut so low as to reveal the fullness of her breasts, she was the perfect picture of loveliness. She was two years older than Jane, of medium height and with a curvaceous figure, her dark hair arranged in knots of shining ringlets on either side of her face. The elegance of her clothes made Jane feel countrified and drab in comparison. Clearly she was still the same vain, egotistical person she remembered, excitable and temperamental, and seeing her again—with three years and an oceanful of misery standing between them—made Jane realise just how much she had changed.

The hunger and terror she had lived through during those awful days of the siege—when she had conditioned her mind to think no further than how to cope with the daily sufferings of those who depended on her for their survival—had taken away what was left of her youth, of her vibrancy for life. She had emerged older, more serious, and when she looked at Isabel—beautiful, self-assured, and seemingly untouched by the unpleasantness of war—then, in a rush, a wave of bitterness rose up and threatened to overwhelm her.

Anne stepped forward to greet Jane with genuine warmth. Being the same age as Jane, her character was vivid and energetic, and she was frequently chastised by her mother for her mischievousness. She had an abundance of unruly auburn hair and soft brown eyes. They had been close friends since they were children, although after the outbreak of the war their visits to each other's homes had ceased. Isabel smiled broadly at Edward, but scarcely glanced at Jane.

'You look surprised to see me, Edward.'

'Perhaps that's because I am.'

'And Jane,' she said, as Jane moved to stand beside Edward.

For a long moment Isabel and Jane stared at one another. A wall of antipathy seemed to spring between them and resentment and jealousy began to rise in Isabel's eyes—but each knew they would have to be nice to one another whilst at Deighton.

'Hello, Isabel,' said Jane. 'How nice to see you.

Forgive me if I seem surprised. Edward did not tell me you would be at Deighton.'

'That, my dear Jane, is because it is as much a surprise to me as it is to you,' said Edward, bowing politely over his cousin's bejewelled hand, his lips scarcely brushing her white flesh. 'When did you arrive, Isabel?'

'Two days ago,' she said with just a touch of petulance, putting on an injured air and seemingly annoyed by his lack of enthusiasm over her presence at Deighton Hall. 'You did say I would be welcome any time, Edward, when you called on my mother and myself at Beestone Lodge when you were in Derby last month.'

'Of course,' he said graciously. 'Military matters have kept me so much occupied of late that it quite slipped my mind. Do forgive me.'

Jane noticed that this was said in such a way that she was sure he had not invited Isabel to Deighton. However, noticing the warmth in his eyes when he looked down at his cousin and the smile that moved across his handsome face, she thought he did not appear to be displeased to see her. Quite the opposite, in fact, and she was surprised at the rush of resentment she suddenly felt.

'I had an overwhelming desire to escape the confines of home for a while,' said Isabel. 'I would have journeyed to London, but because of the danger to travellers at this time Mother was set against it. Besides—I hear it has become such a dreary place since the theatres closed and all form of amusement was banned. I know not whether to blame your vindictive Mr Cromwell and his puritanical beliefs,

Edward, or the King for declining to accept Parliament's terms and prolonging the war—for like everyone else I long for peace.'

'I trust you are well, Isabel—and the journey to Deighton was not too fraught with difficulties,' said Jane politely, feeling the last thing everyone wanted at that moment was to become embroiled in a discussion which could only cause Lady Blanche great distress, considering Edward's position as a cavalry leader in the Parliament Army.

'No. I had quite a pleasant journey on the whole—and Beestone is not too far from Deighton. I must commiserate with you over the demise of both James and your father, Jane,' Isabel said on a more sympathetic note as she remembered her tragic loss, for she too had felt a stab of regret on learning of the death of James Marlow. He had been such a handsome man. 'What a terrible loss for you to bear.'

'Thank you, yes. It has been a distressing time for all of us at Bowden.'

'One which I hope will be eased for you here at Deighton,' said Lady Blanche kindly, beginning to lead the way up the wide stairs to the first floor, where the impressive long gallery and rooms where the family dined and received guests were situated. 'Now come along and take some refreshment before I show you to your room. You have no maid with you, I see, Jane?'

'No. Everything was in such confusion after the siege—with few servants left at Bowden, those who did remain were needed to take care of Maria and my sisters.'

'Then I shall see to it that one of my own is

appointed to you. How is Maria coping with your father's death?'

'As well as she is able. My sisters are a great consolation to her.'

'Yes, I'm sure they must be. They are all to come to Deighton for the wedding?'

Jane felt herself flushing—she had forgotten for the moment her real reason for coming to Deighton. She became aware that all eyes were turned on her, including Edward's, and that a faint smile curled on his lips.

'Yes, of course.'

'Then I shall look forward to seeing them. It will be good to have young children in the house again.'

'Lady Blanche,' said Jane suddenly, having no wish to sit and make conversation for a further half-hour before she could escape to her room. 'Would you mind terribly if I went directly to my room?'

Lady Blanche looked at her in concern. 'Of course not, my dear. No doubt you are tired after your journey.'

'Yes—I confess I am,' she replied, conscious of increasing weariness; still feeling terribly depressed at having to leave Bowden, her forbearance was beginning to wear thin. 'It has been a long day.'

She was shown to a chamber at the front of the house, which overlooked the lake and the wide expanse of moor. The walls were hung in tapestries and it was dominated by a huge four-poster bed with hangings of deep blue silk, heavily embroidered in gold and silver thread, the principal motif being the swan.

'I thought you would like this room, Jane. It's

familiar to you—the one you always liked when you came to stay because it overlooked the lake and you could watch the swans. It's such a warm room and so light. The sun is on it for most of the day. Of course you will move to a suite of rooms on the second floor when you and Edward marry.'

Sensing Jane's unhappiness, she went over to her by the window where Jane stood looking out at the view.

'I know how distressing all this is for you,' she said gently, 'but I cannot tell you how much it means to me having you here—and that you and Edward are to marry at last. He told me about the letter your father wrote before he died—how, in the event of his own and James's death, Edward was to be your guardian and his heir. I confess I thought little of it then. After all, how could any of us have known that dear James was dead?'

'I understand why my father did what he did—that it was his way of taking care of us—to protect the future of Bowden and the future security of his family. I also know he held Edward in the highest esteem, despite their divided loyalties to the country. But. . . Lady Blanche,' she said hesitantly, looking her straight in the eyes, thinking how like Edward's they were, 'I must be perfectly honest with you. I—it is only right that you should know that when Edward took up arms against the King—when he made no effort whatsoever to contact me—I considered our betrothal to be at an end. For three years I did not hear from him. No word. No letter. What was I to think?'

'Oh, my dear, if only I had known.'

'How could you? You had your husband's death to contend with—and you were away with Anne for some considerable time staying with your brother's wife at Beestone. But I was more than grateful for your letters—and Anne's. I was extremely angry and hurt that Edward should neglect me in such an abominable manner. As his future wife I deserved better.'

'Yes, you are right and I cannot blame you for being angry. But do not judge him too harshly. I know that, despite the long separation between you, you always remained the woman he intended to marry. It was never his intention to cause you any unhappiness.'

'How could I have known that when he did not write? It was only when he appeared at Bowden quite unexpectedly, and made me aware of my father's letter and his wishes, that I relented.'

'And how do you feel towards him now?'

'I—I am confused. He—he is a stranger to me. I feel that I do not know him. I am finding it very difficult coming to terms with everything that has happened—and I cannot forget that we stand on different sides in the war.'

'Yes—yes, I understand that. You see, in the beginning, when I learned he was to take up arms against the King, I felt very much the same. My husband and I raised our children to think for themselves—to be true to themselves—but when Edward told us of his intention to support Parliament—which I know was not a decision taken lightly—it hurt us deeply. He was convinced of the righteousness of Parliament and no amount of remonstrance could sway him from his committment to his conscience.

'His father and I reasoned and argued with him, for it grieved our hearts that he should be against the King. But so deeply did we love and esteem him that we had little choice but to accept his decision— to respect his views—if we wanted to remain a united family.' She looked at Jane hard. 'We may be divided by the rebellion that beset the country, Jane, but not as a family. Loyalty to each other and family tradition are paramount to all else. Can you not find it in your heart to think as we do—to revise your opinion of him?'

Lady Blanche watched the many conflicting emotions pass over Jane's face as she struggled to accept what she had said. She herself had been reared in the tradition of great ladies, who acknowledged the teachings of their parents that women were the weaker sex, accepting without question that it was a man's world—which was not unusual, considering the standards of the time.

She was an intelligent woman, though she had been a submissive wife, obedient to her husband throughout his life, and on his death had transferred these traits to her son, who was now Lord Talbot and must be treated with all due respect, despite the fact that his allegiance was to Parliament and not the King. However, there was a certain amount of constraint between her and her eldest son, but she held her peace and continued to live as she always had as the war went on, without bitter words.

Jane looked at her steadily and nodded, sighing deeply, finding peace in her promise of surrender to Lady Blanche—bitter though it was.

'I—I will take your words to heart, Lady Blanche. I promise.'

The mid-September day was sunny and mild with autumnal colours of copper and gold beginning to burnish the leaves on the trees. From where he sat in relaxed mood on the grass in the garden, his back leaning against a low stone wall and his long booted legs stretched out in front of him, Edward was content to watch Jane from beneath hooded lids as she walked along the paths with Anne and Isabel.

She had been at Deighton for three days now and he was happy to see that some of the strain, which had been present on her arrival, was beginning to disperse. He observed that her lissom figure moving along the garden paths was no longer tempered by weariness, and that she was beginning to take pleasure in her surroundings, pausing now and then to pick a flower and place it in Anne's basket, which was suspended from her arm.

In sultry mood, he thought back to when he had first seen her after the siege at Bowden, how slender and young she was, how large were her eyes and how fearful she had looked. His journey to Bowden to relieve the siege and inform her of her father's death had begun out of a sense of duty and ended in passion, for as he looked at her now, her bearing poised and dignified, he felt something mysterious and weakening moving inside him—a feeling not unwelcome—one mingled with desire.

The day was fast approaching when she would be his wife, and he knew, as he sat with the sun warm on his face, how she would look, how she would grace his bed, how warm she would be curled next to him, how her body would mould to his and how her pale silvery blond hair would flow sweetly over the pillows like a silken cloth. He also thought with growing regret how soon he would have to leave her to resume his military duties.

Little had he known, when he left the Low Countries with the intention of settling down at Deighton and assisting his father in running the estate, that the onset of the Civil War in England would be the beginning of a new chapter in his military career. He had quickly become engulfed in the violent struggle that gripped the country, which he considered must be the greatest tragedy in the history of England, begun when King Charles I had managed to squander what respect many had for the monarchy with a series of blunders.

In the beginning the King had triumphed, winning many battles, but the years had seen the rise of Oliver Cromwell, a man of power to be feared and a strong military leader. The formation of his New Model Army, which was made up of the most committed of troopers ever to don the red coat and whom he had trained himself, turning them into a formidable fighting force—its success over the Royalist forces at Naseby being proof of this—showed clearly that the tide had turned away from the King.

Edward was heartily tired of campaigning, of fighting and long marches in all weathers, of enduring great hardship when conditions were so bad he often wondered if he would survive it. Hopefully it wouldn't too long before a settlement was reached and he could think of retiring from the army and spending his time at Deighton.

When the ladies moved towards him, he rose at Anne's request that he walk a little way with them—but he quickly sensed the mood of the conversation, thinking he would have to be blind as well as deaf not to feel the tension that existed between Isabel and Jane.

'I must say how changed you look, Jane, how thin you have become,' Isabel commented.

Dressed in scarlet velvet, Isabel's beauty was quite vibrant, making Jane feel extremely colourless in comparison.

The friendly words were belied by a poisonous undertone, which Jane detected and reminded her that nothing had changed, that she was still the same Isabel who had unashamedly and unsuccessfully pursued Edward in the past. But her unkind remark, laced with spite, attracted Edward's attention and he cast Isabel a stern look of reproof. His face remained impassive, but in his eyes a spark flashed, grim and formidable.

'The responsibilities thrust upon Jane's shoulders during the siege were heavy enough to bow even the sturdiest back, Isabel,' he said harshly. 'There are few women I know who could have withstood as much. After the deprivations of the past weeks—of starvation staring her in the face day in and day out—it is hardly surprising her health has suffered.'

Jane cast him a look of gratitude, happy that he had so readily defended her, but when she looked across at Isabel she intercepted a long measuring look that carried something far stronger than contempt.

Edward paused when a footman came up to him, informing him that a messenger had arrived with a letter of some importance. After he had excused himself to the ladies they resumed their walk in silence, the moment one of awkwardness in which Isabel struggled to compose herself.

'How like Edward to speak up for you, Jane,' she said at length, speaking in a high, strained voice. 'He is always the perfect gentleman, don't you think? I used to see him often when his duties took him to London—and I have to tell you that he was fêted in all the great houses. The ladies are quite wild about him, you know.'

Jane cast her a casual glance, smiling tolerantly. 'No, I didn't. But I'm sure you're right,' she replied, refusing to be overawed by Isabel's condescending superiority. She hated to think of her as a rival— and yet how could she not? In an extremely sensitive state after her recent experiences, she felt a touch of uneasiness. She might be physically exhausted but mentally she was alert.

Isabel had gone out of her way to imply that she and Edward had seen much of each other on the times when they had both been in London. How much truth there was in this she could only guess at, for with Parliament's ban on all pleasurable activities, and Edward's military commitments, she would have thought he'd have had little time for socialising. But it did suggest they had become close.

She wasn't sure why she found the knowledge so painful, why it should affect her so much when she was not in love with Edward—except that it might be her pride that was hurt, to hear another woman speak in such familiar terms of the man she was to marry. He did not appear to resent the proprietorial manner Isabel always showed him, but then, Edward did not show his feelings, and where Isabel was concerned his manners were impeccable—apart from his sharp reproof of a moment ago, before the footman had announced the arrival of a messenger.

'Why are you not marrying at Bowden, Jane? It does seem peculiar to me that a bride should not be married from her home.'

'The people of Bowden have no liking for Parliament and feelings are raw and extremely hostile following the siege. If I were to marry Edward in Bowden Church, the rebellion would be great indeed. It is a situation we both felt we had to avoid. My family will travel to Deighton for the ceremony—which I believe is to take place before Edward returns to the army.

'I see,' said Isabel stiffly. 'But why the haste? With the deaths of both your father and James, is a respectful period of mourning not to be observed?'

'No. I did suggest it—but Edward is of the opinion that in times of war such matters can be overlooked, however rigid the rules regarding mourning are in all families in times of peace. He is keen to have it over and done with as soon as possible.'

'Then I'm sure you'll be very happy together.'

'Let us hope so for both our sakes,' Jane replied drily.

'But of course the most important thing in his life is his career—not that I've given much thought to either cause—although my family, as you know, support the King. But I firmly believe Mr Cromwell thinks highly of Edward—as does Sir Thomas Fairfax. When this hurly-burly is done he will come out of it very well, I dare say.'

'Dear me,' said Jane, looking at her in wry humour. 'You make him sound quite mercenary, Isabel.'

Isabel frowned crossly. 'Do I? That was not my intention. You misinterpret my words, Jane.'

'I'm sorry—but I don't think so. You insult Edward, Isabel,' she chided. 'I believe I know him well enough to know that in supporting Parliament he obeys his conscience rather than to gain particular ends. You make it sound as if he is merely supporting Parliament to be on the winning side for self-gain.'

'No. I merely implied he was wise in choosing to fight for Parliament, that is all.'

They continued to follow Anne who walked on ahead, through the garden, stopping from time to time to cut a late bloom and to place it in her basket.

'You've never been to London or seen much society, have you, Jane?' Isabel asked after a moment.

'No—and nor have I any desire to.'

Isabel looked at her in shocked amazement, unable to understand why anyone in their right mind had no wish to visit London. 'Have you not? Then unless you have partaken of its pleasures you have lived the life of a nun. Do you mean you have no desire to see a play at the theatre, to go riding in Hyde Park or to sail on the river?'

'Dear me, Isabel.' laughed Jane. 'If London is as exciting as you say it is, then I am extremely surprised you could bear to leave it for the dullness of Derbyshire.'

Isabel pulled a face, for she'd had little choice but to do just that. 'I told you—what with the war and everything there's little excitement there now. Having instigated a programme of moral reform, the Puritans have made London quite unbearable.' She sighed as Anne began strolling back towards them. 'It cannot be compared to the gay, lively place it used to be—and I cannot see how Edward can possibly be associated with such depressingly dull people who do not care for pleasure or enjoyment in any form.'

'You mean there really are no theatres to go to— no dancing or trips on the river to enjoy?'

'No. Although there is more tolerance given than is commonly supposed, with theatre productions continuing in private and clandestine ways. But soldiers often raid the establishments and arrest the actors.'

Falling into step beside them, Anne joined in the conversation. 'Sadly the ban is not confined to London but is in effect throughout the length and breadth of England, which was once such a merry place. We can no longer indulge in simple, innocent pleasures without being told it is a sin. Why, even the maypoles have been pulled down—those harmless structures around which people would dance to celebrate our festivals. How they can be an offence in the eyes of God eludes me.'

Jane smiled at her, linking her arm. 'You're right, Anne. Even Christmas is not the same any more. Its festivities have been suppressed and instead we are faced with a day of fasting.' She sighed deeply. 'A miserable prospect, don't you think?'

She stared at the house directly ahead of her which was soon to be her home, a feeling of melancholia creeping over her. Was this to be her life now, she wondered, with rigid rules to be adhered to? As a representative of Parliament, would Edward expect her to obey his will when they were married? Fear touched her heart, which Isabel's sharp ears detected when she next spoke.

'I wonder what Christmas will be like at Deighton Hall this year,' she murmured absently. 'There will be no waits or wassailers, no mummers acting out St George and the Dragon.'

'With Beelzebub and the Prince of Paradise as the main characters,' Anne followed on with a sigh of regret.

'I don't suppose there will be any plum pudding or wassail bowl being filled again and again with spiced ale, either, as is always the custom for the people of the neighbourhood to partake of. I suppose Edward will insist we abide by the new laws which have been imposed upon us.'

'I do believe Edward takes a more moderate view on such matters,' remarked Isabel with a malicious smile, pleased to hear Jane sound somewhat disgruntled. 'He was always one to enjoy himself as much as the next man—and I do not believe for one minute that he's changed.'

'Maybe not,' retorted Jane sharply, feeling tired and irritated by Isabel's high flaunting voice. 'But he will have to adhere to the rules like the rest of us, nevertheless.'

'Why—what's this?' murmured Isabel, her eyes narrowing with a glitter of malice. 'Do I detect a hint of regret in your tone? Perhaps marriage to Edward is not such a happy prospect after all.'

Beginning to look a little uneasy at the tone of the conversation, Anne hurriedly suggested they take a walk down to the lake. Jane readily accepted—and was thankful when Isabel haughtily declined, remarking that she was quite worn out by all the walking and would go back to her chamber to rest a while.

'Take no notice of Isabel, Jane,' smiled Anne sympathetically when they were alone. 'She's envious because you are to marry Edward and not she. After the wedding I think she will return to Beestone Lodge immediately.'

Following in Anne's wake down the narrow path to the lake, Jane couldn't help wishing Isabel wouldn't wait until after the wedding to return to her home. How much happier she would be if she returned forthwith. But musing over Edward, she found herself smiling, for she was discovering things about him that surprised her—like now, when he had spoken so quickly in her defence.

Since coming to Deighton Hall, she had also discovered he possessed a sense of humour, and there were times when he would make her laugh—which was something she hadn't done in a long time. At dinner, with promptings from Anne, he would delve into his fascinating store of news and incidents of his military experiences at home and abroad, regaling them with stories for them to comment upon and enjoy. She sighed, quite confounded by him.

Chapter Seven

Shaded by willows sweeping the water, Jane was sitting contentedly by the lake. Even as a child she had been irresistibly drawn to it by the swans, for large numbers would congregate on the wide expanse of water for breeding and the summer moult, most of them remaining throughout the year.

Quite enchanted, she watched two Mute swans, a cob and its partner, with bright orange-red bills and black knobs, glide sedately by, carrying their downy young on their backs, hardly creating a ripple on the still surface of the lake, whilst Anne, with her legs folded modestly beneath her skirts, quietly and with deep concentration on her face, plaited the strong stalks of reed grass dexterously together to form a garland. It was early evening and the sun was low in the sky, shining down onto the glassy surface of the lake.

Neither of the girls were aware of Edward's presence until he was upon them. He stood looking down, unable to tear his gaze away, thinking how pretty they looked, a perfect picture of demure elegance as they sat on the grass. The birds were singing in a sky dotted with white clouds and a dappled herd of cows grazed contentedly in the pasture across the lake.

In her cool beauty Jane was sweet, curving and graceful like the swans on the water. Lulled by the sultry warmth and the gentle lapping of the water on the bank, he sensed her passivity. Dressed all in yellow with her skirts spread about her like a giant sunflower and her unbound hair, a curious mixture of bright shades of silver and pale gold, coiling down to her waist, her face held a sensuous purity as she gazed wistfully at the water.

He was glad she hadn't elected to wear the dark-coloured dresses of mourning, and he was happy to observe that the pale, spent look was disappearing from her face, and that colour was beginning to glow in her cheeks. Only when he stopped beside her did she glance up at him, her face soft, her eyes sparkling.

Feeling her heartbeat quicken, Jane greeted him with a little smile, squinting her eyes in the sun's fading brilliance. He seemed relaxed and she watched as the gentle breeze played with his short dark locks and saw how warm his gaze was as he looked down at her. His shirt, white and loose, was open to halfway down his broad chest, tucked untidily into the waistband of his black breeches. Quickly she averted her eyes.

'You looked far away,' he said softly. 'Of what were you thinking?'

'Oh—of how beautiful the swans are,' she answered softly, falling in with his mood and watching as two more went gliding serenely by. 'They are such splendid birds, don't you think, although quite mysterious. I have been told by Anne that they usually pair for life—or until the death of their partner. Are you aware that there are those who say they carry the souls of our ancestors?'

'Yes. Which is why my own chose the swan as their emblem. One of them is reputed to have borne it on his pennon at Agincourt. Their whiteness has been associated with purity and their spirits forever elude us. They are linked with innocence and grace—but they are also remote and unattainable.'

Edward looked down at Jane, calmly meeting her gaze for a long instant, aware of her sparkling amber eyes, wide and innocent, studying him. He smiled softly. 'You look like Venus sitting by a silver pool, and yet you also remind me of a swan, graceful and innocent—not unlike a swan-maiden. Will you promise me not to change into a swan and fly away?'

'If I could do that, then I would have done so on the first day of the siege,' she replied softly, 'and I could only do so if I were immortal.'

Still looking into the dark depths of his eyes, Jane could feel herself being drawn into his mesmeric gaze. Overcome by a perplexing emotion, a rose flush spread over her milky-smooth complexion, for she was shy suddenly, and looked away, feeling a moment of panic when he sat on the grass close by her. Anne—having overheard their words and observed the intimacy that had sprung up between them—took this as a cue to leave them alone.

'Anne! You need not leave us,' Jane exclaimed with sudden panic, her eyes entreating her to stay.

But Anne laughed merrily, her eyes sparkling mischievously, ignoring her plea. 'Oh—but I think I must. A betrothed couple reunited after so long a parting must have time to be alone together before they marry.' Without another word she placed her finished garland playfully on her brother's head and skipped off in the direction of the house to find her mother.

'We are hardly a couple of star-crossed lovers,' Jane retorted sharply, feeling that the peace of a moment earlier had been broken.

Anne's words caused Edward to chuckle softly as he reached up and removed the garland from his head, stretching out and placing it on the water and watching as it floated away from the bank.

'Nevertheless, it is an appealing thought,' he murmured, stretching out on the grassy bank and turning sideways, lazily lounging on one arm and admiring her lovely profile as she continued to watch the swans glide on the calm water of the lake.

'I would say there is another star in the sky, my lord. One which outshines me in your eyes, for it would seem you are quite dazzled,' Jane remarked, still chafing over her conversation with Isabel, and the overly familiar manner she always adopted when she spoke of Edward.

To her chagrin, instead of looking guilty or abashed, Edward raised a quizzical eyebrow and smiled infuriatingly.

'By that I can only assume you are referring to Isabel. Am I correct?'

Jane found his teasing smile intolerable. 'If you like.'

Edward became thoughtful, aware of the feelings that had prompted that remark, that Isabel had little liking for Jane—and that for all her attempt at civility, Jane liked Isabel no better.

'You don't like Isabel very much, do you?'

'She has never made it easy for me to like her—and she has never gone out of her way to claim my friendship. She has made it abundantly clear to me that she wants you for herself.'

Edward smiled at her mercilessly, well pleased that Isabel's attentiveness had succeeded in rousing such emotive feelings within his betrothed.

'Is it possible that you are a little jealous of my cousin, Jane? Is that it? Isabel has always been one to make an impression, I grant you, but I would have thought that such an emotion was beyond you.'

'I am not jealous, Edward,' said Jane indignantly. 'Far from it. But nor am I stupid. If I am to be your wife I will not be made a fool of—not by Isabel or any other woman who makes sheep's eyes at you.'

'Then you may set your mind at rest. I am very fond of Isabel, but she is my cousin—and I have never thought of her as anything else.'

'But you are attracted by her.'

'No. At least not in the sense you imply.'

'Are you telling me it's all in my imagination?'

'I think you make too much of it. Certainly nothing has ever happened between Isabel and me to substantiate your accusations. She is very beautiful—and I would be lying if I said anything to the contrary. But she is of no consequence. It is you I am to marry. Not Isabel—and I am not dazzled by her. You far outshine her in my eyes,' he said softly, his gaze focusing on her mouth, a generous mouth, a mouth made to be kissed.

'Thank you,' said Jane, feeling his warmth, his masculinity and the power of his body stretched out so close to her own, finding that being so close to him was having a strange effect on her. She felt altogether too vulnerable and unsure of how to respond to him as she tried not to show surprise or emotion, but she felt a peculiar fluttering in her stomach and a sudden lightness of heart.

He was so essentially worldly that she felt stimulated in a way she never had before, and she was not surprised that women like Isabel were attracted by him, for there was a strong element of physical sexual allure that she had never encountered in any other man.

Edward laughed softly at the maidenly blush that coloured her cheeks. 'My dear Jane. Are you not aware that I am attempting to indulge in a form of seduction? I tell you that you are one of the most beautiful women I have ever seen and you merely say "thank you".'

Frowning, Jane looked into his eyes seriously. 'Please don't jest, Edward.'

He ceased to smile. 'I never jest about serious matters.'

'It—it's just that I'm not used to being seduced by anyone.'

'I am thankful to hear it,' he replied, never having doubted her innocence, for her lack of experience showed in her maidenly blushes and discomposure whenever he tried to come too close to her.

'I—I am not practised in such things,' she said

hesitantly, feeling warm and embarrassed beneath his bold look, but not unpleasantly so.

'That can easily be put right on instruction,' he said softly, meaningfully, for sheltered from inquisitive eyes by the curtain of long, trailing tendrils of the willow trees, it would take only a short time for him to turn her from a virtuous, innocent girl into a warm and passionate woman.

Jane's eyes seemed to be caught by his. They conveyed strange things to her, stirring her instincts as they had when he had kissed her on his arrival to Bowden Manor. He was smiling, but in his dark eyes a glow began, causing her to look away in confusion.

'Wh—what is a swan-maiden?' she asked suddenly, in an attempt to bring some normality back to her rapidly beating heart. 'I—I cannot say that I've ever heard the expression before.'

'What! Do you mean to tell me you've never seen the tapestry along the gallery depicting one of the stories that abound about swan-maidens?'

'No. But then, there are so many tapestries hanging at Deighton Hall that it has quite escaped my notice.'

'Then I can see I shall have to tell you. The tales which abound in legend and myths are many and varied, but the one most familiar to me is the one told to me by my Irish nurse when I was a boy,' he said, watching her face as he spoke. 'It is of an Irish legend, of a young man who was one of the fairy people, who dreamt he saw the most beautiful girl in Erin and fell in love with her. After searching for her, he came upon a group of young maidens and she was one of them. It transpired that she spent alternate years as a girl and a swan—but it was only as a swan that she could be won. The young man returned the following summer to find the group of swans, and on calling her name she came to him. After he changed himself into a swan, they flew away together and were happy ever after.'

Wrapped in the timeless lull that had fallen with the early evening, the dimming light filled with hazy grey shadows, Edward fell silent, smiling into Jane's eyes, which were wide with wonder. She looked quite enchanted, for as she listened to him a curious passivity stole over her so that she was almost deprived of identity.

'There. That is one of the legends that exists of a swan-maiden. Laugh at it if you must, for my nurse was full of such nonsensical stories.'

'That may be—but I cannot laugh at it. It's a beautiful story and I believe it implicitly.'

'There is another story of another swan-maiden, who can also change her form at will—providing she has an essential garment which is usually a feather robe. In this the young man who falls in love with her and hides the robe to ensure she will remain with him forever. They marry and live happily together, until one day she finds the robe. She cries as though her heart is broken—unable to resist her fate, she is compelled by an overwhelming urge to change back into a swan. She flies away into the unknown to join her own kind, leaving her husband brokenhearted.'

Jane looked at him a little sadly. 'How sad. I think I prefer the first story.' But then she brightened, smiling at him from under her lashes a little coyly. 'You astonish me, Edward. With your natural aptitude for telling stories I think you have missed your role in life. Any children we might have will have no need of story books with you to hand. When shall we be married?' she asked, the touching tales about the swan-maidens reminding her of her own situation, stirring her out of the fantasy world into which Edward's sonorous voice had sent her—only, unlike the young men in the stories, her betrothed was not in love with her.

'Why?' he asked, sitting up and raking his fingers through his unruly hair. 'Does your enquiry mean you are eager for the ceremony to take place?'

'Of course not,' she replied sharply. 'I am merely asking so that I can write to Maria. It will take three weeks for the banns to be read, will it not?'

'Normally that would be the practice—but I cannot wait three weeks. I should have told you that I have obtained a special licence. We are to be married on Thursday week.'

Jane's face whitened and she stared at him aghast, anger replacing her confusion of a moment before.

'Thursday week! Why—that is little more than eight days. Yes, Edward,' she protested, 'you should have told me. But why? It—it is too soon. If you are in such haste to return to your military duties, why can we not postpone the wedding until you are next at Deighton? Unless, of course, you are afraid I will fly away like the swan-maiden in the story.'

'Then I would be forced to hide your feather mantle which would change you into a swan—and in so doing prevent you from flying away,' he teased gently.

Jane flushed, hot and indignant, her eyes becoming

locked on his as she refused to let herself be mollified. 'But there's the difference. The young men in
the stories were deeply in love with their swan-
maidens—whereas you and I do not suffer from the
same affliction. So tell me, Edward. Do my wishes
count for nothing? Am I not to be consulted in anything to do with our marriage?'

Edward looked at her hard, his face becoming set
in lines of smiling challenge, making it perfectly
clear to Jane when he saw the rebellion spring to her
eyes that she understood he would not be gainsaid.

'In this, no. After the ceremony I shall have to
leave almost immediately. The visitor who came
earlier brought me a message making it abundantly
clear that it is imperative I go to Windsor, where
what remains of my old regiment is being integrated
into the New Model Army. I have to leave as soon
as possible.'

'Then for that I suppose I should be grateful,' Jane
retorted sharply.

Edward smiled, his manner infuriatingly calm and
superior.

'I said *almost* immediately. Not so soon that I
shall leave without first sampling the delights of our
marriage. That is one pleasure I shall not be deprived
of,' he said softly, his words full of meaning, for
whether she loved or hated him he had one need,
which was to bring her to life, to make her yielding
and soft, pliant to his touch, to chasten her rebellious
heart and cast away the invisible cloak of depression
that shrouded her. He would lead her into the depths
of passion, showing her what joy, what total fulfilment could be achieved by the merging of two

bodies, so that when he finally left her she would crave his return.

His words caused Jane's anger to increase. Tossing her head, she glared at him defiantly. 'No doubt you will take that which pleases you, my lord—but I can tell you it will be no pleasure for me.'

Jane's instinct told her she must go—yet Edward was set on her staying. Quickly she rose, but he caught her foot and pulled her down. She lay on the ground, momentarily stunned by the force of his assault and as mute as the swans on the lake. He lay close beside her, poised above her and blocking out the sky, the light, her surroundings, so that she felt a rush of helplessness and was aware of nothing else but his overwhelming presence. His eyes held a burning glow of intent, but deep in their depths there was something else she had never seen before, something that defied analysis and made her afraid.

'How can you know you will not find my love making pleasurable, my pet,' he said, his eyes fastened on her trembling lips, 'until you've sampled it?'

Panic seized her but she was powerless to escape. 'Please, Edward. Let me go. You would not force me?'

'If I have to,' he murmured huskily, the subtle fragrance emanating from her body firing his desire.

He held her hands above her head, his face poised above hers, close, looking deep into her eyes, his warm breath caressing her face. Lowering his head, he covered her mouth with his own, his lips insistent, parting her own and kissing her slowly, long and deep. She strained to resist the feel of his hands on her body, his mouth on hers, but her weak flesh began to respond and at last she yielded, her lips answering his in mindless rapture.

She became languid and relaxed with sensuality, uttering a moan and a sigh of pleasure. Sensations like tight buds were opened and exploded into flowers of splendour, growing stronger and sweeter. She felt the hardness of his body pressed close to her own and a melting softness flowed through her veins, evoking feelings she had never experienced before or thought herself capable of feeling.

Edward lifted his head and looked down at her with burning black eyes before his mouth claimed hers once more. There was nothing gentle about this kiss, not like the first. This time it was hard and brutal, making her realise the tender kiss had been but a ploy to what would inevitably follow if she remained.

She tried to fight, to get away, but she was filled with a like need, wanton and shameless and, closing her eyes, her treacherous woman's body curved to his. She arched her long white neck as he buried his lips, warm and soft, in the creamy hollow of her throat, trailing them down to the partly naked gentle swell of her breasts above the delicate lace collar of her gown before finding her lips once more, sending her soaring into a void of violent pleasure.

Her fear was gone and she was devoid of will. Time ceased to exist and nothing that had gone before mattered to her then. Her body glowed and throbbed with delicious need, and she was drowning in a sea of pleasure as all her dreams of love burst into shattering reality.

When Edward pulled back she was not aware of it at first, but her disappointment was real when she realised he was no longer kissing her. She opened her eyes to see him looking down at her, and he watched as she struggled to return to the conscious world. Gently he kissed her again.

'You are wanton, my Jane,' he murmured with his lips against hers. 'Wanton and unable to protect yourself from your own desires. You say you are inexperienced in matters of love—and yet your body seems to know how to respond perfectly.'

His soft words and quiet smile brought Jane quickly to her senses—angry with him as much as she was with herself for yielding to his will so readily, shamelessly, telling herself she should have known better.

'You must forgive me, Jane,' he said smoothly, rising quickly to his feet. 'I got quite carried away by your charms. I had to stop lest I forgot myself altogether and tumbled you here and now—which would never do. A week is not too long to wait until you are my wife.'

Mingled rage and horror at her own reaction brought Jane staggering to her feet, angrily brushing away his outstretched hand. Edward's seductive dark eyes met hers and she realised her body had provided the information as to its willingness to comply with his needs as he had wanted. She stood looking at him with her cheeks burning, trembling, fuming, unable to conceal her feelings, the gentle amusement he did not attempt to hide in his eyes making her blood boil.

'How dare you!' she cried in outrage. 'How dare

you! I thought you were serious when all the time you were merely amusing yourself by playing with me. I am no common trollop to be tumbled at will— unless, of course, molesting respectable females is the usual thing with you. You—you are disgusting— and if I were a man I would call you out and have you horsewhipped.'

Edward sighed a smile curving his handsome mouth. 'And there was I thinking you wanted me to make love to you.'

'Save your breath, Edward. I am not interested.'

Turning from him, no longer able to look upon his handsome face without reaching out and slapping the insolent smile from his lips, hearing him laugh softly behind her, she hurriedly ran towards the house, the memory of his burning kisses, of his hands as they had caressed her body, and all the dark and secret pleasures they had aroused in her, filling her with fresh paroxysms of anger. Not even when she reached the sanctuary of her bedchamber did the humiliating sickness leave her.

When Jane saw Edward the next morning in the hall as he was preparing to go out, her stomach tensed at the memory of what had occurred between them by the lake. As he approached her she looked into his eyes, which were startling and distracting— making her feel surprisingly weak. Helplessly con- fused, she was still trying to sort out her thoughts, for so many conflicting and unfamiliar emotions were at war within her—anger, humiliation, hurt pride—but also frightening and exciting emotions that were bewildering, weakening her resolve to remain

detached from him to the point where restraint ended
and submission to his will began.

After yesterday, when she hadn't wanted him to
stop kissing her, no longer could she maintain her
indifference towards him, or ignore the strange forces
that were at work between them, drawing them
together. Their marriage was to have been an act she
would undertake without love because her father had
asked it of her, but being in his presence so much
of late—and her weakened state brought about by
his kisses—then she was at a loss to know what to
think. How could she not love him and yet desire
him at the same time?

What had he done to her? What had happened to
her? She had fallen to sleep the previous night dreaming of his naked body making love to her, and she
remembered how she had woken with frustrated
desire and how she had thrust her face into the pillows with shame afterwards, outraged that she should
feel this way—and hating Edward for being
responsible.

He had called her wanton and shameless, and he
was right, for even now she wanted him to repeat
what he had done to her—and more. They were not
romantically attached and yet she was not so naïve
as not to recognise that his kisses of yesterday had
been given out of passion rather than duty. His
behaviour towards her had been both playful and
serious, and he seemed to delight in her confusion.
When she thought of her marriage which was to take
place a week hence, when she would once again
experience the same pleasurable sensations he had

woken inside her, then she flushed and trembled like a giddy young bride.

Edward looked at her, his eyes softening at the tantalising picture she presented in her pale green dress, the fabric shaking like a leaf in the breeze blowing in through the half-open door. The tender pink flesh of her lips looked so appealing that he was tempted to savour them as he had yesterday— a temptation he resisted, for now, when other members of the household might appear at any moment, was neither the time nor the place.

Her hair was arranged in sleek coils about her head, making her face look naked, giving it the appearance of fragility and wantonness, a striking contrast that touched him. In no way did he regret what had happened between them the previous day, but it had only succeeded in increasing his impatience for their marriage to take place, when she would no longer be free to run from him as she done then in her outrage at his tender assault on her virtue.

'I would like to speak with you, Jane—before I leave to meet with my bailiff,' he said, pulling on his leather gloves.

'Of course.' His voice was quiet, tender almost and she stood before him with her hands clasped decorously in front of her, preparing herself for what-ever he had to say. She had the courage to look directly at him, seeing his eyes were expressionless. Unconsciously she fixed her gaze on his mouth, the mouth which had succeeded in raising her to heights of such rapturous delight, and the memory made her pulse rate soar and caused her to flush guiltily, making her realise just how fragile her control was over her emotions. She wondered if he could see her tremble.

'I wish to apologise for my behaviour by the lake yesterday. It was without excuse. It was quite wrong of me to take advantage of you like I did.'

His frankness startled her. 'You—apologise?'

'Yes. I behaved badly. Am I forgiven?'

'Why—I—I—yes. Of course.'

'Being raised to behave like a lady, with decorum and restraint, you were right to be outraged. But do not deny your womanliness, Jane. However, I have to say that I was quite surprised by your passionate response,' he teased her gently.

'If you think I am too responsive, then perhaps you should find yourself a Puritan miss to marry,' Jane replied coolly.

He grimaced. 'I am no Puritan,' he said, his lips curling distastefully around the word, 'nor do I want a Puritan wife. I was delighted to find your lips hot and sweet and that you were not cold and unresponsive to my caresses—that you welcomed my touch. Your reaction pleased me greatly. You are extremely beautiful—you cannot blame me for being carried away by it.

'I have been so preoccupied with the war of late—with fighting battles and keeping the soldiers in my regiment in order—that I was quite distracted on finding myself alone with you. However, I promise to keep my ardour in control until we have said our vows in church and you are my wife—no matter how difficult that may be. So take care not to drive me to distraction, Jane, lest I forget what I do,' he murmured, his dark eyes dancing wickedly.

His voice was soft and deep, and completely irresistible. Discomfited, Jane looked away, finding it harder and harder to maintain her cool reserve when his overpowering physical presence reminded her so vividly of their close embrace and made her head spin.

A groom appeared to tell him his horse was saddled, and he left her then with a smile and a bow, which he made with such flourish that he could have been mistaken for a King's man. She watched him go, utterly bewildered, before sighing and going in search of Anne.

Jane first noticed that all was not well with Anne when she returned from Deighton the following day with her mother, after visiting the sick and needy. Lady Blanche had much on her mind and appeared not to notice that Anne was agitated and out of sorts, nor did Isabel, who had spent the morning riding about the countryside—no doubt in the hope of meeting Edward, Jane strongly suspected, who was overseeing the work at one of the mines.

'Jane,' said Anne, taking her aside when dinner was over, 'it is imperative that I speak with you at once on a matter of the utmost importance. It cannot be put off any longer,' she whispered urgently.

'Why Anne! What on earth can it be that makes you appear so agitated? Come—let us take a stroll around the garden and you can tell me what it is.'

'No, Jane. We must go somewhere more private.'

Jane looked at her with concern. She really did look worried about something. 'Then come with me to my bedchamber. No one will disturb us there.'

Not until the door was closed did Jane turn and look at Anne, who stood wringing her hands in consternation—quite distraught.

'Now—tell me what is wrong, Anne.'

'Oh, Jane. Something quite extraordinary has happened. Today when I went into Deighton with Mother I—I saw Simon—Simon Butteridge—James's friend. You do remember him, don't you?'

Jane felt her heart skip a beat and fear gripped her. She stared at Anne in growing alarm, for after leaving Bowden she had thought he would be well out of the area by now.

'Simon?' she whispered, her voice scarcely discernible. 'Of course I remember Simon. How could I possibly forget someone who was such a dear friend to us all? You have seen him?'

Anne nodded. 'Yes. He—he was in the market place dressed in such dreadful clothes that it's a wonder I recognised him. But I did, of course. I could never forget Simon, Jane—you know that.'

She spoke with so much passion that it caused Jane to look at her curiously. Her face was ashen, her brown eyes enormous—and there was no mistaking the warm, rapturous glow of excitement in their depths, which caused Jane's heart to sink with disappointment, for she well remembered how Simon had succeeded in captivating Anne's young heart—as well as her own, in those early, halcyon days before the War. She also recalled how Simon's eyes had glowed fondly when he had asked after her when they had met in the church at Bowden.

'Oh, Jane—he has been wounded in a skirmish and is very ill indeed.'

Jane frowned, remembering he had told her he had been wounded. He had tried to reassure her that it was only slight and was nothing to get alarmed about, but she remembered how she had not been entirely convinced at the time.

'He is ill?'

'Yes. Clearly his wound has become infected and needs tending urgently.'

'Was—was he alone?'

'No. He—he was with another man—who supported him. But—oh, Jane—what can be done? He is in such danger. If the local Parliamentary troop should capture him, he will be imprisoned for sure.'

Swallowing hard, Jane shook her head slowly as she tried to digest what Anne had told her, at the same time realising that Edward had dominated her mind so completely that not once in twenty-four hours had Simon entered her thoughts.

Chapter Eight

'I never stopped thinking of Simon, Jane,' said Anne in her gentle voice, her doe-like eyes fixed on her friend's. 'The feelings he stirred in me before the war were those of a child—I realise that now—for they have been heightened by absence and my dreams of him. However, the man I saw in Deighton market place today was a hundred times more thrilling than the one I remember. He is no longer an easy, bright-eyed youth, but a man—lean and bronzed by long campaigns—hardened by war. He is the same Simon—yet so very different now he is a man. He was dressed as a peasant, but he had the bearing of a prince.'

Jane stared at her, remembering that look of old on Anne's face, of quiet, thrilling expectancy, which had always gripped her when she had been in the presence of Simon Butteridge.

Pain tore through her heart on hearing Anne speak so lovingly of Simon—the man she herself had dreamed of also, dreams that had sustained her throughout the long days of the siege when she believed that her pledge to marry Edward was no longer binding. But all that had changed for, unlike Anne, she was no longer free to voice her thoughts. The despair that swamped her was as bleak as the wind that blew on top of the moor in winter, and the impact sent her tumbling down into a chasm as black and deep as Grindly Mine up the valley.

'Did Simon tell you that I saw him at Bowden after he had been involved in the skirmish—the day I left to come here?'

Anne was greatly surprised to hear this. 'Why— no. Did you, Jane?'

'Yes. He was hoping to find James or my father at home—to request their aid. Sadly he did not know of their demise and was deeply shocked to hear of it.'

Quickly she told Anne of their conversation in the church and that he did not appear to be troubled too much by his wound—unlike Captain Digby, who was obviously much weakened by his.

'Tom, my father's steward, assured me he would direct them to a safe house until Captain Digby was strong enough to travel.'

'If Captain Digby is the gentleman he is with, then he does seem to be much better—and they did say they had been sheltering somewhere for the past few days. Despite the infection of his own wound and the misery this is causing him, Simon is eager to continue on his way—to rejoin the King as soon as possible.'

'Where is Simon now, Anne?' Jane asked, knowing she must concentrate on the practicalities of the situation and not be weakened by what was in her heart.

'I—I gave him directions to go to Old Hall Farm up the valley on Grindly Moor. I know it's a long way for them to climb, but they had one horse between them so it should not be too difficult for them to reach it. I know Mr Jarvis, the farmer, is a loyal supporter of the King and has often sheltered fugitives in the past.'

Jane stared at her in surprise. 'How do you know this?'

'From Mother. Far from being passive since the outbreak of war, she has often aided fugitives—hiding them, feeding them, and ministering to their wounds before helping them on their way to the next safe house, whether it be south or west. Despite Edward's decision to oppose the King, my mother's confidence that her own opinions are the right ones has never faltered.'

Jane continued to stare at her in disbelief, feeling nothing but admiration for Lady Blanche. 'Does Edward know about this?'

'Good gracious, no. He would be furious.' She moved closer to Jane, her voice urgent and compelling when she next spoke. 'What are we to do, Jane? Simon desperately needs someone to take care of him.'

'Yes,' she agreed, 'you are right. We must go to him. Does Mr Jarvis not have a wife who will minister to him?'

'No. He is a widower and lives alone.'

'Then what about your mother, Lady Blanche? Does she know about Simon? Did she see you speaking to him?'

'No. It was market day, so I was browsing among

the stalls while she visited one of the houses when I happened to come upon him. I—I thought of telling her, but there is so much constraint between her and Edward at this time that I did not wish to make matters worse should he find out.'

'I see,' said Jane, having noticed the strained atmosphere that existed between Lady Blanche and her son, despite her assertion that they were a united family, that love and loyalty towards each other were paramount to all else. 'Then you are right. I think it best she knows nothing of this. Please God we can keep it from her—and Edward,' she whispered, knowing his rage would be great indeed if he should discover what they were doing. 'Can any of the servants be trusted, do you know?'

'That I cannot say—but Seth, the head groom, can be. He always accompanied Mother on her missions.'

'That will be useful—we cannot go up the valley alone without raising curiosity and suspicion. We will require all our ingenuity, Anne, if we are to see Simon. Although if Isabel knows we are to go riding, there is every danger of her wanting to accompany us.'

'Then let us go now,' suggested Anne eagerly. 'It is the perfect opportunity with Edward travelling to Hopton Hall to call on Sir John Gell. He is not expected to return until late tomorrow morning at the earliest—although I am at a loss to know why he should wish to associate with a man whose moral weaknesses abound, whose reputation for adulterous affairs is quite shocking considering the Puritan element of Parliament.'

Jane knew this to be true, for Sir John Gell had

been an acquaintance of Edward's for many years—
and his father's before that, although their divided
loyalties at the beginning of the War had created a
rift between them. Sir John, having secured most of
Derbyshire for Parliament during the early months
of the War, was one of the leading lights of the
Parliamentary cause in the North Midlands. However, Jane experienced a quiver of fear; she was not
unaware that he had proved extremely successful in
keeping his native county virtually free of Royalists.
It was imperative that Simon recovered his health in
order to find his way back to the King's army.

'Yes, now would be a good time. It won't be dark
for hours yet. But what about Isabel?'

'At this moment I believe she is soaking in a hot
tub—and Mother is resting.'

It was too good an opportunity to miss. 'Then let
us ask Seth to accompany us up to Grindly Moor.
The horses can be got ready whilst we change.'

Accompanied by Seth, Jane and Anne rode up the
valley to Grindly Moor. The stream which they followed, having hewn its way over the centuries into
a deep gully, tumbled over its rocky bed. Its gentle
flow was deceptive, giving no evidence now of the
turbulent spirit with which it would become possessed after the winter months, when the sun would
melt the deep drifting snows high up on the moor
and unlock the frozen earth, creating a force of water
that would go crashing and thundering down the
valley, advancing to the swollen waters of the River
Derwent.

Old Hall Farm stood on the edge of the moor, a

small isolated farm—a relatively new dwelling, built in grey stone with mullioned windows and a heavy stone-slated roof, a style of domestic building that was gradually becoming part of the personality of the Peak District.

Carrying a bag containing salves and medicines— most of them of a herbal nature made by Lady Blanche in the stillroom at Deighton Hall—the small party rode into the farm yard, hurriedly dismounting and, their arrival anticipated, were met on the door-step of the house by Mr Jarvis, an elderly, hardworking sheep farmer who had lost both his wife and two sons in the space of five years.

His wife had died of a fever and his sons had been killed fighting for the King—one at Edgehill and the other at Marston Moor. He was an ardent supporter of the King, who never turned a fellow of the same conviction from his door—not even should his own life be put in danger.

After confirming that Sir Simon and Captain Digby were sheltering inside his house, quickly Mr Jarvis showed Jane and Anne inside, leaving Seth with the horses. The dim light filtering through the grimy windows to the untidy interior caused them both to blink and adjust their eyes. Clearly it was the abode of a man who lived alone, for it was full of jumble and clutter, without the orderliness a woman brings to a home. They followed Mr Jarvis up the stairs to a small room high up in the eaves. It contained an assortment of odds and ends, leaving little room for the straw matress laid on the floor in one corner, but at least it was reasonably clean and warm.

Simon lay stretched out on the mattress with his

eyes closed. Captain Digby slumped on a stool beside him, but rose and bowed his head politely when Jane and Anne entered.

'How is he?' asked Jane, her eyes coming to rest on Simon's face, alarmed at how flushed he was with beads of perspiration standing out on his brow.

Captain Digby shrugged and, though he looked weary, it appeared he had recovered from the worst of his own wound.

'Much worse. He has a leg wound which has become infected. He feared as much when he left you at Bowden, miss, but he didn't want to say anything for fear of worrying you unnecessarily. Over the days we've been on the road it was clear it was getting much worse. He keeps slipping in and out of consciousness and, as you see, he breathes with difficulty.'

Overcome with concern, Anne brushed past Jane and sank to her knees beside the mattress, taking one of Simon's hands in her own and brushing back a stray lock of fair hair from his face. Feeling the gentle contact, Simon opened his eyes, moving them vaguely about the room, his feverish, glittering gaze passing over the worried faces of his visitors, a feeble smile moving on his lips in recognition. However, Jane saw that she was not the one who captured his attention, but Anne. A look of intense joy spread over his features when he looked at her and his fingers tightened around hers.

'Jane! Anne!' he sighed, the effort causing him to close his eyes. 'Dear Lord—I think I must have died and gone to heaven—for surely these are the faces of angels. As you see, I did not get far from Bowden,

Jane,' he breathed, 'but I'll soon be well and on my way again.'

'Of course you will, Simon,' said Anne. 'We have brought salves with which to dress your wound—and some of my mother's remedies to help bring down your fever.' She looked at Captain Digby. 'Where is he wounded, Captain Digby?'

'His leg—his left thigh, that is.'

'Then would you mind uncovering it so that it can be cleaned and dressed.'

'Aye—glad to,' and when Anne rose, stepping back to make room for him, without further ado he soon had the wound exposed—a dark sword wound full of pus, the edges grossly swollen and the flesh around it red and inflamed.

The hideous appearance disturbed them greatly, although Jane was used to such sights, having tended many wounds like it during the siege. But Anne had not so strong a stomach and turned her head away. After a long moment of trying to compose herself, and taking a deep breath, she turned and applied herself to helping Jane, knowing this was not the time to be squeamish.

Bent on the urgency of the task in hand they did what was necessary. With clean water supplied by Mr Jarvis, and working in the light of a wax candle held by Captain Digby, they cleaned the wound as best they could, smearing it with pungent-smelling ointment before dressing it with clean bandages, thankful that Simon had slipped away into unconsciousness and remained quiet throughout the operation.

After several minutes he opened his eyes, enabling Anne to pour some of her mother's powders mixed in warm water into his mouth, in the hope that it would help reduce the fever. Side by side Jane and Anne stood looking down at him. Again he closed his eyes, his face seeming to shrink into the pillow. After several more minutes his breathing seemed to become easier but his flesh was still burning.

Jane glanced out of the small window, becoming aware of darkness beginning to fall over the moor for the first time, and that they must return home before they were missed.

'Come, Anne,' she said softly. 'There is nothing more we can do for Simon tonight. See—it is almost dark outside. We must return home.'

A sudden spasm of pain tore over Anne's features and she jerked her head round to look at Jane. 'I cannot leave him, Jane.'

Jane thought she must have misheard her. 'But you must. You cannot remain here. Mr Jarvis and Captain Digby will take care of him until we are able to return. Is that not so, Captain Digby?' she asked, noticing that Mr Jarvis had left them.

'Aye. I can't speak for Mr Jarvis. He has his animals to tend—but we've been through much together, Sir Simon and I. We'll neither of us leave the other until we're back with the army.'

Jane smiled her thanks. 'There—you see, Anne. You have no need to worry. Leave some of the powders for Captain Digby to administer should Simon wake during the night.'

'But what if he doesn't wake? He might die, Jane,'

she whispered urgently. 'I must stay with him until the crisis has passed.'

'You can't,' Jane cried, shaken by Anne's words, for she knew there was much truth in what she said: there was every possibility that Simon's condition would deteriorate—that he might die.

'He is ill. He needs me. I will not be apart from him at this time. And besides,' she said, looking to where Captain Digby was slouched once more on the stool beside the bed, 'it seems to me that Captain Digby is in need of sleep himself.'

'But I cannot return to Deighton Hall alone.'

Anne was adamant. 'Yes, you can. I'll return in the morning. Take Seth back with you and have him return at first light. That way no one will know I have been anywhere other than in my room all night.'

Seeing the hard gleam of determination in her eyes, and the square, stubborn set of her chin, Jane thought how infuriatingly like her brother she looked. Knowing that her mind was set on staying with Simon, that it was useless trying to persuade her to return home, Jane sighed and turned towards the door without further protest.

Riding back down the valley in the gathering darkness to Deighton Hall without Anne, Jane was overwhelmed by such an acute sense of loss that there was no room for anything in her heart or mind but this one vast disappointment, which was becoming like a terrible pain. It made her realise that ever since she had first met Simon at Bowden Manor all those years ago she had been living in a dream, a dream which had been shattered. But how she wished she could slip back into that dream, she thought wistfully, instead of having to live in a world of reality.

Simon was gone from her forever. But, she asked herself, how could he be gone from her when he had never been hers in the first place? Had James not warned her about his character, that he had the reputation of a philanderer? She sighed, for now she knew that her brother had been right to warn her. But she could not blame Simon, for had he not brightened up her youth? His visits had been something to look forward to—and when he had gone had been something her tender young heart had cherished. His charismatic charm and debonair manner had thrilled and delighted her, for he had been so very different from the serious-minded, authoritative Lord Talbot she was to marry.

But it was over, she knew that now, for had she not seen with her own eyes how things were between him and Anne? In his weakness it was Anne his eyes had sought in the little room at Old Hall Farm. Anne, who was to remain with him throughout the night, who had held his hand, who loved him.

Blinking back a tear, she fixed her eyes on the tall chimneys of Deighton Hall in the distance, shaking herself out of her depressed state, for she was filled with apprehension about leaving Anne behind, trying to figure out how she could possibly allay suspicion that Anne was not at home from both Lady Blanche and Anne's maid, who always assisted her when it was time for bed.

*   *   *

It was dark when they rode into the stable yard. Jane left Seth, who assured her he would return for Anne at first light and bring her back to Deighton Hall. Quickly Jane went into the house, breathing a sigh of relief when she entered her room without encountering anyone, knowing that Lady Blanche would already be in bed, for more often than not she retired early.

Later she went to Anne's bedchamber in search of her maid, who was just turning down the bed for the night. Jane casually told her that Anne was in her room, that they were engaged in conversation and she would put herself to bed later, so there was no need to wait for her. If the maid thought this odd she didn't show it, quite happy to do as she was told, for it meant she would have more time to spend with her young man in Deighton.

That night Jane spent in a feverish state of apprehension as she waited for the dawn, praying that Simon's fever would abate and he would recover from his wound. She thought of Anne sitting in silent vigil, hoping she would make it back to Deighton Hall without raising anyone's suspicion that she had been out all night.

Just before dawn she fell into a fitful slumber and when she again opened her eyes it was to see the sun was well risen. Angry with herself for falling asleep at the crucial time when she should have been up to wait for Anne, she scrambled out of bed and into her clothes of the previous evening, as they were to hand, uncaring that they were her riding clothes.

Hurriedly passing a brush through her hair, she slipped out of her room.

The great house was quiet apart from the occasional stirrings of the servants in the domestic quarters. Gliding as silently as a ghost along the passageway towards Anne's bedchamber, she had to pass the top of the stairs, where she was brought to an abrupt halt when a voice rang out, shattering the silence of the great house.

'Jane! What the devil are you doing prowling about the house at this hour?'

Jane started violently, stopping in her tracks and looking down the stairs to see Edward's tall figure climbing up them, his black brows drawn together in puzzlement. Having just returned home, he had discarded his coat on entering the house and his shirt above his black breeches was open to reveal his firm, strongly muscled throat. He looked tired, as though he had been riding for half the night, and his dark hair fell untidily about his face.

His surprised arrival put Jane at a disadvantage; for a moment she was thrown into such confusion and panic that she could do nothing but stare at him in shocked amazement, watching as he came closer, her breath caught in her throat and her heart thumping so violently she was certain he must hear it. She wanted to turn and run back to her room and yet she was unable to move.

'I—I—Edward! You startled me.'

'Obviously.'

Still Jane could not move. She stood as insensate as a marble statue, clutching her hands to her sides, unaware of the enchanting picture she presented to her betrothed. Not expecting to meet anyone at such an early hour between her own and Anne's bed-chamber, in her haste she had omitted to fasten her bodice properly and her hair flowed down her back unbound.

Her face was white, her eyes enormous and bruised with mauve shadows. But she was lovely, achingly so, and at any other time Edward would have drawn her into his arms and embraced her. But he held back with a sense of unease and suspicion, his instinct telling him she was engaged on some misdeed.

His mind went back to the time when he had been at Bowden Manor, when he had met her returning from an early morning walk on the day of their departure. She had looked at him then as she did now, like a rabbit caught in the sudden glare of a poacher's bright light. He frowned, sensing all was not as it should be.

He had just come from the stables; having seen Seth rubbing down one of the horses, he had thought it odd at the time but, eager to get to his bed after a hard ride from Hopton Hall, he had put it from his mind. However, Jane was dressed for riding. Had she been riding already—and if so, where to and why at such an early hour?

The passage of time it took for him to reach her might have been an hour or a second—Jane had no way of knowing, for time seemed to stand still. But when he stopped in front of her he seemed extraordinarily tall as he looked down at her upturned face, his expression grave and inquiring.

'Why—what is this, Jane? No kiss? No warm

embrace or words of greeting? 'Tis poor welcome for your betrothed who has hastened back lest you felt deprived of his company. I have been thinking of you constantly on my journey back.'

'Then I am honoured. Although you have scarcely been gone twenty-four hours, my lord, so I think I can stand the deprivation.'

'Come. Your answer is evasive. Are you not pleased to see me?'

'Yes—of course. I—I did not expect you quite so soon, that is all. You were not expected to return until later in the day.'

He nodded slowly, staring at her with a brooding look, speaking quietly. 'That was to have been the case—but why do I have this peculiar feeling that it is probably a good thing that I have returned early? I have a feeling—an instinct, if you like—that you are up to something.'

Jane shifted uncomfortably and did not look at him. She dared not look at him, but she was vividly conscious of his close scrutiny. Panic attacked her every nerve.

'Why—I cannot think what you mean,' she said nervously. 'However, I suspect the reason for your early departure from Hopton Hall was not to hasten back to my side but because Sir John was either not at home or has been called away, for I am aware that he is a man of great importance and must have many duties.'

'You are right, he was called away. But enough about Sir John. I am more concerned with you and why I should find you wandering about the house at this hour in a state of semi-undress,' he said, his eyes flickering over her attire. For a moment there was a sudden softening of his expression when his eyes lingered on her partially exposed bosom, but then his face hardened again.

Jane flushed when she realised her bodice was partly undone, revealing the soft white fabric of her undergarments. With nimble fingers she hastily fastened the tiny buttons.

'You seem to be in the habit of rising early, Jane. Perhaps when you are my wife we will find a cure for your insomnia—one which will make you reluctant to leave your bed.'

His words were spoken quietly and with meaning, and aware of their implication Jane flushed hotly, but before she could find words to reply he continued.

'I recall another time, at Bowden Manor on the day of our departure. You rose early that day—to take a walk, I remember you saying on your arrival back at the house. But, unlike that day, there is an absence of sparkle to your eyes—or your cheeks— which, had I not known better at the time, led me to suspect you might have been keeping a tryst with an admirer.' There was no mistaking the dry, sarcastic note in his voice.

'But—but that is quite ridiculous,' Jane cried, drawing a sharp intake of breath, beginning to look confused beneath his steadfast gaze.

'Is it?' he queried, raising a quizzical eyebrow and carrying on speaking relentlessly, his tone hardening. His features were stern as he searched her face, his eyes dark, irate and penetrating, and he addressed her as he would a subordinate.

'I would say that, looking as you do, you have

had little sleep. That like myself you have been absent from your bed for most of the night. What is it this time, Jane? I see you are dressed for riding; perhaps you decided to take an early morning ride and have just returned—although if that be the case, I hope you were decently covered,' he said, referring to her state of semi-undress of a moment before. 'Would I be correct in thinking that the horse I saw Seth rubbing down on my arrival at the stables had been ridden by you? Is that it?'

His voice sounded patient and perfectly reasonable, but his eyes were like cold steel and loaded with suspicion, making Jane's heart contract and leaving her in no doubt that anger and mistrust simmered beneath the surface. An expression of guilt covered her face, for she did not like deceiving him in this manner—which came as some surprise to her and which she thought curious, because until then it had not mattered to her that she offended him or what he thought. But, strangely, it did matter now and she could not bear to think he would despise her.

What would he say if he knew she was helping Simon and that his own sister had spent the night at his bedside? No doubt his wrath would come down on them all at Deighton Hall and he would forbid Anne ever to leave the house again. She preferred not to dwell on what her own punishment would be. His face was grave, his lips pressed together, and she wondered what had happened to the man whose passion had almost overwhelmed her down by the lake, for at that moment he was a stranger to her, without any softness or affection.

He was studying her, his dark eyes narrow and

piercing, searching her features for an answer to his question while vainly she sought for a plausible excuse, hoping that nothing of her inner feelings showed in her face. He had told her he had seen Seth rubbing down one of the horses, so she could only assume that Anne had returned to the house unobserved and was now in her chamber.

She could not betray her by divulging to her brother that he was mistaken and that it had been his sister who had ridden the horse. To save any unpleasantness she thought it best to own up to it herself—giving no consideration to the consequences should she be found out to be lying. Edward's eyes compelled her to speak, and with an effort she forced a tremulous smile to her lips.

'Yes—you are right, Edward. I couldn't sleep and thought a gallop might make me feel better.'

'And did it?'

'Yes. I—it was quite invigorating up on the moors.'

She spoke with a curious little appeal in her voice, trying to deceive him, and she might have succeeded had she not been standing so close that he could see the truth mirrored in her eyes as she turned her head half-away. He reached out, placing his fingers firmly on her cheek and forcing her to look at him again, forcing her to look at the hard lines of his face, his set jaw, and she felt sick, horribly sick suddenly, that he sensed her lie and knew exactly what she was guilty of.

A thought that Jane might have seen Simon Butteridge crawled into Edward's mind, as it had on that previous occasion, and he was angered by it—

not so much by the fact that she might have assisted him in his escape, but that he had found a way into her heart over the years he had been absent. He did not particularly care one way or the other what happened to Simon Butteridge, but it did matter to him that Jane might have become enamoured of him and was playing him for a fool.

Not wishing to accuse her of anything merely on suspicion that would widen the rift between them, the rift he thought was beginning to close, he decided it was prudent to put an end to the conversation. But he would be more watchful of her movements in the future.

'Have a care. Do not oppose me, Jane—and don't ever lie to me. I can stand most things, but I cannot stand lies. I much prefer silence. You will do well to remember that if there is to be harmony between us in our marriage. There must be trust between us. Return to your chamber—although I cannot imagine why you should be visiting Anne or my mother at this hour of the morning, for neither of them are known to rise early.' His eyes narrowed suddenly and he smiled lazily, gently mocking her. 'Unless you were looking for me—assuming I had returned from Hopton Hall, of course.'

'You assume too much,' said Jane with a flash of anger.

'Do I? I read hostility and dislike in your eyes, Jane, which, I admit, I find bewildering at times, for it is often confused by murmurings and blushes which lead me to suspect that beneath it all you are not averse to me—or my attentions, despite your boldness—and assumed indifference to have me believe otherwise, which, I believe, is a front to conceal your meek and pliable heart.'

'Then let me assure you there is nothing meek or pliable about me or my heart,' retorted Jane heatedly, trying not to look at him, to meet those penetrating eyes, half-afraid that she might soften in her anger, already too well aware of the beguiling quality of his smile.

With a smile twisting his lips, his hand came up to caress her cheek and touch her tumbled hair, and she trembled, for there was a clouding of desire in his eyes she was beginning to recognise, which made her heart beat wildly and a softness, a glowing, to radiate her body and stir the desire he was capable of arousing in her.

'Excuse me,' she said quickly. 'I—I must go back to my room.' Quickly she stepped back from him and, shaken, turned and hastened back along the passageway to her own room, lest she lingered a moment too long and he had a mind to repeat what had happened between them down by the lake. What he said was true, for where he was concerned she was all confusion.

When she reached the sanctuary of her chamber it was not the previous night's events which disturbed her and dominated her thoughts, or Anne's reckless decision to remain at Old Hall Farm with Simon, but her own strange thoughts and feelings for Edward that were beginning to consume her.

As she gazed wistfully down towards the lake where the swans were preening their white plumage, and other birds were swirling and crying above the water's glassy surface, she found her thoughts carry-

ing her away. What did the strange feeling mean that
came over her whenever he came near her? Why did
her body tremble so and why, at times, was it so
very hard to meet his eyes?

She found it absurd, incredible, almost, that she
wanted to be near him, to feel him close—and for
him to hold her as he had by the lake. What could
it mean, this chaos and disruption he had brought to
her heart?

Chapter Nine

A dark scowl creased Edward's face when he turned to make his way to his own bedchamber. Had Jane deliberately lied to him? he asked himself. Speculation about her activities and what her relationship was with Simon Butteridge would continue to plague him until it had been explained. But perhaps his fears and suspicions were groundless, that he was wrong to doubt her, and that she spoke truthfully when she told him she could not sleep and rose early most mornings. And yet the feeling of unease continued to gnaw at him, for she had been going in the direction of Anne's or his mother's bedchamber, which he thought curious, because it was well known that neither of them rose early from their beds.

His mother! What was important about his mother was that she had gained much in public esteem during the many years she had lived at Deighton Hall, but he sighed wearily, for he was not unaware of her past activities in aiding Royalists.

Despite his time spent away from Derbyshire he

knew more about what went on at Deighton Hall
than she, or anyone else, gave him credit for. She
had a passionate and loyal heart and after his father's
death she remained faithful to the Royalist cause.
When he had declared for Parliament it had caused
her much sadness, but there had always been such
deep family feeling among the Talbots that—as was
not the case in many families torn apart by differing
beliefs—they refused to let it drive them apart. His
mother's actions were her own affair—and he was
thankful she conducted them with discretion and
subtlety. Naturally he had misgivings, but he loved
her too well to censure her.

But what of Jane? If she had been visiting his
mother at this early hour, then for what reason? And
how active had she been at Bowden Manor over the
years in assisting the Royalist cause? Before he had
returned he would have said it was beyond her, that
she had been little more than a child and inexperienced in such matters. But the siege had been savage
and brutal, having forced her to grow up quickly.
Was it possible that she was involved in secret acts
of heroism he knew nothing about—that the life she
had led had taught her to be more clever and devious
than he gave her credit for?

The thought angered and frustrated him. Which-
ever cause she chose to support was her own affair.
He would not ask her to choose. But he would not
have her engaging in any activity that would
endanger her life or cause him embarrassment. His
own position made it necessary for her to behave
with discretion, and if she was to become his wife

then he would see to it that she conducted herself as such and kept her opinions to herself.

For Jane, the day had started like a nightmare when Edward had come upon her on the stairs, and she could not shake off the suspicion that he knew something was amiss. It was an immense relief to her when Anne slipped into her chamber to tell her that when she left Simon he seemed a little better, and that she hoped to return some time during the day. Jane was overjoyed to learn there was every chance he would recover from his wound, but the very thought of going back to Old Hall Farm and risk being found out by Edward filled her with dread.

As it turned out neither of them managed to escape Edward's watchful eye that day, and so they had to be content with sending Seth up to Grindly Moor with food and for news of Simon's condition.

The following day Anne—in a perpetual state of anxiety and obviously quite wretched—could stand it no longer.

'I must go, Jane,' she said when they found themselves alone. 'I'll go mad if I don't go to him.'

'Be patient just a little while longer, Anne, I beg of you. Be content for now to let Seth go to Grindly Moor. By his own account Simon is getting better. He'll soon be strong enough to leave.'

'And what then?' Anne cried with sudden anguish. 'He cannot walk far. Somehow another horse will have to be found if they are to stand any chance of returning to the army.'

Jane sighed, for what she said was true. Although

where they were to procure a horse from without taking one from the Talbot stables was quite beyond her.

'Let us think of that when the time comes, and be content for now knowing that he's getting stronger with each day. Maybe Seth will be able to come up with something.'

Appeased for the time being, Anne once again settled down, awaiting the moment when she could slip up to the moor unobserved—the opportunity presenting itself later in the day when Edward was occupied in his study. Accompanied by Seth, she also managed to slip away the following afternoon, her excuse being that she was to ride into Deighton, but when she was returning home she took a tumble from her horse, badly spraining her ankle. Lady Blanche was adamant that she should rest her foot until after the wedding.

'Oh, Mother.' Anne wailed in despair. 'I simply cannot remain in the house until then. I ride side saddle and my mare is as quiet as a lamb.'

'No, Anne,' said her mother firmly. 'If she is as docile as you say, then she would not have thrown you in the first place. I know very well how tedious you find riding slowly and in no time at all you would be galloping all over the moor. You are not to mount another horse until after the wedding.'

When Anne with her foot raised upon a stool, at last found herself alone with Jane, she gave vent to a huge sigh of frustration. 'Jane, what is to be done? You must go to Simon and explain what has happened.'

'Forgive me, but I cannot, Anne. I have told you

it is dangerous for either of us to go up on to the moor. Edward already suspects something is wrong, I know it—which is why he is keeping such a watchful eye on me. If he should find out I've been riding up to the moor to visit Simon, then his anger will be terrible indeed.'

'I don't care,' Anne cried, sounding unusually selfish in her anguish. 'Oh, please, Jane—just this once,' she begged. Seeing the disapproval in Jane's eyes, she scowled and flung down the book she had been reading in a fit of childish temper. 'Oh, how I curse my wretched ankle—and my horse for throwing me,' she wailed angrily. 'I'm dreadfully afraid that now Simon's so much better he will leave without my knowing it. I've written him a letter, Jane. Please take it for me.'

'Seth can do that just as well as I, Anne.'

Seeing the petulant droop of Anne's lips, Jane was afraid she was about to burst into tears—and there was such despair in her eyes that at last she conceded, although she had no idea how she was going to get past Edward's watchful eye.

A measure of disquiet existed between Jane and Edward following their meeting on the stairs, and a few days of dubious calm passed. He was relaxed and attentive, yet Jane recognised the signs of an icy, silent inquisitor. Whenever he spoke to her his words, however ordinary and commonplace they sounded, inevitably threw her into a state of confusion. He watched her as if seeking the answer to some burning question.

Subject to his close scrutiny she began to feel

uncomfortable and alarmed and felt herself pale at the the thought of what he would do if he should discover the part she and Anne were playing in aiding Simon. No amount of lying, pretence or explanation would be able to extricate them from his wrath.

The tension was relieved when Maria, with Susan and Penelope, arrived at Deighton Hall for the wedding, which was almost upon them. Jane was overjoyed to see them again and to absorb all the news from Bowden.

Sadness stared out of Maria's eyes, the grief she felt over the death of her husband apparent, but as she accustomed herself to Deighton Hall she observed Jane with a great deal of concern.

She was happy to see there was more colour to her cheeks than there had been when she had left Bowden Manor, and the sadness her father's death had caused her seemed to have lifted a little. But she was still a long way from being the girl she had once been, when her laughter had been spontaneous and she had been so full of life and energy. Maria perceived a struggle going on within her, which she had no doubt had something to do with her meeting with Simon in Bowden Church.

'I have to say you are looking a good deal better, Jane,' she commented when they were strolling down to the lake with Susan and Penelope, who, intent on feeding the swans, excitedly ran on ahead. The air smelled of wet grass after the recent rain, and the sun's rays peeped out from behind dove grey clouds, bathing the surrounding moorland in a golden glow. 'Deighton clearly suits you.'

'Yes. Who would not like Deighton? It is very beautiful.'

'Forgive me for mentioning it, Jane, but I cannot help noticing that things do appear to be a little strained between you and Edward. I had hoped that after some time spent together you would have become closer.'

Jane stared ahead. 'Then I am sorry to disappoint you, Maria. We are as far apart as we ever were.'

'Do you think your resentment might have something to do with that—that it is apparent to him?'

'Resentment! My resentment is nothing compared to his stiff and unyielding manner. He is so stern, so unbending, that I confess there are times when I am afraid of him.'

'Afraid? Oh, come now, Jane,' admonished Maria gently. 'Of Edward or yourself? After making up you mind to dislike him, perhaps you are afraid lest you bend too much and find yourself becoming partial to him. I have given much thought to our conversation on the day you left Bowden Manor—and how affected you appeared to be by our meeting with Sir Simon Butteridge. Having had time for reflection, do you still feel the same as you did then?'

'I no longer know what I feel for Simon. Having seen him since, I have to say things are so very different.'

Maria halted in her tracks and stared at her in shocked amazement. 'Simon? You have seen him?'

'Yes. He is sheltering at a farm upon the moor. He has been ill but is recovering now, thank goodness.'

'And—and you have been seeing him?'

'Only once. Edward's watchfulness has made it

virtually impossible for me to leave the house without having to face a barrage of questions. I have to content myself with the news Anne brings me.'

'Anne?' Maria asked, beginning to look quite bemused.

'Yes. We saw him together the first time. He was suffering from a leg wound acquired in the skirmish, which had become grossly infected, and as a consequence he was extremely ill. Fearing he might die, Anne insisted on remaining with him throughout the night I returned to Deighton Hall, but the following morning I rose early, hoping Anne would have returned home. I was going to her chamber when I encountered Edward. Because I was unable to explain my actions, he clearly suspects me of hiding something from him and has not let me out of his sight since. Anne had to visit Simon without me.'

'Jane—you must stop thinking of Simon,' Maria said, falling into step beside her, clearly shocked by what Jane had told her. 'No good can come of it. And as for Anne—well—what can I say? Her foolish insistence on remaining with him all night in a farmer's house up on the moor is highly reprehensible. I shudder to think what Edward's reaction would be were he to find out.'

'I know,' Jane answered softly, for this thought worried her also. 'But you need have no worries on what my feelings are concerning Simon any more, Maria. You see—I am not the object of his affections. It is Anne who attracts him, Anne who holds that special place in his heart.'

Clearly this was all something of a surprise to Maria. 'You must excuse me if I appear a little bemused, Jane—but I was not expecting this. What are Anne's feelings for Simon?'

'She adores him,' Jane said simply, amazed that this knowledge no longer hurt her.

'I see. Then God help her should her brother find out about this,' whispered Maria, shocked by what Jane had disclosed. 'No matter how far the relationship has progressed between them, he would never consent to a union between them.'

'I fear you're right, Maria. A man of Edward's inflexible will would sooner send Anne to a convent than allow her to marry a man of Simon's sort. That is why it must be kept from him. Perhaps when Simon has left Derbyshire and returned to the army—when he is no longer accessible to Anne— then maybe it will all blow over and she will forget him.'

Maria frowned. 'If her heart is set on him, then I very much doubt it. Oh, foolish girl to let herself fall in love with him. Men as appealing as Simon Butteridge are dangerous and can destroy a young girl's reputation, bringing her nothing but anguish so that she's no longer her own person.' She cast Jane a thoughtful glance. 'But what of you, Jane? Has this affair between them hurt you very much? After all, you loved him, too.'

'I thought I did—but now I realise that what I felt for Simon was merely a young girl's infatuation. It wasn't love. Oh, Maria, I was such a fool.'

'No,' Maria laughed, linking her arm as they followed Susan and Penelope. 'That is something you'll never be. You made a mistake, that is all. We're all entitled to do that occasionally. But I'm glad you realise it, Jane. One day, when you are married to Edward, you will be able to see just how lucky you were that things turned out the way they did. I trust Edward. He will do all he can to make you happy— I do know that. Come now,' she said, smiling a little when Jane cast her a look of doubt. 'Do not tell me you continue to carry the hatred and bitterness you accumulated for him over the years in your heart. Tell me he is no longer a stranger to you.'

'No. He is no longer a stranger.'

'And despite your initial resentment and what you said earlier—when you accused him of being stiff and unyielding—tell me you have softened towards him, just a little,' she coaxed gently. 'Could the reason why the affair between Anne and Simon doesn't hurt be because you're already a little in love with Edward?'

Jane smiled a little sadly, but her cheeks became suffused with a wave of crimson. 'I confess I have softened towards him a little,' she answered softly, astonishing herself by admitting it. 'But love! No— I think not.' Maria smiled with greater understanding than Jane realised.

'There will be time enough for that when you are married. But take my advice and look to the future. Love is one of the most precious gifts—and you have so much to give each other. Don't waste it on bitterness. Do not spend too much time gazing at the sun to make you blind as to what is in your heart, Jane,' she said, having observed her abrupt change of colour. 'I do not know if you realise it, but when I see you look at your betrothed, I see you are not as averse to him as you once were.'

Knowing this to be the simple truth, Jane was silent. Thinking of Simon suddenly, her heart was empty—as if for a time it had shone and burned like the sun, and the delirium of joy it had brought her was slowly burning itself out, the fire never to be revived. The very image of his face, the mention of his name, no longer had the power to stir her heart as it had. And now, despite her efforts to drive him out, it was Edward who invaded her heart and mind; Edward who had taken over her life and was beginning to make a deep impression on her; Edward who affected her in a way Simon never had.

'Love matches are rare,' Maria went on. 'Most young ladies marry husbands of their parents' choice—but you and Edward have the added advantage of knowing one another from an early age. When the wedding is over and you have had time to get to know each other well—as only husbands and wives do,' she said, lowering her voice a tone in a conspiratorial whisper, for she considered what went on in private between a husband and wife to be of a delicate nature, and not a matter to be discussed freely, 'then I'm sure you will look at things differently.'

Knowing Maria referred to the more intimate side of marriage between a husband and wife, Jane's face flushed immediately and she looked away. Although she was unprepared for the physical side of marriage, she was not so innocent as not to know what happened and what was required of a wife. Through whisperings with friends as she had been growing up, she had been told that that side of the relationship, when a woman surrendered the privacy of her body to her husband and how it always afforded him pleasure—no matter how distasteful and shameful she might consider this to be—then she should not expect too much other than to give him that pleasure.

This confused Jane, for after experiencing Edward's kisses and his embrace, she had felt pleasure and had even found herself responding in a way that would have shocked the young ladies of her acquaintance who had told her that. But Edward already seemed to know her so well, how to set her pulses racing with his sheer animal magnetism and how to rouse her with his first touch. And yet how much more difficult it would be for her to submit to his demands when he became her husband, when there was so much acrimony between them.

Often of late she found herself half-waking in the dark, her mind adrift in some exotic dream, to feel her body soft and melting in a way it never had before, half in anguish and half in inexplicable delight—to feel her muscles tense and trembling, and a mysterious excitement in possession of her limbs. She sighed, extremely confused. There was still so much she had to learn.

Happy to spend this time with her sisters and feeling a sudden lightening of her spirits, Jane stood at the water's edge with Maria, watching Susan and Penelope taking great delight in throwing bits of bread the cook had given them to the swans. At first they held back, trepidation to move forward on their glowing young faces as the birds flocked together in excited anticipation of this unexpected treat. But growing increasingly bolder, they edged closer, laughing and squealing with delight, holding their bunched skirts in front of them with one hand to prevent them becoming wet as the birds flapped on the lake, while throwing the bread with the other. Maria laughed at their joyous faces.

'At least there will be little chance of them becoming restless at Deighton. It's good to see them so happy.'

'See!' squealed Susan, shrieking loudly and dancing back to cling for protection to her mother's skirts when one huge cob came skimming across the surface of the lake, its wings raised above its back in a spectacular display of aggression.

'Gracious—how angry and aggressive he is,' shrieked Maria. 'I do declare he resembles that surly tyrant Mr Cromwell.'

'Aye—or one of his compatriots much closer to home,' laughed Jane with almost uncontrollable mirth.

His eyes fixed on the little group as he approached along the path towards them, their shrieks piercing the air, Edward began to smile. Jane's remark and its implication that it was himself she referred to was not lost on him, but he was in no way offended. His feet stepped lightly, making no sound to warn them of his approach. They stood beneath a canopy of willows, the chequered light dancing on their happy forms. Their laughter was infectious and he was drawn towards them compulsively—especially to the woman who was very soon to be his wife. He was relieved to discover she had not lost her ability to laugh after all.

He was bewitched, utterly enchanted by this new picture of Jane as she laughed loudly with pure, ringing tones, her lovely face suffused and shining with happiness, her amber eyes wide and her soft

lips parted and lifted with laughter. Her dress was
of a soft blue silk, the skirt full with a tight waist.
It was cut low on the shoulder and finished with a
delicate muslin colour with cuffs to match. Her neck
rose white and graceful and her hair shone as though
the sun's light had become locked inside.

Until that moment he had not fully realised the
extent of the emotions she aroused in him, but seeing
her like this, so carefree and uninhibited, he knew it
was going to be no simple matter leaving her behind
when he had to go to Windsor so soon after their
wedding.

Feeling the intensity of his regard, Jane turned and
fixed him with a steadfast gaze, and as she did so
she recognised something in his expression she had
not seen before, something gentle and reverent—and
yet compelling and burning, causing her heart to
lurch. She flushed, realising he must have heard her
remark, and turned away in embarrassment. Observing the offending swan moving away from the rest
he smiled, standing beside her, almost touching her.

'You appear to be in the habit of creeping about,
Edward,' she commented, her eyes bright with laughter, her natural vitality shining through in the glowing
sparkle of her eyes.

'How else does one learn what others are saying
about oneself?'

'Usually people who listen at keyholes do not hear
anything to their credit.'

Edward directed a glance of wry humour at her.
'Nevertheless, they often hear secrets that may be of
benefit. I apologise if I intrude—and I have to say,
with regret, that you are right. Like the swan, aggres-

sion is part of my nature, as many of my friends
would very quickly inform you.'

'You do not intrude, Edward—and I, for one, will
not hear a word said against you,' Maria said with
a laugh.

He bowed his head slightly in her direction,
favouring her with one of his most charming smiles.
'Thank you. I am happy to know I have at least one
friend in the enemy camp—in a manner of speaking,
of course,' he teased. 'I am glad to see your daughters
are enjoying themselves, Maria.'

'Yes. I was telling Jane how much they love it
here at Deighton Hall. They are quite excited about
the wedding so they can visit more often when you
are married.'

'To see me or the swans?' Jane smiled.

'I must admit they are an added attraction—but
it is you they miss, Jane. You they will come to see.
You must have observed how much they adore their
big sister, Edward?'

'I have indeed—and who can blame them?' he
murmured, encapsulating Jane in the warmth of his
gaze. 'She will make a beautiful bride. It is unfortunate that I have to leave so soon after the wedding.'

'And so it is. It is a great pity. But if you are to
go to London then perhaps you should think of taking
Jane with you,' suggested Maria, ignoring the look
of horror Jane threw her way. 'I'm sure London
would be good for her. Why—she would shine in
society and no doubt charm and impress all your
illustrious friends who would appreciate her worth.'

'No, Maria,' said Jane quickly, shocked that she
should suggest such a thing. 'I shall be perfectly

content to remain here at Deighton. Edward has told
me he hopes to be home for the winter months—so
I am sure I shall be able to stand being deprived of his
company for so short a time. And you are mistaken if
you think I would shine in society. I have no desire
for such company—and nor am I quick-witted
enough for social repartee. Now, please excuse me,'
she said, picking up her skirts and turning from them.
'I promised Anne I would sit with her for a while
before dinner. You know how bored and irritable
she has become since her fall. I am sure she will be
wondering where I've got to.'

When she had left them, Maria looked up at
Edward as he watched Jane's retreating figure. She
saw how his expression had changed to one of concern and that his eyes were quiet and sombre, making
her realise how worried he was about her stepdaughter.

'I fear Jane is angry with me,' she said softly.
'Maybe I should not have suggest her going with
you to London—but I do feel it would be good for
her at this time. Deighton Hall is a wonderful place
and I know she has grown extremely fond of it. But
it is so close to Bowden—not far enough away for
her to put the unpleasant memories of the siege,
which still haunt her, from her mind.'

'I realise that. But if I were to take her with me,
she would be among strangers—and my military
duties at Windsor would keep me from her. How
does she seem to you, Maria?'

'Better, I think—more relaxed, and I'm sure with
a little more time she'll be restored to something like
her former self.'

Quickly Maria moved towards her squealing daughters, who were in danger of falling into the lake with the swans.

'Come and help them feed the swans, Edward,' she begged, laughing as she handed them more bread. 'Otherwise I fear we shall have no peace.'

To placate Anne, Jane agreed to visit Simon the next day, choosing a time when Edward was occupied with his steward in his study and Maria and Isabel were entertaining Susan and Penelope. With Seth to accompany her she took the path up to Grindly Moor, galloping hard, for she did not wish to be gone for longer than was necessary.

As she arrived at Old Hall Farm, Simon came out to meet her, the sun shining through the feathered layers of his fair hair. He walked with a slight limp, but she was relieved to find him much better than the last time she had seen him. He smiled and held out his hands, grasping her own, his eyes clear and shining down into hers—but it was plain he had been waiting for Anne to come to him and was unable to hide his look of disappointment on seeing that Jane came alone. But it was gone almost as soon as it had appeared.

Quickly he drew her inside the cottage, away from prying eyes. Jane found his hands so warm and gentle—not firm and strong like Edward's. She thought it odd that they did not excite her and could not believe how she had once hungered for his touch, how it had once filled her with honey-sweet delight. His eyes were as engaging as they had always been—pale and blue, not dark and sardonic like heart, when once his very nearness would have set her all a-tremble.

Now there was only quiet friendliness. Simon was part of her past that was full of beautiful, aching memories, and there had never been anything between them but happiness. Acknowledging Captain Digby who was reclining beside the hearth, she smiled up at Simon.

'I'm sorry to disappoint you, Simon. I know you were expecting Anne.'

'You know how happy I always am to see you, Jane. But is something amiss?' he asked in his anxiety. 'Is Anne unwell?'

'Anne is very well. Do not be concerned, Simon. It is just that she took a tumble from her horse, suffering nothing more serious than a sprained ankle,' she said quickly when alarm sprang to his eyes. 'Lady Blanche forbids her to leave the house until after the wedding. But here,' she said, producing Anne's letter from her pocket and handing it to him, 'she has written you a letter explaining everything.'

Simon's shoulders seemed to droop as he took the letter and his expression became one of sadness. 'Then it seems I shall be denied the pleasure of bidding her farewell.'

'Why? What do you mean? Are you leaving?'

'We must now that I'm sufficiently recovered to do so. The longer we remain the more we endanger you—and Mr Jarvis. We must find our way back to the army—to the King—and help salvage what is left of the cause. I fear since Naseby his strength has been badly depleted and he will be in need of every man he can get.'

'So—it is so bad?'

He nodded. 'It would seem Cromwell can do no wrong. His Ironsides sweep away all who impede them. In these latter days the Royalists have been overwhelmed. England is now ruled by Cromwell— backed by other Parliament Generals. Sympathy and loyalty towards the King is waning.'

'But it can be rekindled, Simon. The King will rally people back to his side. You have to believe that.'

He shook his head dolefully. 'I wish I could. I wish I had your faith.'

'But what will you do?'

'Fight—to the finish, if need be, and if I am to escape then I shall go into exile abroad—as many other Royalists have done already—and prepare to fight another day.' He smiled a little ruefully. 'For- give me, Jane, for talking like this. You mustn't come again. Should Lord Talbot discover you have been coming here, it will make things extremely difficult for you. His displeasure will be great indeed. He would not take kindly to you helping a Royalist soldier.'

'A Royalist soldier who is also my friend,' she said with a sudden spurt of rebellion. 'And after all, isn't that what I am—a Royalist? My own father died fighting for the King's cause—as did Edward's father.'

'That I know—but when you are married you will be answerable to your husband.' He frowned down at her as a thought suddenly occurred to him. 'You do not dislike Lord Talbot, do you, Jane? If so, it is a sorry beginning to a marriage.'

'No. I do not dislike him, Simon. It is his allegiance to Parliament, to Cromwell, I hate.'

'Whatever his reasons for adhering to Parliament, it is clear to me he is deeply and sincerely committed to it. He believes he works for the good of the realm.'

'And I say that if he works towards an England to be ruled by Cromwell then it is far better for the realm not to be saved. I must do all I can to help you, Simon. James would never forgive me if I didn't. And besides, you must have another horse if you are to make it back to the army.'

'Leave that for me to worry about. I'm sure I shall acquire one from somewhere.'

'And Anne? What shall I tell Anne? She worships you, Simon. And you—you love her, don't you?'

Pain filled his eyes when he thought of Anne. 'Yes. Anne is the gentlest of all my dreams. Perhaps if the war had not come—making me choose between the King and Parliament—or perhaps if Lord Talbot and myself had chosen to fight for the same cause, then maybe there would have been a chance for us. As it is, there can never be any future for Anne and I together. Her brother would never consent to a union between us.'

Jane knew this to be the truth but would not admit it, for she had no wish to cause him unnecessary pain when he was on the point of leaving.

'Perhaps when the war is over everything will be different, Simon. Edward is not as he always seems—and he is marrying me, don't forget. And am I not the King's most loyal patriot?' she smiled.

Chapter Ten

It was after Jane had left Deighton Hall for her ride that Isabel, finding the constant chattering of the two small girls extremely irritating, began to regret not going with her—although, when she thought of it, Jane had given her little time to make up her mind and had left the house with undue haste. Intending to catch up with her, she excused herself to Maria and hurriedly went to change into her riding clothes, only to discover when she reached the stables that Jane had already left with Seth.

Taking the same route, she rode in pursuit, becoming curious when she saw them ahead of her riding up towards Grindly Moor, for Jane was riding her horse hard, as it there was a purpose to her ride, rather than the quiet canter into Deighton she had talked of.

Having a faint suspicion that Jane might be up to something, Isabel rode at a discreet distance, watching when they stopped at Old Hall Farm and Jane went inside. Isabel hovered expectantly in the shadow of some rocks until after a time Jane emerged to join Seth, who was waiting patiently with the horses. Curious, her eyes took in Jane's companion, not recognising him at first, not until he turned and she looked upon his face fully for the first time, recognising his handsome features and fair curling hair, even though it was many months since she had last seen him.

The impact of the implication of Jane's furtive meeting with Sir Simon Butteridge up on the moor was like a sudden surge of triumph to Isabel. Unable to believe her good fortune that she had stumbled upon something quite unexpected, with a malicious glitter to her eyes, and looking like a cat set to spring, she rode back to Deighton Hall in jubilant mood.

Riding down the valley from Grindly Moor with a hastily written letter from Simon for her to give to Anne secure in her pocket, Jane thought she saw a rider ahead of her, but being preoccupied about her meeting with Simon—and with racking her brains as to where another horse could be acquired without resorting to taking one from the Talbot stables—she thought nothing of it then. It was not until she was seated at the dinner table at the appointed hour with everyone else that she remembered the rider with disastrous effects.

'Did you enjoy your ride, Jane?' asked Isabel, looking strikingly lovely, her eyes candid and alert as they surveyed Jane from across the table. 'I changed my mind about going with you, but seeing you and Seth already riding up the valley towards Grindly Moor, unfortunately you were too far ahead for me to catch up with you. I had to content myself with riding into Deighton instead—which,' she said with feigned puzzlement, 'come to think of it, you told me was to be your destination.'

Edward looked at Jane sharply, alert, suddenly, and puzzled as to why she hadn't mentioned her ride on the moor when he'd spoken to her earlier.

Summoning all her self-control, Jane favoured Isabel with a sweet smile. 'Then it's a pity you didn't come, Isabel. I did intend riding into Deighton, but changed my mind at the last minute. I couldn't resist riding up the valley to the moors. They're lovely at this time of the year—when the heather is at its best. There's no finer place.'

'Well—perhaps next time,' smiled Isabel. 'By the way,' she said after a moment's thought, paying great attention to cutting her meat, as if the question she was about to broach was only a polite enquiry. 'I've been meaning to ask you, Jane. Whatever happened to that young man who used to visit Bowden Manor before the war? Sir Simon Butteridge, I believe his name was. He was rather handsome, as I recall— and a close friend of James's.'

Jane's heart almost ceased to beat as she stared at her, seized by a feeling of panic, for that was the moment when she realised it had been Isabel she had seen riding away from Old Hall Farm—and that she must have seen Simon, otherwise the question would not have been asked.

Was her enquiry deliberate, she wondered, asked with malicious intent, and if so, what did she hope to achieve by it? Was she out to incite Edward against her? Moved by fear, suspicion, self-defence, her instinct for danger came to the fore. Her expression showed nothing of her inner turmoil when she replied, knowing she had little choice but to lie, which, having been raised to always tell the truth no matter what, was not something that came easily to her.

'Simon! I—I really have no idea. Why do you ask?'

Isabel shrugged, as though it was of little matter, but Jane suspected differently and she cast Anne a look that told her to act normally, not to give anything away.

Isabel shrugged casually. 'Oh—no reason. I merely wondered if you had seen him of late, that was all.'

'Considering I have been besieged inside Bowden Manor for quite some time—and that Simon is with the King—wherever that may be—how could I possibly have seen him?'

Jane knew Edward was watching her. Not a muscle flickered or moved in his handsome face, and when Isabel had mentioned Simon his expression had registered nothing more than a mild surprise. But he watched her with such a hard intensity, searching for the faintest sign that would tell him what he wanted to know.

'You remember him, don't you, Edward?' Isabel persisted, determined not to let the matter rest.

'Yes. We met on several occasions. He's the son, of Lord Butteridge of Oxfordshire—who raised a troop of horse for the King back in forty-two.'

'And what was your opinion of him? Was he to your liking?'

He shrugged. 'His reputation as a soldier cannot

be faulted. He is impulsive and courageous—easily recognised on the battlefield by his flowing fair hair. I remember James thought highly of him and valued his friendship. But as for myself, I did not know him well enough to form an opinion of him one way or the other.'

'Oh, come now, Edward. He must have made some kind of impression on you. On the times when I have seen him at some occasion or other in London before the war, I well recall he had a reputation for high living and colourful, fancy clothes and large feathered hats. He led a charmed life and was incapable of restraining his excited enthusiasms. He won many a lady with his charm and manner.'

'He has a reputation for gallantry, I grant you, but it cannot be merited off the battlefield. My first impressions of Sir Simon were not favourable. He did not recommend himself to me in the slightest. It is well known he has the ability to make friends easily—but whether he has the equal capabilities of keeping them I very much doubt.'

'Of course he does, Edward,' said Jane, stung to indignation and rising quickly to Simon's defence, very much aware of the hurt Anne must be feeling by her brother's harsh attack directed against the man she loved. 'Your remarks are extremely ungenerous. Simon was a good friend of James's—as he became to my whole family. By your own account you admit you do not know him well, so how can you pass such unfair judgement as to his character?'

Edward looked at her hard, both angered and disappointed by her readiness to defend Simon. 'Yes— maybe you're right, Jane. Perhaps my remarks were over-critical—but I have found nothing satisfactory in his character. However, I will vouch for James's sound judgement in choosing many things—including his friends—so he must have seen some good in Sir Simon. Allow me to satisfy your curiosity as to what became of him, Isabel,' he said, glancing at her briefly before again locking his eyes on Jane's. The look he directed at her left her in no doubt that he knew she had been lying when she said she hadn't seen Simon more recently than she wanted anyone to know about.

'By all accounts he was injured in a large and brutal skirmish when the King rode north not so very long ago. He escaped and, I believe, is still a fugitive somewhere in the area.'

Isabel's eyes opened wide in feigned surprise. 'Really? And is he being searched for?'

'I believe so.'

Isabel allowed her gaze to flicker to Jane, who looked as though she had been struck dumb—and Edward's expression as he glared at his betrothed was like a marble mask. Looking down at her plate she smiled to herself, well satisfied that her enquiry about Simon Butteridge had had the desired effect.

Jane felt herself growing colder by the second. Her eyes clashed with Edward's across the table and he saw fear in them as well as guilt. That was the moment when he knew beyond all doubt that she had seen Simon Butteridge; that she knew all about the part he had played in the skirmish and about his injury; and that on the morning of their departure from Bowden Manor—when she had entered the house with a mournful smile on her lips, with her cheeks flushed and her eyes aglow——she had just left the side of the man she was in love with.

This knowledge filled Edward's heart with a cold and impotent black rage, jealousy and resentment causing his eyes to convey to her the sheer magnitude of his anger. Jane's heart contracted painfully, for the realisation that he knew what she was guilty of made her body tremble. Fear crept over her, making her more afraid than she had ever been in her life—— and she dreaded the moment when she would find herself alone with him.

The moment was one of extreme awkwardness, the tension in the air felt by them all. Jane was aware of everyone's eyes on her——both Anne's and Maria's filled with apprehension, for they were both aware that she had been lying when she had coolly denied knowing anything about Simon's whereabouts, and Edward's thunderous expression told them that he was not ignorant of this fact either.

But Lady Blanche, sensing something disagreeable might be about to develop from the discussion concerning Sir Simon Butteridge——her only knowledge of this young man being his name——wishing to avoid any unpleasantness, relieved the situation by beginning to discuss the wedding, which was to take place the following day.

As Jane feared, soon after the meal had ended she was summoned to Edward's study. A distraught-looking Anne, hobbling painfully on her injured foot, met her just emerging from her bedchamber, determined not to let her face her brother's wrath alone——

especially when, as she saw it, Jane was not the one to blame.

'I must see Edward and explain. He must be made aware of the truth of the matter.'

'No, Anne. Edward would not see it in the same light as you and I.'

'But I must. I cannot allow you to carry all the blame. I must tell him you went to see Simon on my account.'

'You mustn't. Don't you see? If Edward discovers how you have secretly been seeing Simon—and if he has so much as an inkling of a suspicion as to how you feel for one another—his anger will be severe indeed and the situation made a hundred times worse.'

'Surely not.'

'Yes. As things stand at the moment, he merely believes I have been aiding him in some way. Unbeknown to me at the time, Isabel followed me up to the moor today and must have seen me with Simon. I thought I saw a horse and rider ahead of me when I left him, but thought little of it then. It must have been Isabel. After her enquiry into his whereabouts and discussion about his character, then I strongly suspect it will not be long before Edward puts two and two together and sends out a search party of his own.'

Anne gasped in horror. 'Oh, Jane! What is to be done? We cannot allow Simon to be caught and imprisoned.'

'Then while I speak to Edward, go to the stables and inform Seth what has transpired—although, should Edward discover the extent of his involvement in this, his position here as head groom could be threatened.'

'No. He would never dismiss Seth. He is aware of his Royalist sympathies, which are shared by most of the servants here at Deighton Hall. Besides, Mother would never allow Seth to go. He has been with us for a long time. My father thought very highly of him.'

'Then I am thankful to hear it. I would hate to think I was to be the cause of his dismissal. I know your ankle still pains you, Anne, but you must try and reach him. The situation has become quite desperate. Tell him to go to the farm and warn Simon and Captain Digby to be on their guard. With any luck they will be off the moor before the local soldiers can be informed and a search is launched.'

Anne didn't need to be told of the urgency of the situation. Her ankle was indeed painful, but she would happily walk barefoot over hot coals without complaint to save her beloved Simon from capture.

Jane entered Edward's study with a vague feeling of anxiety, trying to prepare herself for the storm she knew was coming. He stood behind his desk, looking at her, his lips drawn tight and his dark eyes as hard and cold as his expression. She had almost forgotten how tall and broad he was, and how frightening in his strength. Her heart quailed as she crossed towards him, trying to appear calm, for above all she must not seem ill at ease. But how she wished the interview was over and done with.

'Well? What have you to say for yourself?' he asked harshly when she was close. 'You know why you are here, so I think you have had enough time for

your fertile imagination to invent an explanation—
calculated to try to appease my anger, no doubt.'

'You, my lord, seem very quick to suspect
the worst.'

'And you, madam, to deceive. You already knew
Simon Butteridge was a fugitive before you left
Bowden, didn't you?'

She nodded, the quiet anger in his voice having
an unnerving, weakening effect on her. 'Yes.'

'And yet you did not see fit to tell me.'

'I—I had no reason to tell you. If I had, then no
doubt you would have sought him out and ordered
him to be imprisoned.'

'What a poor opinion you must have of me,' he
scorned coldly. 'Contrary to what you might think
of me, I am not in the habit of hunting down Royalists—especially when one of them happens to have
been as close a friend to James as I was myself.
Besides this affair between us is not about which
side we happen to find ourselves fighting on. How
long have you known about the skirmish—and
Simon's part in it, Edward?'

'Captain Dugdale made me aware of it when I
arrived at Bowden.'

'Then why did you not inform me? He was highly
esteemed by all my family. Did you not think I had
a right to know? Why did you conceal it from me?
For what reason?'

'Out of consideration for you—fool that I was.
When I saw you at Bowden after the siege—knowing
how much you had suffered, and myself being the
bearer of the sad news of your father's death—I
considered it to be in your best interests to do so. I

now realise that I should have told you and cautioned you against seeing him—should he try and contact you.'

Jane stared at him. 'Caution me? But—but why?'

'Because I wished to avoid what has happened. I know not where you have been meeting, nor do I wish to know. But I will not be taken for a fool and nor will I be cuckolded before I am even wed. Do you admit that you have been seeing him?'

Swallowing hard, she nodded, knowing it was useless trying to deny it. 'Yes.'

'How often?' he demanded harshly. 'Once? Twice? Every day since he made his presence known to you? Come—tell me.'

'Apart from the time I saw him at Bowden—twice. That is all.'

'Twice! So you say. So you would have me believe.' Turning from her, he slowly walked around his desk to stand before her, looking down at her, the darkness of her eyes accentuated by the almost transparent whiteness of her face. His eyes were hard and implacable as they became locked on hers. 'You will not see him again. Is that understood? I forbid it.'

Edward's anger and his attack restored Jane's courage at a stroke, for was she not a fighter? Had she not endured worse than this during the siege? She stared at him defiantly, her fists clenched by her sides.

'You forbid it!' she flared. 'I shall see whomsoever I please. Do you think you can dictate my every single thought and act of my life—or choose my friends? I am not one of your subordinates and nor am I under any obligation to explain myself to you or anyone.'

As he towered over her, Edward's nostrils were pinched, his face taut and his eyes blazing with sudden rage. His composure—or what was left of it—finally broke, and his hands shot out and gripped her shoulders hard. When at last he spoke, his tone was merciless and cutting.

'Yes, you are. In your stubborn determination you may succeed in getting your own way with others—but that is about to end. When you are my wife, madam—in less than twenty-four hours, let me remind you—you will not forget that I am your husband and you will accord me that respect. You will acknowledge me as such and render full obedience to me. I cannot govern your freedom of thought, nor would I wish to, but I will not be played false. Nor will I have you defying me in such spectacular fashion. How long did you think you could keep this from me—that you were sneaking out behind my back to meet Simon Butteridge—up on the moor, it would seem? How long, Jane?'

'For as long as I had to,' she cried, continuing to glare at him with defiance.

'Why? Because you both love and serve the same cause? Because you saw me as a threat? As the enemy? Answer me this. When I arrived at Bowden, you told me you considered our betrothal to be no longer binding. Could that be because your relationship with him had developed into something stronger over the years—that there is affection between the two of you? Your furtive behaviour of late leads me to suspect that what is between you is more than mere friendship.'

'You know the circumstances of my relationship with Simon. He was James's friend and a frequent visitor to Bowden Manor prior to the war. There is nothing more to tell you. You know the rest.'

'Indeed I do. But what concerns me is the extent of your relationship with this man. Do you deny you met him on the morning of our departure from Bowden? The morning you lied to me—hoping I would believe you when you told me you had been walking.'

'No, I do not deny it. I met him quite by chance in the church. Before that I had no knowledge of the skirmish or that he was even in Derbyshire. I swear it.'

Edward relinquished his painful hold on her shoulders and she stepped back, her hand creeping up to her throat, her shoulders throbbing from his fierce grip. She bent her head, unable to meet his frightening, accusing eyes boring into hers relentlessly, shaking her head slowly, feeling a pain like she had never felt before in her heart.

'There is nothing between us. There never has been. He is a friend—a good friend, that is all. Your accusations are unfounded and unjust.'

'Are they? Can you be sure of that?'

'Yes,' she answered, truth in what she said. And yet she knew that if he had asked her this question just a short while ago she would have found it difficult to deny. Then, in her naïvety and innocence, she had allowed Simon to occupy her every waking moment because she believed she loved him above all else.

'Then dare you look me in the eye and tell me you have never felt anything for him other than friendship? When I look at you—at the uncertainty in your eyes—I see you would have had it differently.'

She was unaware that it did so, but thinking of Simon had brought a change to her face. There was a softening to her features and her eyes, and when she raised them to meet Edward's renewed rage surged through him and he cursed with fierce impatience. He was consumed with bitterness; he now realised he loved her unalterably, that he would always love her, and it was ironic that after meeting her for the first time after three years and falling for her charms, he had thought to woo her as he had never done in the past, to initiate her into the delights of love, and to hope she would come to love him in return.

Bitterness increased his anger and, unable to stop himself, he reached out and scooped her roughly into his arms.

'Damn you,' he hissed in an almost inaudible voice. 'Damn you and Simon Butteridge to hell. By God, lady, I swear that when you become my wife and share my bed you will think of him no longer. There will be no more secrets between us—and I shall never be satisfied until you surrender yourself to me completely and absolutely. I shall crush your skull with my bare hands if necessary to rid him from your mind.'

As he drew her closer and his head bowed to her face she tried to resist, writhing against him and beating her hands against his hard chest, striving to be free of his grip, knowing he was a man who must conquer, who must win whatever the odds against him. But her struggles were like the feeble wings of a caged bird flapping to be free of its iron cage, for his arms held her like a vice.

'Let me go,' she implored. 'Please—Edward— let me go.'

The eyes that looked down into her's were pitiless. 'You cannot dismiss me so lightly, Jane. I want you too much to let you go now.'

She felt his hot breath on her flesh and experienced the same rush of helplessness as before when he held her, the same yielding softness—and the image of Simon which had fleetingly occupied her mind was gone in a blur of savagery and passion as Edward's mouth ground down on to hers, silencing her protests, his lips possessive and demanding, holding her utterly captive. He kissed her like a starving man, hard and with a passion almost beyond his control in his angry determination to obliterate Simon from her mind completely, wanting to hurt her with all the hurt that was inside him.

Jane found his kiss devastating. She ceased to struggle, and her lips, cold and unresponsive at first, did not stay that way. His hand caressed her breasts, straining beneath her dress, until she grew weak against him and moaned softly. She felt a passion that swept her along on a tidal wave of rapture and ecstacy. Suddenly, tired of fighting, somehow her arms were around his neck, her fingers fastening themselves in his thick black hair.

She returned his kisses with a fierceness that shocked her, but she ceased to care as she discovered a whole new meaning of the word desire, seeking his mouth hungrily, with an intensity that surprised them both. They clung to each other, unaware of everything but this urgent need they had for each other.

Jane's mind was wiped free of everything but Edward's lips on hers and the dark abyss into which she was sinking. She experienced a thrill such as she had never known. It was madness and passion, savage in its intensity, and so consuming that she was certain she would lose consciousness.

When he released her suddenly she staggered on finding herself free. Reaching out her hand, she gripped the edge of the desk for support. An irrepressible force had been unleashed inside Edward— all the more terrible because normally he had absolute control of all his actions. Jane was visibly shaken by the force of his assault—and shocked by the primitive intensity of emotions he had released inside her that had made her respond like some shameless wanton from the streets.

Breathing quickly, Edward looked at her, her eyes wide and filled with a confused assortment of emotions. Her full, soft lips trembled and the late-afternoon sun glowed warm and red through the window, washing over her body moulded into her dress. He was consumed by a burning desire to take her here and now, knowing he would experience a fierce pleasure when he finally made her his own. But, knowing it was madness to think like this, he turned from her abruptly, raking his fingers through his hair. Jane saw he was shaking and that sweat stuck his white shirt to his back. She turned from him.

'I—I must go,' she whispered.

Hearing the soft rustle of her dress as she made a move towards the door, he turned and regarded her seriously, the fury of his passion having gone from his face. Because of the mental torment he was being made to suffer owing to her devotion to Simon Butteridge, a moment ago he had wanted to hurt her, but now he almost regretted the impulse that had made him draw her into his arms and kiss her, for he realised that in doing so he had made it impossible for him to go to Windsor and leave her at Deighton.

This woman, who would be his wife in such a short time, was beginning to seep into his very soul. She had branded him, burned him with a fire that had made him forever her slave. Never again would he be free of her. He loved her with a fierceness that was new to him, and he knew that if that love was not returned then he would be condemned to live in hell itself.

'Wait,' he commanded.

Close to the door Jane paused, waiting to hear what he had to say.

'I intend leaving for Windsor after the ceremony tomorrow. I have changed my mind about leaving you here at Deighton Hall. You will accompany me when I leave. I think it's as well to have you near where I can keep an eye on you. You will stay with Sir George and Lady Marchington, my uncle and aunt, in London.'

His words caused renewed life to flow back into Jane's body. She turned quickly and her eyes flew to his in astonishment. 'London!' she exclaimed. 'But I have no wish to go to London.'

'That is unfortunate. You have from now until tomorrow afternoon to prepare for the journey and a few weeks' stay in the capital.'

Jane stood her ground, defiance in every line of her body, unable to believe he would force her to leave Deighton. 'No. I will not go. You cannot make me.'

'Enough,' he commanded harshly. 'I am in no mood for argument.' He moved towards her, looming over her, trying not to dwell on how tender her lips had been, how soft and red they now looked as a result of his kiss lest they unmanned him. 'Whether you wish to go or not is of no consequence. You have only yourself to blame, you know. In the face of your outrageous behaviour—and, I might add, at great inconvenience to myself—you leave me with little choice but to take you with me.'

Angry, hopeless tears of frustration stung the backs of Jane's eyes. 'I won't go with you,' she said in one final protest.

'You really have no choice in the matter, my dear,' he said, reaching out and opening the door.

Jane left him then and returned to her room like a sleepwalker, too dazed and numbed by what had just happened to think straight. She did her best to forget all he had said, all he had accused her of, telling herself that tomorrow should be one of the happiest days of her life, but the memory lingered like a bitter taste.

It was not until she was alone that she gave way to all the misery that filled her. Closing her eyes, she let the tears that had been building up from the moment Edward had released her spill down her cheeks, and throwing herself onto the bed she gave herself up to all the wretchedness and pain that filled her heart. She sobbed into her pillows as though her heart would surely break.

But even in her wretchedness she was conscious of the shame she felt towards herself, shame when she thought how easily her body had betrayed her, knowing she would have given herself to Edward willingly, regardless of what he had accused her of where Simon was concerned.

But as her sobs lessened she found her traitorous thoughts turning towards his kiss, remembering how hard and demanding his lips had been on hers, and the way his hands had caressed her. The memory made her tremble and her whole being was flooded with a warmth that gave her a sharp, dazzling awareness of the love she felt for him. It was so strong that it swept through her with an intensity that made the tears freeze on her cheeks, and she lay, with her eyes wide open, shocked by the truth.

Chapter Eleven

The house became a hive of activity as preparations were made for Jane's departure for London. It came as a surprise to everyone that Edward had decided to take her with him, intending for her to stay with Sir George and Lady Marchington, Lady Blanche's eldest brother and his wife. Isabel, their niece, always stayed with them on her visits to London and mentioned that she had a mind to go there herself very soon, seeing that Jane would be there for company.

It was a prospect Jane did not look forward to, especially since she had discovered how much she loved Edward, which explained why she was consumed with a warm glow whenever he came near her, why she wanted to be with him—and why she was now glad he wasn't leaving her behind.

Apart from Jane, everyone was too preoccupied with the wedding to notice how quiet and moody Anne had become all of a sudden, how pale she looked, for her concern over Simon was almost tearing her apart. Jane would tell her little of what had transpired between herself and Edward when he had summoned her to his study, but Anne had a strong feeling that he was angry with her for concealing Simon's whereabouts from him, and that what had occurred had something to do with him insisting on Jane accompanying him to London.

Anne was sorely tempted to confront her brother to defend Jane, to tell him the truth of the matter, but thought better of it. Jane was right. It would solve nothing and only make matters much worse than they were already. She had managed to give Seth the message that he must warn Simon against staying any longer at the farm on Grindly Moor, and by his account Simon and Captain Digby had left almost immediately—but it would not be until after the wedding, and Edward and Jane had left for London, that one of the horses out of the Talbot stables would be missed.

Anne was saddened that Jane was to leave Deighton Hall immediately after the wedding, because she would have no one to talk to who understood all she was going through. Her inability to write to Simon, to let him know how much she missed him already and all that was in her heart, made her quite desolate—until Jane suggested that she accompanied her to London. Anne brightened at once, and after speaking to her mother, who was not averse to the idea, persuaded Edward to agree.

Looking out of the window of her room towards the lake on the morning of her wedding, Jane leaned against the casement, dreamily watching the swans swimming about on the surface of the water, thinking back to the day when Edward had told her the stories of the swan-maidens. Having a little time to herself in the midst of the wedding preparations, she remembered the tapestry Edward had told her about. Going to the gallery, she walked along its length until she came to the one she was looking for.

It was not as large as some of the tapestries lining the walls, but the work was one of beauty, ranging from colours of rich vibrancy to subtle cool delicacy, depicting a lakeland scene, the main theme being the swans, large and small, some in the process of changing from swans into beautiful swan-maidens, pure white against a backdrop of dark green trees and the purple and mauve hues of the hills.

Coming into the gallery and seeing Jane looking at the tapestry, Lady Blanche came to stand beside her.

'It's beautiful, is it not, Jane? It was worked by Edward's great-grandmother and her ladies. There is evidence of her embroidery throughout the house— as you've no doubt seen for yourself. But this tapestry of the swans is of particular beauty, detailing the story of the swan-maidens as you can see.'

'Yes. Edward told me—although I'm surprised that, after coming to Deighton all these years, I've never heard the stories before.'

Quickly she recounted the two stories Edward had told her that day by the lake, expressing her sadness for the latter when the swan-maiden had been compelled to change back into a swan and fly away back to her own kind, leaving her brokenhearted husband behind.

Lady Blanche smiled. 'How like Edward not to finish the story.'

'Oh! You mean that was not the end?'

'By no means. In due course the swan-maiden, in the form of a swan, bearing a feather mantle, returned to her bereft husband. Slipping off her own robe which changed her back into a maiden, she help him put on the mantle which she had brought, and in so doing he too changed into a swan.'

'And no doubt they flew away together,' laughed Jane softly, pleased to know the story had a happy ending.

'Precisely. So you see—it does not have such a sad ending after all. Now, come along, my dear. I think it's time we got you into your wedding clothes. It will soon be time to leave for the church.'

Because of the recent death of Jane's father, the marriage between herself and Edward, which was to take place in the parish church of St Edmund, was not to be a public affair, denying the people of Deighton the splendid spectacle that would have drawn people from all the surrounding parishes, when the church would have been filled with the cream of Derbyshire gentry and the celebrating would have been magnificent, for weddings in the country areas constituted one of the main features of social life.

Clad in a gown of gold satin, embroidered with gold and sewn with tiny pearls that hung like teardrops from the fabric, Jane, a still, quiet figure, stood beside Edward at the altar with a few close members of family behind to witness the ceremony. As a symbol of virginity her hair had been left unbound, and brushed lovingly by Maria until it shone like a beacon in the church, the grey light filtering through the windows giving it an illusion of warmth in the cold interior.

Before they had left the house Edward had sought her out, utterly bewitched by her bridal beauty. She had looked at him with a quiet, serene contentment. His breath caught in his throat, for he was sure that no one had ever been so lovely. Something like terror had moved in the region of his heart as he prayed to God to make him worthy of her, to bring her all the peace and happiness she deserved.

'I must compliment you, Jane,' he had said, speaking the words almost beneath his breath, looking at her as if he could not gaze too long. 'When I said you would make a beautiful bride it was an understatement. You were lovely then—but now you are quite magnificent. I am relieved to see that after what occurred between us yesterday you are still prepared to marry me—to tie the knot so keenly desired by both our families.'

Jane looked at him, loving him, wanting to tell him that as a result of what had occurred between them yesterday something had happened to her, something quite wonderful. But it was all so new to her, something she was still trying to come to terms with herself that she was unable to put into words just then.

'I have to. I gave my promise, my sacred word of honour, to you and to my father. I will not go back on that.'

And now, with her hand in Edward's—the first time she had touched him since he had released her from his embrace the previous day—with the revelation of her love she had no misgivings. When the priest put the traditional questions to her she spoke her vows with clarity, raising her head and looking directly at the man she was marrying as he, too, gave his responses in rich tones.

Dressed in his buff coat, he appeared every inch an officer in the Parliament Army, darkly handsome and self-assured. His eyes met hers, the expression in them unreadable, but he was surprised to see how her face glowed with an inner light, and that her hand in his was warm and trembled slightly. There was a contentment about her, which signified she was resigned to her marriage to him—but he was also puzzled by it.

When it was over, Edward's strong hand closed around hers and he kissed her, lightly, so that she scarcely felt the touch of his lips. And then they walked out of the church she had entered as Jane Marlow and left as Lady Jane Talbot.

Time seemed to go so quickly that before Jane knew it the wedding breakfast was over and she was seated in the carriage bound for London. Lady Blanche had pleaded with Edward to delay his departure for a few days but he was adamant, telling her he could remain in Derbyshire no longer, and that the arrangements he had made with the local Parliamentary troop—which was to escort them as far as Derby where they were to spend the night—could not be changed.

Owing to lack of maintenance due to shortage of money—for the funding of the war effort had taken its toll in every parish—roads were appallingly bad throughout the country, and so hazardous, not only from poor conditions but also lawlessness. Unprotected travellers were frequently set upon by the hordes of beggars and wandering bands of deserting soldiers that roamed the country at this time. It was hardly surprising that few civilians journeyed far.

And so it was quite a cavalcade that set off from Deighton Hall, with baggage strapped on to the coach wherever there happened to be a space. Not only was Anne accompanying Jane and Edward, but also Isabel, who was returning to her home, Beestone Lodge, on the outskirts of Derby, where they were to spend the first night of their journey. Maria and her daughters were to remain with Lady Blanche for a few more days before returning to Bowden.

Derby was a town with neither castle nor stone walls, being defended instead by a construction of earthworks which so far remained unopposed. It had become Sir John Gell's Parliamentary headquarters at the start of the Civil War, its garrison housed in the Town Hall which had been built in Tudor times.

It was almost dark when they reached Beestone Lodge, where Isabel's parents were waiting to greet them warmly. The atmosphere between Jane and Edward had been somewhat strained since leaving Deighton Hall, which, Jane suspected, could have something to do with Isabel and Anne being with them. She very much hoped things would be different between them when they were alone together, that perhaps their relationship would be improved now they were married. But if she had any notions of spending a romantic night in the arms of her husband then she was to be sadly disappointed.

Edward had to pay a visit to Sir John Gell at the garrison headquarters, having important military matters to discuss, but he had no intention of being away from his bride for longer than necessary. The hour was already late when he excused himself, giving Jane no more than a perfunctory glance before leaving the house.

Being a keen-eyed observer on how matters stood between Jane and Edward, Isabel noticed the disappointment cloud Jane's eyes when he left and she gave her a quelling glance, clearly glad to see the coolness that existed between them and losing no opportunity to exacerbate the situation.

'I should not be too expectant of Edward's company tonight, Jane,' she said smoothly, accosting her as she was about to join Anne in the adjacent room and speaking for her ears alone. 'Sir John is a very good friend of his, whose reputation for liquor and his eye for the ladies is well known. I very much doubt that Edward will be able to tear himself away from such convivial company tonight—and that he will not put in an appearance until you are due to resume your journey to London tomorrow.'

Isabel conveyed the meaning of her words to Jane perfectly, causing her to colour with astonishment at her outspokenness and to quell the hurt that rose inside her, for the thought of Edward in the arms of some harlot was almost more than she could bear. Jealousy and anger knifed through her and she faced Isabel, highly incensed and refusing to be influenced by her spiteful words.

'Then if that is to be the case I shall bid everyone goodnight and retire. The journey has quite tired me out. I understand perfectly that if Edward has military matters to discuss with Sir John then clearly he must speak to him tonight if he wishes to make an early start for London tomorrow. But what you imply, Isabel—that Edward is so weak as to be tempted to partake in Sir John's activities, however unsavoury, on his wedding night—and said in so frivolous and thoughtless a manner, I find distasteful.

'For all his faults, Edward is a gentleman and sincere in all he says and does, and I would not injure him by insulting his character in such an abominable manner. If I were to believe the truth of your insinuations then I too would be insulted. As it is, I do not. Goodnight, Isabel.'

Jane turned from her and immediately went to bid everyone goodnight, seeing nothing in Isabel's insinuations other than her own malicious intent. Of course Edward would return later, he had to. He would not seek to humiliate her in such a hurtful manner.

And so she waited, the thought of what was to come filling her with excited pleasure and sweet anticipation, and a nervous trembling came over her. Edward's embrace of yesterday had had her completely at his mercy, leaving her unfulfilled and impatient for what must inevitably follow, when she would surrender herself to him totally.

The night passed slowly as she fell in and out of sleep, her ears straining to hear his footfall on the landing outside her door. But when the dawn light invaded her room she knew with cold reality that Isabel had been right, that Edward had found other attractions to keep him from her bed on their wedding night.

Swamped with disappointment she wanted to cry, to give way to her despair. She felt humiliated as well as puzzled, for when he had kissed her so violently the previous day he had made her believe he would lose no time in claiming his rights. But she now knew that when a man kissed a woman with such passion it did not mean that his heart was involved. She was a fool, a stupid fool, to think that because her own feelings had changed towards him he would feel the same. But she had been wrong.

Anger that she had allowed herself to succumb so readily to the embrace of this hard and unfeeling man who was now her husband—who would no doubt satisfy his carnal appetite only when he was good and ready—made her draw herself up proudly. He would never see how much he had hurt her, how she had waited in vain for him to come to her. She would not give him that satisfaction.

As Isabel had predicted, Edward arrived back at the house the following morning just before they were to depart for London. Already dressed for the journey, Jane had yet to go downstairs and saw him arrive from the windows of her room which overlooked the drive. Her eyes were on him instantly and her heart quickened on seeing him, but she would not go down just yet. She would wait. Let him come to her. Again she waited, and the longer she waited it became more and more apparent that patience was not one of her virtues.

Finally, unable to wait any longer, she went downstairs. Hearing the sound of Isabel's gentle laughter coming from one of the rooms she moved towards it, standing in the doorway and looking in on the scene that met her eyes, feeling a flare of resentment and jealousy. She missed nothing. Isabel and Edward were the only two people in the room.

Isabel, she saw, was unusually animated, and there was a predatory alertness to the way in which she leaned towards Edward, speaking confidentially, her mouth close to his ear. Edward appeared to be in excellent spirits. What was the topic of their conversation? What was it she was saying to him that caused him to smile and bend his head so close to hers as he listened attentively to her words—from which she was excluded?

Isabel's eyes held far too much eloquence and she saw by her whole attitude that it made little difference to her that Edward was now married. Although within the society in which she moved perhaps these things didn't matter, thought Jane angrily. Her whole manner spoke in a language any woman who was not a fool would understand.

Observing the easy familiarity between the two of them caused a terrible pain to wrench Jane's heart and she desperately wanted to turn and go back upstairs, but pride and anger urged her to move forward, to confront this errant husband of hers who had treated her so outrageously. They turned simultaneously when she stepped into the room, and she had the satisfaction of seeing Edward look momentarily abashed.

'Please leave us, Isabel,' she said stiffly, determined to take Edward to task. 'I wish to speak to my husband alone.'

Without a word Isabel left the room, but as she passed, Jane observed how her eyes held a malicious sparkle and her lips were secretly smiling—a smile Jane had a great desire to smack from her lips. Stiffened by pride she managed to dominate her anger, determined to show no emotion as she faced Edward, forcing herself to ignore the dark appeal of his eyes, his mouth, which she had longed the whole night through to kiss her own, and his hands to caress her. She longed to run into his arms and yet at the same time wanted to strike out at him. Oh, why did she have the misfortune to love him?

In full possession of herself and the light of battle gleaming in her eyes, she stood facing him, waiting expectantly for some explanation for his absence, but one wasn't forthcoming. He moved towards her and greeted her with a smile and a few commonplace words—even placing a quick kiss on her cold cheek, the only intimate contact there had been between them since their marriage. She seethed inwardly, hating herself for her stupidity, for she resembled a doting dog waiting for a pat and caress from its master, only to be dealt a rebuff instead.

'Good morning, Jane,' he said airily. 'You slept well, I trust?'

'Perfectly, thank you. No doubt my lord found a more comfortable bed on offer in the town,' she said boldly.

'On the contrary. The bed I slept on was too small and damned uncomfortable. My cousin was just telling me that it serves me right. That I would have found a softer resting place here at Beestone Lodge—had I returned,' he said, speaking with appealing softness and smiling at her under drooping eyelids, letting his eyes dwell appreciatively on her lovely face.

'Cousin indeed!' scorned Jane, refusing to be mollified by his silk-like voice and seductive dark eyes. 'There was nothing cousinly in the way she was looking at you. Even the most naïve of wives would not be fooled. To whose bed was she referring do you think, Edward? Mine or hers?'

Edward's eyes hardened as they became fixed on her hostile face, for he had been prepared to find her displeased and slightly vexed by his failure to return to the house, not this angry vixen with fire-spitting amber eyes.

'What the devil are you talking about? Are you accusing Isabel of propositioning me—a married man?'

'Oh, come now, Edward,' she taunted. 'I do not think you are such a simpleton that you didn't know she was doing precisely that.'

He shrugged, drawing away from her a little, determined not be drawn into a disagreement when they were on the point of leaving for London. 'You are being ridiculous, Jane. We have been wed scarcely twenty-four hours and already you are showing all the signs of becoming a jealous wife.'

'No—a humiliated one. I have not the faintest idea where you spent the night or with whom—and nor do I wish to—for I am sure I would find the details quite sordid. But after swearing before God to love and cherish me—kindly have the courtesy to tell me why you chose to spend our wedding night away from me? Do I not deserve an explanation for that at least—if you have one to offer?'

Edward's dark brows rose and one corner of his mouth lifted in a mocking smile. 'So—you noticed. I am flattered. You must forgive me, you see—I thought maybe my absence would meet with your satisfaction.'

'Yes—thank you, it did,' she lied, giving him no indication of how much she had suffered. 'But it might have been a little more considerate of you not to have absented yourself from my bed on our wedding night quite so openly. Your conduct and indifference to my feelings was callous and out-rageous. It is clear you gave no thought to me what-soever.'

Jane stood looking at him in such a way that almost shamed him. But Edward was angry at having to defend himself, even if he couldn't blame her for being furious. She was right, his conduct had been quite outrageous, but he was unable to offer her the true reason as to why he had not returned to Beestone Lodge. His face was inscrutable, but in the dark depths of his eyes something flickered like a raw flame.

'Then what can I say, Jane? I am truly sorry for any embarrassment my actions may have caused you—but had I known you would be waiting for me so ardently, then nothing would have kept me from your bed.'

'I did not invite you to make love to me—merely to spare me from humiliation,' she said, with an edge to her voice like finely honed steel.

'You are right. I know what you must be thinking—but things are not always as they appear to be.'

'Then explain yourself, Edward—if you can.'

He studied her calmly and coolly for a long moment, as if considering what to say next. His brow puckered in a scowl and he appeared to choose his words with care. He averted his eyes, as if he had something to hide, which Jane took to be a confirmation of his guilt.

'Well?' she prompted impatiently. 'Could it be that your conscience is troubling you, my lord?'

'My conscience is clear,' he answered harshly, a pulse in his temple beginning to beat violently as he tried to contain the rage that was threatening to erupt inside him at any moment—and his desire, for even in her scorn and defiance she looked so damned lovely facing him that he had to suppress the urge to move towards her and take her in his arms. 'I told you I had urgent military matters to discuss with Sir John. Unfortunately, they took rather longer than I expected—and by the time we had finished the hour was extremely late, too late to ride back to Beestone Lodge alone.'

'And being aware of Sir John's reputation, no doubt you found yourself in more congenial company—with someone who was no doubt more appreciative and responsive to your lovemaking. Oh, I quite understand, so please spare me any concern you might feel, Edward. It really doesn't matter. The damage is done and no doubt Isabel will feed off it at my expense for many months to come.'

Stung to anger by her accusations, Edward's eyes narrowed dangerously and his lips twisted with scorn. 'I am no saint, and in the past I have freely partaken of life's pleasures, that I admit,' he said tersely. 'But no matter what your fertile imagination has conjured up regarding my activities last night, you are quite wrong, you know. I slept alone. I have no intention of breaking my marriage vows. So do not sit in judgement on me, Jane. Especially not in the light of your own activities where a certain gentleman is concerned. I will not have it.'

At a glance he saw she didn't believe him and he turned from her, struggling to overcome his anger lest he reach out and throttle her in her obstinate determination to believe the worst in him. But then he turned, and seeing the pain behind the fury in her eyes, which she wore like a protective shield, the last of his anger died away.

His look became thoughtful and he could see she was visibly struggling against her anger. Her youth and vulnerability reached out to him, seeing this, a softness entered his gaze. As though mesmerised by the close proximity of her beauty, and annoyed by his inability to smooth the situation, he sighed, moving towards her, intending to take her into his arms, but when she saw what he was about to do she stepped back as if she'd been stung, afraid that if she weakened now he would expose the pitiful, hopeless love she carried for him in her heart.

'Don't touch me,' she flared. 'Don't you dare touch me now.'

Abruptly Jane turned away from him and left the room, much too hurt and angry to see that his words and his cool manner sprang from a bitter jealousy. It had been revived and had deepened on seeing Sir

Simon Butteridge arrive at the garrison in Derby in
a miserable line of Royalist prisoners recently
rounded up, en route for London, to be paraded
through the streets before being incarcerated in one
of the city's infamous prisons.

Simon had been robbed of his hat, so it was his
hair which had first drawn Edward's attention to
him, and the dignity with which he held himself,
which seemed to set him apart from the others, even
though he was bound with match cord. He lacked
the ulcerated fetter sores which plagued most of the
other prisoners—about fifty, in all—and unlike the
others whose bleeding feet were tied around with
rags, he was still in possession of his boots, which
told him his capture was recent. By the time he
had marched to London, dragged at a rope's end—
a journey which would see some die from exhaustion
and hunger and others, who endeavoured to escape
along the way, cut down mercilessly—he would
resemble the rest.

Edward had been on the point of leaving the town
when the prisoners were brought in, but on seeing
the man he believed had captured Jane's heart, he had
cursed resoundingly and turned about, going back to
seek the company of Sir John once more, downing
formidable quantities of liquor in an attempt to
deaden his senses, to blot the man and his miserable
situation from his mind.

In no time at all he was as drunk as the proverbial
noble lord he was, but on recollecting that Simon
Butteridge had been James's friend, as close a friend
as he himself had been, he was swamped with a
terrible guilt and self-loathing that he had done

nothing to alleviate his misery—and in so doing had in some way betrayed James.

On returning to Beestone Lodge the following morning, his heart marked with a burning resentment for Simon Butteridge, he refused to even consider mentioning the incident to Jane, for she would more than likely dissolve into floods of tears and hasten to Derby to be by his side, to do all she could to set him free, regardless of any embarrassment to himself. But if Edward thought he could banish the man and the matter from his mind then he was mistaken, for the image of Simon Butteridge would continue to haunt him for many weeks to come.

As a result of partaking of too much of Sir John's hospitality, his head ached and his body felt as though it had been stretched to its limits on the rack, owing to the crude pallet on which he had finally collapsed, but he could give Jane no reasonable explanation for his absence from her bed. Lord knows, before he had seen Butteridge he had intended returning—his desire to make love to her, to possess her, being uppermost in his mind. But after that he couldn't.

When they came together he wanted to love her as tenderly as any man could love his wife on the first night of their lives together, but feeling as he did, with anger and resentment boiling inside him against Butteridge for stealing her heart, he knew there would be no gentleness in him that night. Better to wait than to risk further contention.

As the coach taking them to London left Beestone Lodge, Jane would have experienced a feeling of

unease had she seen the hard light shining ruthlessly
in Isabel's eyes; her resentment and bitterness
towards Jane had grown considerably since her
marriage to Edward. All the years they had been
betrothed she had never for one moment believed
him to be genuinely and deeply in love with Jane,
and for that matter had never considered her to be of
much importance—and even now she was convinced
that nothing was changed.

The fact that he had chosen to stay away from her
on their wedding night sent out the message that
their relationship was not as it should be—and that
there might be other nights he would wish to spend
away from her. She smiled maliciously; not averse
to causing a little mischief now and then, she had
already decided on going to London herself
very soon.

On their journey to London Jane saw little of Edward
as they travelled, for he preferred to ride along with
their escort for most of the way than occupy the
confines of the coach with herself, Anne and the two
young maids they had brought to attend them. When
they did meet at the coaching inns along the way to
rest and stay the night, she behaved with discretion
and treated him in a cool, friendly enough manner,
and made to further reference to his continued
absence from her bed. Her chamber was always
shared by Anne, and if she thought it strange that
Edward hadn't come near her since their wedding, it
was too delicate an issue for her to comment upon—
furthermore, she had other things on her mind.

The further they travelled from Derbyshire the

more Jane became increasingly worried about Anne. She seemed to withdraw into herself with each passing mile. Sitting beside Jane hour after hour in the carriage, she was motionless, staring out of the window at the passing scenery and yet seeing nothing. She was quiet, her face pale, and in her loneliness and despair she thought of nothing and no one other than Simon.

Wrapped in her own misery of unrequited love, Jane could only pity her, for whereas her relationship with Edward offered hope now they were man and wife, that the path they were to travel together could only get smoother, where Anne was concerned there was no such hope. The future to her eyes was as bleak as the moors around Deighton on a winter's day. However hard she might dream of sharing her life with Simon, should Edward find out then it would be a pathway to tragedy.

'I would die for Simon, Jane,' whispered Anne into the dark one night when they lay abed at a wayside inn, her voice full of longing. 'Just for one look, to have him hold me and kiss me once—I would forfeit everything I own. Even my life.'

Unable to offer any words that could be of comfort to her, Jane reached out her arm and squeezed her hand, praying she would emerge from her melancholy state when they reached Marchington House and she had other matters to occupy her mind.

When they reached the outskirts of London, no matter what Jane had told Isabel about having no desire to see the city, she was like a wide-eyed country girl as they passed through the suburbs towards

Clerkenwell, north of the city. The setting sun trailed its golden rays across the unfolding landscape and a silvery mist hung over the London skyline on the horizon, its church spires and parapets providing a jagged edge. Edward had sent word on ahead to Sir George and Lady Marchington to expect their arrival. They were greeted warmly and ushered inside Marchington House where refreshments awaited them.

Ardent Royalists, Sir George and Lady Marchington were an elderly couple, Sir George a quiet man, small of stature and of copious build, his wife slightly taller, extremely slender and with a regal bearing. She had no reservations on meeting Jane, whom she had never met but had learnt much about from Blanche over the years, and Anne, of course, over whom she cast a worried glance, thinking she looked a little peaky. When she commented on this Anne laughed lightly, telling her if she was a little pale then it could only be put down to the long journey from Derbyshire.

In the bustle of their arrival her aunt accepted this to be the reason, but Edward cast her a sharp look of curiosity and concern. His aunt was right, Anne did look a little pale and her eyes lacked lustre. There had been a noticeable absence of her usual high spirits for some time now—since before the wedding, in fact. He must have a word with Jane. Perhaps she would be able to provide a reason for his sister's melancholic state.

Chapter Twelve

I'm so glad you were able to come to London, Jane,' Lady Marchington said when they were all in the drawing-room after dinner, 'such as it is in these unfortunate times. I have to say it is not the best of times to visit. Sadly, it is not the same as before the War, when the King and his Court gave us all so much to gossip about. Then there was a constant round of masques and balls, but now there is nothing to look forward to. Why, so many houses lay empty—deserted by families who have gone to fight.'

'Nevertheless, I am looking forward to going into the city, Lady Marchington.'

'I shall see to it that passes are obtained,' said Edward from where he was standing with his uncle in front of the fire, twirling the amber liquid of his brandy around his glass. Seeing Jane's enquiring look, he smiled. 'They are essential for passing in and out through the gates,' he explained.

'Then I suppose that is one favourable aspect of your being a Parliamentary officer we should all be grateful for,' she said, the irony underlying her words not lost on Edward—although it seemed to be on everyone else, which he was relieved about, for the last thing he wanted was for his aunt and uncle to sense the discord that lay between them, a discord he was determined to rectify at the earliest possible opportunity now they had reached London. Nevertheless, her remark brought a dark scowl of displeasure to his features.

Jane turned again to Lady Marchington. 'Did you not think of moving to the country, Lady Marchington?' she asked. 'Would it not have been safer with London being a Parliament stronghold?'

'George and I chose to stay. We're too old for such an upheaval, and besides, no matter what hardships are cast our way I refuse to be daunted. I will not be intimidated in my own home. Although it doesn't do to be too outspoken, otherwise one is in danger of being thrown into prison without a moment's notice. There are drawbacks, of course. Food is so very expensive and coal almost unobtainable—except at exorbitant prices. Puritanism is sweeping across London like a blanket of smog and Marchington House—as well as those of other Royalist sympathisers—is regularly searched.'

After responding to some remark from his uncle, Edward smiled indulgently across at his aunt where she sat on the sofa beside Jane, with Anne across from her.

'Not recently, Aunt, I hope. I thought I'd sorted all that business out before I left for the north.'

'Yes, thank you, Edward. I have to say we have not been searched for quite some months now. So you see, Jane,' she said, her eyes twinkling merrily, 'it does help having a nephew in the Parliament Army—however misguided I believe his allegiance to be. I'm only thankful his brother William did not follow suit. Still—we're not the only family in the land who suffer from divided loyalties. I'm just happy that we're civilised about it and have remained close.'

'Yes. Lady Blanche said much the same thing.' Jane smiled. 'I hope you don't mind Edward foisting myself and Anne on you, Lady Marchington. I'm afraid we gave you short notice of our arrival.'

'Not at all, my dear. It will give us great pleasure entertaining you at Marchington House. It will also give us the opportunity of getting to know you—and I'm always happy to see Anne, she knows that,' she replied, smiling fondly at Anne. 'Of course, Edward always was one to spring surprises—turning up when one leasts expects him. But we're always happy to see the dear boy. And I dare say that having just married you he couldn't bear to be parted from you—and having met you I cannot say that I blame him. He failed to tell us how outrageously pretty you are. Are you to stay with us tonight, Edward?'

'No, Lady Marchington,' said Jane quickly, casting her husband a taunting, smiling glance, indignant at his continued aloofness towards her—and her own weakness in allowing him to ensnare her heart with such little effort, feeling that she would have to use all the powers of her allurement to melt the indifference of this man who seemed to be encased in ice. 'He has pressing military matters to attend to and must leave for Windsor directly. Is that not so, Edward?'

Dismayed by the prospect of being apart from him, her eyes held a challenge, a challenge that was irresistible and which Edward rose to. With a grim smile on his lips he directed a glance across the space that divided them that was not lacking in interest, and a wicked gleam flashed through his black pupils.

Lady Marchington sighed, slightly disgruntled. 'And no doubt you will be so deeply occupied at Windsor getting your new regiment together that you will scarcely give us a second thought.'

'Now you know that is not so, Aunt,' he said smoothly. 'Nothing would give me greater pleasure than to retire from the army and stay at home, for heaven knows there are enough commanders now in the Parliament Army to form their own regiment. But until a settlement is reached I must soldier on. However, never fear. I shall come to see you whenever I have the opportunity.'

'Can you not be persuaded to remain with us until morning?'

With a tilt of his dark brows he smiled, his eyes locked on his wife's. 'I might be—if my uncle can tempt me with another glass of his excellent brandy,' he said, handing Sir George his glass.

After being prepared for bed by her maid and left alone, surrounded by elegant furnishings, Jane was seated at the dressing-table in the bedchamber that was to be hers for the duration of her stay at Marchington House. She gazed wistfully at her face in the mirror, seeing how large her eyes were. How pale her skin was in the dim light, yet how could it be when it was burning? Gently she touched her lips, feeling them tremble, knowing she would feel no greater bliss than the moment when she gave herself to Edward.

When she had left him with Sir George earlier, she had tried to justify her foolish aberration to herself as she had climbed the stairs, trying to delude herself into believing that all she had wanted was for him to stay, just to be near her, even if he slept elsewhere in the house, because when he left for Windsor there was no telling when she would next see him. But she smiled, knowing it was self-delusion, for she wanted him with her—in her bed, where he should be. It had been madness to entice him with words and a look to her room, but he had been unable to withstand her. The alchemy between them was so great he had recognised the message she conveyed.

But would he come—or would he keep her waiting in a torment of quivering excitement and sweet anticipation as he had on the night of their wedding, leaving her to face the cold light of dawn alone?

But then he was there. She saw his image in the mirror behind her. She was still, watching him move closer, silently, and then his hands were on her shoulders, gentle and caressing, before he bowed his dark head and, shoving back her hair, placed his warm lips on her neck. He slipped the garment that covered her off her shoulders, exposing her breasts, the flushed nipples hard and thrusting forward. His lips travelled over them with a velvety softness, burning her flesh with the tip of his tongue. With a quick intake of breath Jane closed her eyes and leaned against him.

'You were expecting me, I think,' he murmured, his lips still nuzzling her neck, the sweet scent of her flesh almost overwhelming him. 'You have an artful tongue, my dear, sweet Jane, and your powers of persuasion are great indeed. Do you not think it wicked to tempt a man away from his duties, his military duties, when his country is in dire need of his services?'

'And do you not think that, on occasion, his duties to his wife are more important than those to his country, my lord?' she breathed. 'But if the man is weak and is so easily tempted, then maybe he should take his wife with him when next he goes off to campaign.'

Edward raised his head, his eyes moving across her face in the mirror before locking on her jewel-bright gaze, the slightest hint of a smile forming on his lips.

'You are shameless. Your mere presence on a battlefield would confound the enemy. It would sap the foundations of any strategic plan.'

'But am I not the enemy? How do you know this is not a strategic plan of my own to confound my husband into lying with me?'

Edward stood up straight, drawing her up to face him, tilting her head up to his and lowering his lips to hers. She made a faint sound in her throat before closing her eyes and melting against him, feeling his lips hard and demanding, aware of her own opening to his. She felt herself going soft, weakening against him, fearing she would swoon with the pleasure he was arousing inside her. With the length of his firm body pressed close to hers she was drowning, dissolving in a sea of passion until she became quite lost.

Withdrawing slightly from his kiss he looked down at her, his lips twisting crookedly in a smile. 'This is how I know,' he answered at last, his mouth against hers. 'Your passionate response to my kiss, and the way you have of trembling whenever I touch you, tells me it is you who is confounded.'

Laughing softly at the mastery he knew he had over her, he sat on the bed, drawing her down beside him and pressing her back onto the pillows, gently kissing her eyes, her cheeks, her lips, his hands sliding under the thin garment that covered her, stroking and caressing her nakedness so tenderly, so expertly, that she gasped, almost crying out for him to stop because she could not bear it—and yet wanting him never to stop. She opened her eyes, looking at him, begging him with her eyes for him to take her.

'You are wanton, my Jane,' he whispered, his breath hot against her cheek. 'Come—say you want me.'

'Yes,' she gasped. 'Oh—yes.'

He divested her of her gown and removed his own clothes with such speed that she scarcely noticed he was doing so. Lying naked before him, she watched as he devoured her slender body with his eyes, throwing back her head in an ecstasy of joy when he bent his head and kissed her arms, her breasts, the firm, flat surface of her abdomen, burning her flesh with his lips as they travelled the length of her body. There were no maidenly blushes, no modest attempt to cover herself as he awoke all the old demons inside her clamouring for fulfilment.

His body was strong and hard, his muscles clearly defined, and when at last he covered her's she threw her arms around him, bringing his head closer to her own. Everything inside her melted and ran as he invaded and possessed her, and his possession was both magnificent and terrifying. His body was huge and powerful, wonderful and glistening with sweat above her; his eyes were dark with passion.

Allowing herself to be carried away to the realms of ecstasy, where torment and delight were one, she clung to him, hearing him murmur passionate endearments close to her face as he satisfied his need. She was powerless beneath him, for there was nothing to save her, nothing she could do as he continued to make love to her, nothing she wanted to do as she responded to him like the wanton he had called her, the steady rhythm of him inside her sending her to heights of unimaginable bliss.

When at last it was over he left her like smouldering ash, her senses in absolute disintegration. She turned from him, her skin continuing to tremble from her contact with him, still burning, still feeling the ecstasy of relief wash over her, and yet, despite reaching a fullness of satisfaction, long after he had left her her senses remembered and she wanted him still.

The night seemed endless as they made love until dawn, when Jane finally slept. When she awoke Edward was beside the bed, already dressed to travel to Windsor. With a kiss and a promise to return to her at the first possible moment he left her then.

Rolling on to her back, she sighed, stretching with languid contentment, thinking of him and the extraordinary things that happened to her when she was in his arms. She shone when she was with him. Her heart and body belonged to no one but him. He became her all, filling her world so that she could not look forward without seeing him.

After that night Edward's duties kept him from her and she suffered an agony of torment as she waited for him to return to Marchington House. With Anne—who spent every waking moment worrying about Simon—she spent her days walking through the surrounding fields and gardens, and one day taking the carriage into the city with Lady Marchington to see the sights.

The massive defences left her agog, for it was a wall of earth, eighteen feet high and eleven miles round the city with a ditch in front, built by an enthusiastic, overwhelming number of Parliamentarian inhabitants in fear of a siege.

London was a handsome city, teeming with people, although stark evidence of the Civil War was everywhere, with the City's Trained Bands marching through the streets and wounded soldiers and beggars abounding. They kept to the main thoroughfares and squares, seeing well-paved courtyards fronting fine houses of rich merchants, avoiding the maze of twisting, mean back alleyways lined with crumbling, squalid dwellings, inhabited by cut-throats and skulking thieves.

After visiting St Paul's Church and the river, with Jane marvelling at the terrific amount of traffic journeying up and down and Lady Marchington pointing out certain places of interest, they travelled along the Strand towards Charing Cross, to Westminster and the sprawling Palace of Whitehall, which had housed the King's court and government.

When they were returning to Clerkenwell the carriage came to a halt, moving to one side of the narrow street to make way for a long line of prisoners of war. This was a familiar sight to Lady Marchington, for prisoners rounded up after a battle were frequently marched to London to be incarcerated in the filthy, disease-ridden hulks on the river or one of the many prisons.

The most she had ever seen paraded through the streets was after the Battle of Naseby. Then about four thousand had been brought in, the prisons too full to take them all. Almost seven hundred had been imprisoned in Lambeth Palace across the river, the rest caged in the open on Tothill Fields.

For Jane and Anne the scene was quite new and filled them with horror and revulsion.

'Don't look if it upsets you,' advised Lady Marchington. 'But I'm afraid it's a common enough sight to see Royalist prisoners being brought into the city.'

Anne and Jane could not look away for these poor men deserved their pity. Tied together with cord, many without shoes and stockings, the prisoners struggled along, dragging their feet in an effort to keep up with the man in front. They were dirty and dejected, reviled by people who lined the streets to see them, while there were those like themselves who looked on with pity.

It was Anne's involuntary cry of pain and disbelief that drew Jane's gaze to one of the prisoners, to his flowing fair locks, though lank and dirty after many days of marching. His head was lowered, but he still bore himself well. Robbed of the trappings of a gentleman, he still managed to look dignified. Profoundly shocked, tears filled her eyes when she recognised Simon, tears of anger and despair on discovering he had been captured after all their efforts to help him make his way back to the Royalist force. Her heart went out to him.

He was not so far away, and when he was about to pass by he raised his head and saw them. His blue eyes widened with incredulity, unable to believe what they saw. He was unable to speak to them, unable to reach out and take one of Anne's gloved hands that gripped the door of the carriage—but true to his character he smiled and a merry twinkle lit his eyes. Jane was sure that if he'd been wearing his hat and his hands had been free he would have removed it and made them a flourishing bow, despite his obvious suffering. Sensing what was happening, Lady Marchingron pulled Anne into the interior of the coach.

'If you recognise one of them, it is imperative you let no one see. It could be dangerous for us all.'

Her words fell upon deaf ears. Before Lady Marchington could stop her, Anne had scrambled out of the carriage and into the street. Quickly Jane went after her, catching her arm and pulling her back, seeing Simon disappear round a bend in the street.

'It was Simon. You saw him, didn't you, Jane?'

'Yes—yes, I did.'

'I cannot bear to see him so publicly humiliated. I must follow him,' said Anne in a choking voice, her face ghost white. 'I have to know where they're taking him.'

Looking about her, Jane saw a soldier on horseback who was with the prisoners. She ran towards him, hoping he would stop.

'Please—tell me where you're taking them?'

The soldier slowed his horse and looked down at her, grinning salaciously into her pretty face. 'Now why would a pretty wench like yourself be wanting to know that? One of those handsome Cavaliers caught your eye has he, love—although he's not quite so handsome now, eh?'

Jane tried to keep calm, trying not to get too close to his restive horse. 'No. Of course not. I'm just interested to know where they're being taken to.'

'The Tower,' he answered before kicking his horse on.

Anne had come to stand beside her, reaching out and gripping her arm with trembling hands, her eyes wide with stark terror. 'The Tower!' she whispered, her voice quivering. 'Oh, dear, merciful God, Jane, I cannot bear it. Its very name conjures up images of absolute horror and cruelty. Still weakened by his injury he will never survive. We—we have to do something. We cannot let him remain in that awful place.'

'We will think of something, Anne. I promise. But come—we cannot stand here. See how we are attracting attention. Lady Marchington is right. It would be sheer folly to claim association with any one of the prisoners.'

Back in the carriage Jane quickly explained to Lady Marchington that one of the prisoners was known to them, but when Anne's overstretched nerves finally snapped and she burst into convulsive sobs, Lady Marchington quite correctly assumed that the prisoner with the fair hair and handsome looks was more than just a friend—that Anne was in love with him.

'Then you must have a word with Edward. He has a certain amount of influence—and if, as you say, he is an officer, then an exchange or even parole may be arranged.'

Anne stared at her aunt tearfully. 'Oh, no, Aunt. Not Edward,' she cried, gulping back her tears. 'He knows nothing about my relationship with Simon. He has no liking for him—and if he should find out how close we have become, then he would make quite sure he remained in The Tower for ever.'

'Is this true, Jane?'

Jane nodded. 'I'm afraid so, Lady Marchington. Edward's dislike of Simon is quite intense.'

Lady Marchington frowned. 'Then that complicates matters. I have always considered Edward to be a sound judge of character, so there must be a perfectly good reason for his dislike.'

'There is absolutely nothing to dislike about Simon,' wailed Anne, springing quickly to his defence. 'He is honourable and a gentleman—and I love him dearly.'

Lady Marchington sighed deeply as Anne continued to cry, her body racked with sobs. In an effort to console her, she reached out and patted her hand comfortingly.

'Dry your eyes, Anne. We'll think of some way of freeing your Cavalier. You'll see.'

As he went about forming a new regiment at Windsor Castle, which was being used not only as a Parliamentary garrison but also as a prison, holding many Royalists, Edward's conscience had been troubling him ever since leaving Derby, when he had seen Simon Butteridge brought into the town as a prisoner. Try as he might, he could not rid himself of the feeling that in ignoring his sorry plight he had somehow betrayed James's friendship.

No matter what his own opinion was of the man, he knew his conscience would give him no peace until he had done all in his power to secure his release.

Unless he met with some mishap along the way it was almost certain he would eventually arrive in London. He scanned the lists of all new arrivals until at last he found what he was looking for. Had Sir Simon Butteridge been a lesser mortal he would have been sent to Newgate or the Fleet, or any of the other infamous prisons in London, but being an officer he had been incarcerated in the Tower.

In making his decision to obtain his release, Edward tried not to think of Jane. Now she was his wife in every sense he wanted her to put Butteridge out of her heart and mind for ever. Thoughts of her made him want her, made the blood pound in his temples, as he longed for the time when he could go to her. He knew how to rouse her sexually, how to make her come alive to his touch, and how to tune her body so that it was in complete harmony with his own.

But what did she think of when he was no longer there? What went on in that head of hers? And what of her heart? Did she belong to him or was she still pining for Simon Butteridge? These were the thoughts that tortured him so that he thought he would go mad as he set about trying to obtain Simon's freedom.

Each day without Edward was an eternity for Jane. She had never thought it possible to to be so happy, to feel such wonderful elation glowing inside her. When she thought of the night they had spent together as man and wife, she smiled and hugged herself, wondering how she could contain her happiness until he returned London. Not since before the siege had there been such a bright sparkle in her eyes and a soft flush on her cheeks. During the whole night Edward had not once mentioned love, and she began to hope that perhaps during this time of separation he would come to realise he loved her as much as she loved him.

Sadly, Anne was not blessed with the same happiness as Jane, who, observing her friend's suffering, became increasingly anxious about her health and state of mind. Each day Simon remained in his awful prison was like torture to her—as it was for herself, but her concern now was as a friend, a close friend, and nothing more. Anne's spirits were low, her face pale and drawn and she had no appetite for food.

She continued to function correctly and tried to appear cheerful, not to give in to her anguish and

refusing to cry—at least not when she was in the
company of others—but alone in her room Jane was
sure Anne spent her nights shedding copious tears
of despair—her red and swollen eyes in the early
morning bore evidence of this.

Somehow it came as no surprise when Isabel arrived
at Marchington House, full of her usual exuberance
and declaring that having reached a peak of boredom
and irritability in Derbyshire, she had obtained permission from her parents to travel to London to be
with Jane and Anne. It didn't take her long to sense
there was an atmosphere of unease in the house. Jane
seemed to be in a perpetual state of anxiety, which
stirred her curiosity, and Anne kept to her room a
great deal.

  She came upon her aunt and Jane in conversation
one day, hearing them mention Simon Butteridge.
Keenly alert, she enquired of Jane if she had heard
anything as to his whereabouts, and if he had succeeded in escaping the Parliament troops searching
for him in Derbyshire.

  Well remembering that other occasion at Deighton
Hall when Isabel had enquired about Simon,
implying in her subtlety that they were romantically
attached and maliciously inciting Edward's anger,
and knowing Simon's imprisonment could not be
kept from her, Jane looked at her directly.

  'He was captured and brought to London, Isabel,'
she answered stiffly

  Isabel looked surprised. 'You have seen him?'

  'Yes. One day when Anne and I were in London
with your aunt, we saw him among a group of

prisoners being taken to the Tower.'

'Dear me! The Tower! No wonder you look so concerned.'

'Yes, I am concerned, Isabel—as I would be for anyone who was as close a friend to my family as Simon.'

Indeed, as the days passed Jane became so concerned about the effect Simon's incarceration in the Tower was having on Anne's general health—knowing she would get progressively worse if nothing was done to have him released—that with Sir George and Lady Marchington's approval she travelled to Windsor to see Edward, to plead with him to intervene, which, in the light of their past differences where Simon was concerned, she did not look forward to.

When Jane told Anne what she intended she brightened, hope beginning to return to her heart, but she begged Jane to plead as a friend for his release, to give Edward no reason to suspect her own involvement with Simon, otherwise he might refuse to consider what she asked.

The coach wound its way through the rich countryside of small villages, field and forest towards the little town of Windsor. Unfortunately, because one of the wheels had come loose on the coach, forcing them to stop at an inn along the way to have it secured, their journey was delayed considerably. It was almost nightfall when Jane saw the ramparts and turrets of the castle, the Headquarters of the Parliament Army, a majestic pile towering over the great park and meadows, the town stretching along the big hill on which the castle was built. The streets were steep, which the horses pulling the coach struggled to climb.

After passing through the Castle Gate into the Lower Ward of the castle and undergoing the inspection of the guards, Samuel—an elderly and faithful retainer of the Marchington family who had accompanied Jane—went to look for someone who could direct them to Lord Talbot. Jane waited in the coach—had she had the interest to look around, she would have seen the castle was like a bustling town within the massive walls, with a patchwork of half-timbered houses and buildings in the Lower Ward. It lacked the uniformity of the Upper Ward of the castle, which housed the royal apartments used by kings and queens throughout the ages—but, with a diversity of buildings around it, the dazzling, magnificent St George's Chapel, the final resting place of monarchs and knights of England past, dominated the Lower Ward.

After several minutes Samuel returned with a Captain of the Guard, a tall, active-looking gentleman with good-looking features and an easy manner. Quickly Jane stepped down from the coach, her heart throbbing madly in her chest, knowing that at last she was to see Edward.

'Can I be of assistance?'

'I am Lady Talbot. Please—would you direct me to Lord Talbot?'

'Of course. I'll be happy to take you to him.'

He took her to a small half-timbered house where he told her Lord Talbot was staying and left her there while he went to fetch him. Feeling her heart thumping in her breast and her blood pounding in her temples, she waited, wondering what his reaction would be on seeing her, every minute seeming like at eternity. Eventually Edward's tall figure appeared in the doorway, eclipsing the moonlight, looking tired but jaunty. He was bare-headed and his dark eyes stared at her incredulously. For the space of seconds he didn't move, but then he came to her and took both her hands in his.

'Jane! My darling girl. What brings you all the way to Windsor at this late hour? How on earth did you get here?' he asked her seriously.

'Samuel brought me. He—he's left to look for rooms in the town with the coachman. He will send word where I can contact him if need be, otherwise he is to return in the morning. I would have been here sooner but a wheel came loose on the coach, which took some time to fix.' She looked up at him uncertainly. 'You—you don't mind me coming, do you, Edward?'

He laughed, scooping her into his arms and kissing her lips hungrily. 'Mind? Dear Lord, Jane. Why should I mind?' he said, his voice soft but vibrant, looking down at her with genuine pleasure. 'Ever since that wonderful night I have dreamed of you. I have missed you like a starving man craves food. But what brings you here? Perhaps you were missing me—is that it?'

'Yes.' She laughed as he drew her to him once more, speaking as he covered her face with kisses, as if he couldn't believe she was there. 'I had to come. I couldn't bear being away from·you any longer,' she said, forgetting, as she abandoned herself in his arms and feeling that she could die of happiness, the true purpose of her visit. But when he released her, she felt a rush of guilt when she remembered Anne's anguish.

'But I have also come to talk to you, Edward. There are certain matters I wish to discuss with you.'

Without taking his eyes off her, he led her to a rather battered sofa with a table placed in front of it with the remains of a meal littering its surface. 'Not now—later. These moments are too precious to waste. Come and eat something—not that there's much left, as you see. I'll order some more food to be brought.'

'No—thank you, Edward. I ate on the way here. I'm not hungry, truly. Perhaps a little wine, nothing more.'

Quickly Edward poured them both some wine and, sitting beside her, continued to look at her in a way Jane found both disturbing and miraculous, for he had never looked at her like this. After taking a few sips of wine, unable to contain himself a moment longer without kissing her again, he took the glass from her and placed it on the table, taking her in his arms and seeking her lips once more, his heart beating so hard against Jane that she knew he was beyond the power to master his desire.

'The days I have been without you have been heavy with longing, Jane. Come, I entreat you,' he said, breathing hard, the perfume of her body filling his head. Taking her hand, he raised her to her feet, for never had he known a love like this and he was impatient to have her lay beside him. 'Come to bed and let me make love to you.'

Jane's heart leapt and lifted her beyond a love stronger than anything she had ever known. She went with him into a small bedchamber and with his aid— and his lips kissing every part of her newly exposed flesh as she removed her clothes, dropping her garments one by one on to the floor—she eventually came to him naked and unashamed. Raising her arms slowly, she unbound her hair, which tumbled in a luxuriant mass to her waist. Seizing a handful, Edward brought it to his lips before finding her mouth once more, slowly lowering her on to the bed and pressing her back against the pillows and proceeding to make love to her.

At first he was gentle with her, his caress tender, but he was achingly impatient—until he felt her body respond to his with a quickness that pleased him. And then the magic, the miracle, happened as before and the joy Jane felt erased everything she had ever known as the attraction that drew her to his man began to exert itself once more. There was something wild about their lovemaking and she allowed herself to be possessed willingly. Edward yielded to the delights her body offered like a man given drink after a long period of thirst.

At first their hunger for each other was intense and insatiable, and when it had passed their lovemaking became tender and gentle, as each slowly roused the other to new heights of passion—then they slept.

Later—when the room was bathed in the dawn light and the castle could be heard coming to life all around them—Jane, slow to wake, stirred within Edward's arms. She couldn't believe he was beside her, but his lean-muscled warm body was unmistakably real. She sighed with absolute contentment, well satisfied, for their union had not only been a coming together of their two bodies in passion, but also of their hearts and minds. Sensing she was awake, Edward opened his eyes and rolled her over on to her back, his dark head poised above her face, his face seductive with sleep and their bodies languid with pleasure.

'My love—my wife. My adorable wife in the sight of God and man,' he murmured against her mouth, and then he kissed her and the kiss that began slowly and tenderly went on and on until they were both aflame, but on hearing the sounds outside the house, reminding him that he would be needed elsewhere in the castle, reluctantly he tore himself away from her arms, speaking with a note of regret.

'No matter how much I wish I could keep you with me, unfortunately I cannot remain here making love to you all day, my pet. I have duties to attend to.' He smiled suddenly, beginning to pull on his clothes. 'Do you realise that since your arrival we have hardly exchanged two words? Come, up you get,' he said, love and laughter in his eyes as he picked up her clothes from where they had fallen and heaped them on to the bed, 'and maybe we'll have time to share some breakfast before Samuel arrives to whisk you back to London.'

Slowly Jane began to dress. Still unable to resist her, Edward bent and placed a kiss on the back of her neck as she fumbled with the buttons of her dress.

'When you arrived you said there were matters you wished to discuss, as I remember—before we were otherwise distracted.' He smiled and raised a quizzical brow. 'What was it?'

His question brought Jane down from the dreaming heights of earlier, bringing the night to a swift conclusion. It was as if the sun had suddenly gone out, for this was the moment she had dreaded.

'Yes—I. . .' She lowered her gaze, unable to go on.

Fastening his shirt Edward paused and frowned, giving her a strange, suspicious look. Something dark and disagreeable was beginning to form in the back of his mind.

'Well?'

His voice was calm, much too calm, which brought a feeling of unease to Jane's rapidly beating heart.

'Look at me, Jane,' he said, his voice very quiet, seeming to sense what it was she was about to ask.

Unwillingly she looked at him. His dark brows were raised and his eyes gleamed hard. Again she hesitated for a moment, but knowing that if she wanted to help both Simon and Anne then she had to see this thing through. She drew a determined breath.

'I—I came to ask a favour of you, Edward.'

He nodded. 'I suspected as much. And whom does it concern?'

'Simon. Simon Butteridge.'

Chapter Thirteen

The name defied utterance, but when she spoke it it fell between them like a cannonball. Jane could hear the noise outside but inside the room there was no sound at all. A lifetime later Edward spoke.

'I see,' he said, his voice like ice.

Jane's heart fell, for he did not resemble the passionate lover of the night. He had been absorbed into the rigidly severe figure of a military leader, a stranger—the space between them becoming a chasm.

'And the favour?'

'You are a man of power, Edward. A man of influence. I have come to ask you to attempt to secure his release from the Tower where I know he has been imprisoned.'

His eyes continued to stare into hers like cold steel. 'You are well informed, Jane. How is it that you know he has been captured, even?'

'I—I saw him being brought into London among a group of Royalist prisoners one day when I was with your aunt. I enquired of one of the soldiers

246

where they were being take to. He—he told me it was to the Tower.'

Edward nodded, his expression severe. 'Then why didn't you ask me last night when you arrived—before preying on my susceptible heart?'

'Forgive me, Edward. I—I meant to. But. . .' She flushed, unable to go on, unable to remind this cold and unfeeling husband of hers of his impatience to make love to her, giving her little time for thought.

Aware of her confusion and following her train of thought, Edward's lips twisted cruelly and with a contemptuous shrug of his shoulders he moved away from her, walking into the other room. 'You don't have to explain,' he growled as she followed him. 'I remember how it was. I was so delighted to see you that my ardour to have you in my bed quite swept you off your feet—casting all thought of Butteridge from your mind.' He cast her a look of sarcasm. 'That is correct, is it not?' He sat down and began pulling on his boots. 'Butteridge is a prisoner,' he said flatly. 'You must accept it.'

Jane's cheeks began to burn with growing anger at his stubborn refusal to be reasonable. 'I will never accept it.'

'Then knowing my opinion of him, why do you think I will try to secure his release?'

'Please, Edward,' she begged, going to stand beside where he sat. 'If not for me—then do it for James.' She saw pain enter his eyes when she reminded him of her brother but went on relentlessly. If she had to resort to emotional blackmail to win him over then so be it. It would be well worth it if he succumbed to her request. 'I know that after

negotiations prisoners are frequently exchanged—
and wounded officers, who are an added burden on
their gaolers, are sometimes paroled—and released.
I beg of you to use your influence as a Parliament
officer.'

'And it is important to you, is it, that he is
released?' Standing up, he looked at her hard, his
voice harsh. 'What better proof of your love for him
could I have than this? The speed with which you
forever spring to his defence is sure evidence of that.'

'Love! But I do not love Simon,' she cried
passionately, prepared to lay bare her very soul if
need be to make him believe her. 'How can you say
that after what we have shared? How long do I have
to go on denying it? Whatever you may suppose, it
is you I love, Edward—you I belong to. It is you I
adore above all others. I admit I have not always felt
this way—but the love I feel now I shall always feel.'

She sighed, knowing his accusations sprang from
a bitter jealousy. If only she could tell him it was
Anne who loved Simon, then maybe he would
believe her. But if she divulged this, then his anger
would be increased a thousandfold and Simon would
remain incarcerated in the Tower indefinitely.

'If I were in love with Simon, do you really believe
I would ask you, my husband, to intervene on his
behalf—to help secure his freedom? I am deeply
concerned for him, that I cannot deny. You already
know he was injured in the skirmish in the north.
As a result of this he became very ill indeed. After
being captured and his enforced march to London,
his health has suffered greatly. His imprisonment in
the Tower will not help matters either. I came here

in the hope that you would understand and help to alleviate my concern. I have to try and help him— for James's sake. I would never be able to forgive myself if I did not try—no matter how much you may hate me for it.' Reaching out, she placed her trembling hand on his arm, feeling how tense he was, tears swimming in her amber eyes. 'Please, Edward,' she beseeched him. 'You must learn to trust me— otherwise our marriage is a mockery.'

Just as her request that he help secure Butteridge's freedom had roused his violent mood, her stricken face now softened him. He loved her too much to allow this to continue to cause contention between them. She was right. There had to be trust on both sides if their marriage was to succeed. His innate sense of justice told him he must try. Fiercely he gathered her into his arms, his coldness and reserve gone.

'I do love you, Jane. You've no idea how much. But maybe my jealousy would not have been so profound had I loved you less.' Sighing deeply, he held her at arm's length, looking deep into her eyes. 'I have not been fair with you, my love. You could have saved yourself a journey. You see—I attended to the matter of Sir Simon's release from the Tower before you came. He will be freed any day now.'

Jane stared at him in silence, astonishment and disbelief registering in her eyes. 'You—you knew he was a prisoner in the Tower?' she whispered.

'Yes. I also saw him in Derby—on our wedding night, which was the reason, I have to admit, why I did not return to you at Beestone Lodge. Oh—I had every intention of doing so, for until I saw Butteridge nothing could have kept my from you that night.'

'Then—then what happened?' she asked, finding what he was telling her absolutely incredible. 'And why did you not tell me you had seen Simon? Had he been captured when you saw him?'

'Yes. I had just left Sir John when I saw him among a group of prisoners. I did not tell you at the time because through my observations of your behaviour—which stemmed from the morning of our departure from Bowden when I imagined you to be in love with him—I firmly believed, had I done so, that you would have rushed to his aid and begged Sir John to release him—regardless of the embarrassment to myself.'

'But—but I still don't understand why you did not return to me at Beestone Lodge? How did seeing Simon influence your decision not to?'

'Because I am a selfish creature. I was angry—and jealous—because I truly believed he held that special place in your heart I coveted for myself. Had I returned to you that night, I could not have trusted myself to love you gently.'

'And so you gave relief to your feelings and returned to Sir John and got hopelessly drunk. Is that not so?' she smiled, chiding him gently, and beginning to understand at last what had been behind his odd behaviour that night.

'Yes. My recollection of my behaviour at the time deserves your severest reproof and is extremely painful to me. I am not proud of the way I acted—but there it is. There is no going back. All I can do is beg your forgiveness.'

'You have it freely,' she replied softly. 'But your

suspicions and accusations where Simon was concerned were not entirely ill founded. Had I been more open with you, trusted you more, then perhaps we would have reached a better understanding before now. But why did you feel you had to have Simon released at all? For what reason?'

'Not out of any act of chivalry or friendship. I do not rate Sir Simon Butteridge very highly in either regard or esteem, you know that. What I did I did for James,' he said, his tone one of deep emotion, 'and for no other reason. When I left Derby without making any attempt at having him released—or to alleviate his suffering—I was swamped with mortification and was the most wretched of men. Knowing how fond James was of him, I felt that in some way I had betrayed his friendship—his trust—which is why, knowing the group of prisoners I had seen in Derby would eventually arrive in London, I made a point of enquiring about which prison he would be sent to.'

'And was it very difficult having him released?'

'No. Not very. As you said yourself, prisoners are being exchanged and paroled all the time.'

Jane looked at him, loving him, extremely proud of the way he had involved himself and taken charge of Simon's release without any promptings from her. And for herself she was deeply ashamed and humbled to learn of his thoughtfulness and loyalty towards her brother.

'Your compassion towards Simon is most generous. He owes you a great deal, Edward, and I am sure he will wish to thank you personally.'

'As far as I am concerned, the act is done with. I

have no wish to set eyes on him again. As far as he is concerned, he will never know the part I played in getting him released.'

'Poor Simon,' sighed Jane. 'You do him an injustice, Edward. I believe that if you were to get to know him a little better you would perceive that he is not wholly bad—that he is more agreeable than he seems. When I saw him last I thought how much more serious he was. He too wishes a settlement could be reached to put an end to the bloodshed. Like so many others, this war has changed him.'

'Maybe. But I shall never know. Let's hope it won't be long now, my love, before the King accepts the settlement Parliament has put to him and I can return to you at Deighton, where I shall spend the remainder of my days raising our children and running the estate.'

From the circle of his arms Jane smiled teasingly up at him. 'You, my lord, are far too active to sink into placid domesticity. I will wager that in no time at all you will be off to fight in some other war.'

'Never,' he said, taking her chin gently between his fingers and looking deep into her wonderful eyes. 'I love you, Jane, and that's the truth of it. You have the power to make me the happiest of men or the most miserable wretch. There must always be honesty and truth between us. Agreed?'

With a little nod and a smile she allowed him to enfold her once more into his embrace, where he held her like some precious, priceless object, and she trembled with a joy so great she thought she would die of it.

'There will never be anything between us again

to keep us apart,' he murmured with his lips against her hair.

Nothing, thought Jane in a most wretched state as she sat in the coach taking her back to London—nothing but Anne's involvement with Simon. For no doubt when she learnt of Simon's release from the Tower she would hasten to be by his side and within no time at all Edward would find out. The inevitability of it made her want to weep, for had he not just said there must be honesty and truth between them? And had she not already broken his trust by keeping his sister's relationship with Simon from him? Oh, why did he have to have such a low opinion of Simon? Why?

Several days after Jane's visit to Windsor, on a mopping-up exercise in an area several miles west of Windsor, an area which had recently seen the storming of Basing House—the fabulous stronghold of the Marquess of Winchester which had acted as a magnet for beleaguered Royalists—Edward rode towards some woods where it was believed a small pocket of resisting Royalists were hiding out.

It was not until he rode into a clearing at the head of his troop that he brought his foaming, broad-chested horse to a halt and sat there in the saddle, staring around him into the dense woods. His soldier's sixth sense had brought him alert. He felt danger all around him. Too late, he realised he had led his men into an ambush. Looking up the hill rising in front of him, he immediately saw the enemy and knew at once that they outnumbered his own small troop. They were an impressive, alarming sight, causing a hard knot to form in the pit of his stomach as they came riding down upon them, yelling and whooping like wild animals and waving their swords, their colours flying in the wind and their arms and armour glinting in the sun.

Edward pulled hard on the bridle to turn his horse out of line. His soldiers did the same, but, knowing they had to fight or perish, Edward drew his sword and turned about and charged, bravely and fearlessly, leaning forward on his horse's neck as a warrior born, his sword extended in his hand. Smashing into the enemy, he took the leading Royalist with a single blow, which lifted him dead or dying from his saddle. Sweeping on, he caught a second in the throat, turning away as he uttered a shrill scream before choking on his own blood and crashing to the ground to be trampled under the horses' pounding hooves.

It was complete mayhem, the fighting fierce and bloody as Edward and his soldiers hurled themselves into the forest of swords, hacking and thrusting viciously at the enemy. Edward fought grimly and tirelessly, bathed in sweat and blood from a few minor cuts. Despite being outnumbered, they were the stronger force and soon gained the upper hand, beginning to drive the enemy back in confusion.

Just before the fight was won Edward's foam-flecked maddened horse crashed into another and again he became locked in combat. The two clanging blades made dancing, lightning sparks as they bounced off each other, that of the enemy high and poised and flashing in the sun before finally swinging downwards and sinking into the soft flesh of Edward's shoulder. He followed this with another blow which knocked Edward from his horse, and his head hit the ground so hard that he was rendered unconscious.

On returning to Marchington House after visiting one of Lady Marchington's acquaintances, and leaving Isabel and her aunt downstairs, Jane went in search of Anne who, having pleaded a headache, had not accompanied them.

Jane was concerned by Anne's continued anguish over Simon's imprisonment in the Tower, but after seeing Edward at Windsor and abiding by his expressed wish that no one should know of his own involvement in Simon's release, then, however cruel this might be, she had kept it from both her and Lady Marchington, drawing a veil of secrecy over her visit to Windsor. No doubt Anne would learn of his release soon enough and no one would be any the wiser as to how it had come about.

Anne was not in her room, and as Jane was about to leave to search elsewhere, her eyes alighted on a note propped up on her dressing table with her name written on it. Frowning, she picked it up, curious as to why Anne should write to her. She recognised her neat handwriting—although it looked as if she had written it in a hurry. The note was short, the contents causing Jane to gasp with horror and incredulity, for Anne wrote:

My dear Jane.

Wonderful, glorious news. By some miracle Simon is to be released from that awful place of confinement. I received his letter just after you left the house. I am so deliriously happy. Words cannot express the joy I feel. I am going to the Tower to be with him and from there will go directly to Dover where we will board a ship for France. I know how shocked you will be, my dear, Jane— but be happy for me. Forgive me, for I cannot help myself. Anne.

Jane was stunned by the contents, for this she had not expected. Anger and disappointment shot through her. How could Anne do this to her? She had given no thought to the impossible situation her impulsive and irresponsible behaviour had placed her in. How on earth could she possibly explain this to Edward? She must go after her. She must be stopped and there was not a moment to lose.

'Oh—foolish, thoughtless girl,' she muttered as she flew down the stairs to find Lady Marchington.

Sir George was not at home so he could not be consulted as to what was the best action to take. Alone in her sitting-room, Lady Marchington looked up from where she was reclining on the sofa in alarm when Jane entered.

'Why, my dear! What is it?' she asked, sitting bolt upright on seeing her stricken face.

'Oh, Lady Marchington, something quite, quite dreadful has occurred and I cannot think what I am going to do. Anne has disappeared from the house. She has gone to the Tower to be with Simon.' Quickly she told Lady Marchington what had transpired, giving her Anne's letter to read, and when she had finished she was as horrified by her niece's behaviour as Jane was.

'Why, this is most shocking. What's to be done?'

'I blame myself,' cried Jane in anguish. 'Knowing how distressed she has been of late over Simon's imprisonment, I should never have let her out of my sight.'

'You cannot blame yourself, Jane. You were not to know Sir Simon would be released today—and I have to say I am curious as to how it has come about.'

'I must go after her,' said Jane, moving towards the door quickly, not wishing to lose any time that was precious. 'There is no time to delay. We were not away from the house very long so she cannot be too far ahead of me. I must find her and bring her back. Should Edward hear of this, his fury will know no bounds.'

'No, Jane. You cannot go like this. You are upset and I must oppose such a move,' said Lady Marchington firmly. 'Word must be sent to Edward at Windsor immediately. He must be the one to go after her and bring her back.'

Jane turned and looked at her in alarm. 'No—I beg of you,' she pleaded in desperation. 'I must try and keep this from him—and Isabel. I am well aware of the mischief she would make should it come to her ears that Anne has run away to be with Simon. Besides—there is no time. Anne will be well on her way to Dover before anyone could reach Windsor. I must find her before she leaves London.'

Lady Marchington relented. 'Yes—yes, you are right, of course,' she agreed, speaking as she hurried out into the hall to order the carriage. 'I shall wait here for my husband to arrive home—and it is best that someone is here should Anne return, having seen

the error of her ways. Samuel will accompany you.
You will be quite safe with him.'

Samuel's duties had become many and varied during the three years of Civil War as the domestic staff
had dwindled, but Jane was so frantic with worry
that she would not be in time to intercept Anne
before she left London, that she didn't care who
accompanied her. Samuel confirmed that Anne had
left the house an hour earlier, ordering one of the
carriages to take her to the Tower. As yet it had not
returned.

As Jane hurried down the steps to the carriage,
begging Lady Marchington to forgive her request for
secrecy, that she must hurry to the Tower before
Simon was released, and failing that she would have
to consider taking the Dover road to intercept him,
she failed to see Isabel in the hall behind her, who
heard her parting words and was about to miscon-
strue them—which would have disastrous effects.
She also failed to see the horserider who had ridden
from Windsor with an urgent message for Lady
Talbot concerning her husband.

Jane derived no pleasure from travelling through the
London streets as she had on the day when Lady
Marchington had taken her on a sightseeing tour with
Anne, and breathed a sigh of relief when they reached
the Tower. The scene of countless horrors, the massive stronghold stood on the banks of the Thames,
looking sullen and gloomy, its grey towers looming
menacingly over the dark water of the river, sending
a cold shiver down Jane's spine. The narrow streets
around the Tower were congested with vendors and

all manner of carts and carriages. The noise was deafening and the putrid smells rising from the gutters and the stench of the river were odious.

Clutching her cloak about her to avoid the outstretched clawing hands of countless beggars, some crippled and maimed by the Civil War, Jane climbed down from the carriage, her eyes sweeping over the crowd searching for Anne, while Samuel went to enquire of a sentry if Sir Simon Butteridge had left the Tower. He disappeared inside and, after what seemed like an age, he emerged some time later followed by Anne and Simon.

Pushing her way past the people who got in her way, Jane hurried towards them, sending up a silent prayer of relief that they had not already left for Dover. When Anne saw her, alarm filled her eyes, for she had not thought Jane would come after her.

'Jane! she exclaimed, quite indignant, for she knew she had come to try to prevent her from leaving with Simon. 'What are you doing here? You should not have come. I—I wrote you a note explaining everything.'

'Yes. I found it,' Jane said sharply, her anger mixed with relief that she had found Anne before she left the city. 'But you should not have left in the manner you did. It was foolish and thoughtless.'

'But I had to. You don't understand.'

'I understand perfectly. You gave no thought for me—or your aunt and uncle. Anne,' she implored, 'you cannot leave like this. You cannot go to France with Simon. It's insane.' She turned to Simon, who stood close to Anne. His face was grave and he seemed much older than before. No doubt his recent suffering had done this to him. 'Simon,' she appealed despairingly, 'tell her she cannot go with you.'

'Yes, I will, Jane,' said Anne stubbornly, clutching Simon's arm tightly. 'I will not leave him now. I am resolved to remain with him.'

Having already tried to dissuade Anne from going with him, Simon took her hands in his own and tried once more, compelling her to look at him, to listen to him. 'Anne! Sweet Anne! Listen to Jane. If you come with me to France, life will not be easy. At times it will be intolerable. There will be many hardships.'

'It will not be easy if I do not go with you. I can see you are still very weak following your injury— made worse by your time spent in captivity—despite your efforts to keep it from me. You need me, Simon, as much as I need you. Do not make me stay—I beg of you.'

Again Simon remonstrated with her, but to no avail. Anne remained adamant. Sighing deeply, Simon looked at Jane.

'You see how it is, Jane? Her mind is set on it.'

'Yes,' she whispered. 'Yes, I do. But I have to say I am more than happy to know you have been released, Simon. H-have you any idea how it has come about?'

He shrugged. 'I have to confess it's a complete mystery to me. I have been paroled on the promise never to fight again and issued with a pass to leave the country.'

'And will you fight again, Simon?'

He grinned and cocked an eyebrow, and for a brief moment some of the old Simon showed through. 'As

a gentleman I can be relied upon to keep my word—
but there are many who would dispute my claim to
be a gentleman.'

'But as a gentleman—will you violate that
promise? I ask out of concern for Anne should you
decide to do so.'

'My word is my bond, Jane,' he replied seriously.
'I was offered the opportunity of serving in the
Parliament Army in Ireland. Of course I declined. I
was also approached by the Spanish Ambassador, to
enquire if I would agree to serve the Spanish King
in the Netherlands. I declined that, too. But when I
was offered a pass to leave the country on condition
that I do not fight—I accepted.'

'And I am going with him of my own free will,
Jane. Simon did not ask me to come here today.'

Jane looked at Simon curiously. 'How did you
know where to write to Anne?'

'I recognised Sir George Marchington's carriage.
He is known to me and I was already aware that he
is a relative of Anne's. But when I sent my letter I
did not think for one moment she would come here
to this odious place. I cannot blame you for being
concerned, Jane. But I do love Anne—more than my
life. The fact that I would sell my soul to make her
happy is justification enough. I have friends in
France. I promise you I will take care of her.'

'And Edward? Have you given no thought to what
his reaction will be to all this? What am I to tell
her brother—my husband? His anger will be terrible
indeed.'

'I am sorry,' said Simon. 'It is not my intention
to cause discord within your family. But if I refuse

to take Anne with me, she will follow on alone. She is stubborn and self-willed.'

'That I know. She is so like Edward. But what am I to tell him—and Lady Blanche?'

'The truth,' said Anne softly.

Simon studied Jane for a long time and very calmly, knowing how difficult the situation was for her. 'When we reach France we will write to them—and I pray Lord Talbot will give his consent to Anne becoming my wife.'

'If Anne's reputation and dignity are to be maintained, then you leave him with little choice, Simon,' Jane replied sharply.

'And you will be able to persuade him, Jane,' said Anne hopefully. 'He will listen to you. I know Edward does not hold a high opinion of Simon—but he's much changed. None of this is his fault.' Sighing, she moved towards Jane, taking her hands and looking deep into her eyes. 'I know how difficult I have made this for you, Jane, and if I could have avoided it I would. But I will not be parted from Simon now. Please be happy for us.'

Jane stepped back as Simon placed his arm about Anne's shoulders, watching as Anne turned and looked at him, her eyes naked and defenceless, and she knew she would not be persuaded.

'Then there is nothing more to be said. Go, Anne—and be happy. And God bless you both.'

As Jane journeyed back to Clerkenwell, her one thought was how she was going to face Edward. How could she tell him what Anne had done?

*   *   *

On Jane's arrival back at Marchington House, Lady Marchington hurried to meet her in the hall, her face lined with concern. She looked past Jane towards the door, disappointed to see she had returned alone.

'Anne? She is not with you?'

Dejectedly, Jane shook her head. 'No I saw her— but she insisted on going with Simon to France. Nothing I could say would persuade her to change her mind. I must go to Windsor directly, Lady Marchington. I have a duty to Edward. He must be told immediately. I cannot keep it from him.'

Lady Marchington nodded. 'Yes—yes. You are quite right, Jane. He has to be told. But—I have to tell you there is another. . .urgent matter. . .that must take you to Windsor.'

'Why—what is wrong, Lady Marchington? Come—tell me. You look quite distraught.'

'Shortly after you left the house a—a messenger arrived from Windsor. I have some grave news for you, Jane.'

A band seemed to tighten around Jane's head as she stared at Lady Marchington, and there was a constriction in her throat, for she feared she was about to be told something quite dreadful which was going to require all her self-control.

'Why? What is it?'

'Edward has been wounded in an ambush—or a skirmish, I'm not sure which. Indeed, I do not know the difference. Military terms have always confounded me.'

Jane stood motionless, as if turned to stone. 'Edward?'

'Yes, my dear. I'm afraid so.'

'How badly?'

'I don't know exactly, but it appears he has suffered a sword wound and was knocked from his horse, hitting his head on the ground. He has been unconscious for two days—and when he showed no sign of recovery, the surgeon attending him, fearing the worst, felt he had a duty to send for you, my dear.'

Pale and stricken, Jane turned towards the door. Anne's leaving with Simon scarcely mattered to her now and vanished from her mind completely. Her one and only thought was to hasten to Edward's side, refusing to consider the fact that she might already be too late.

'Then I must go to him. I must hurry.'

'Jane—wait. There is something I must tell you before you leave.'

Jane halted in her stride towards the door, turning to look at Lady Marchington, waiting for her to speak.

'When Isabel learned Edward had been wounded—and knowing you were not here—she took it upon herself to leave for Windsor immediately.'

'She—she did *what*?' gasped Jane, angry and indignant that Isabel should have the effrontery to rush to her husband's side. 'But she had no right.'

'I know. But I could not prevent her from going.'

Slowly Jane moved to stand before Lady Marchington, an awful thought suddenly coming to mind. 'Does she know about Anne? That she has gone to France with Simon? Because if so, should Edward regain consciousness, Isabel will be sure to tell him. His reaction at this time could be catastrophic.'

Lady Marchington reached out and took Jane's hands in her own to reassure her. 'Fear not, my dear. I did not say a word about Anne.'

Jane emitted a huge sigh of relief. 'Thank goodness. Forgive me, Lady Marchington, for speaking ill of your niece, but Isabel has a habit of causing mischief, and if she were to sink her teeth into this then she would inject all manner of poison.'

Lady Marchington smiled with understanding. 'Don't apologise. There's no need. I know Isabel only too well. Nothing she does surprises me.'

Chapter Fourteen

With Samuel to accompany her, Jane did not delay in setting out for Windsor, unable to bring herself to contemplate the tragedy it would inflict on her life should anything happen to Edward. Pray God—not now. Not when she now knew how much she loved him, how much he meant to her.

It was a terrible, gruelling journey. She swallowed against the constriction in her throat as fear for Edward fought with her rage and indignation that, owing to her absence from Marchington House when the messenger had come from Windsor, Isabel had been there to go to him. Her thoughts tormented her all the way to Windsor for, during the time it took the coach to travel the twenty miles or so, she had time to dwell on, and examine them. Isabel's effrontery in rushing to Edward's bedside caused all the hurt and doubts that had plagued her in Derby to rise up inside her like a reopened wound.

During those two nights when she and Edward had been drawn together in love, she believed all her agonies and fears where Isabel was concerned were over, that what she had thought to be between them was nothing more than a fabrication of her own jealous and suspicious mind. But once again Isabel had stepped in, seeming to take a malicious pleasure in trying to separate her from Edward.

In the past he had stressed that the only link between himself and Isabel was one of kinship—and she had come to believe him. But what did Isabel feel for him? Why else would she hasten to his side if she wasn't in love with him? Unless, of course, in her jealousy and spite it was to humiliate and hurt her for marrying Edward, for it must have been a severe blow to her vanity and pride.

Edward didn't lie. He was far too sure of himself to feel the compulsion to do anything so base. But Isabel was also sure of herself and she had the power to twist most men round her little finger. Perhaps she had seen Edward as a challenge because he always kept her at a distance.

Reaching the castle at Windsor, once again she found the Captain of the Guard on hand. As soon as she stepped down from the coach he recognised her and came to her immediately.

'H-how is my husband, Captain? Is he very ill?'

The Captain smiled crookedly but a deep frown creased his brow. 'He was—but he has been blessed with a robust and vigorous constitution, and if his temper is anything to go by—brought about when he was told his family had been informed of his injury—then I would say he is greatly improved.'

Jane felt a great weight lifted from her and she gave a deep sigh, sending up a heartfelt prayer of thanks to God that he had heard her entreaties to spare Edward so that she might see him, that she might speak to him—and most of all that he might live.

'I am so relieved to hear it. When was he injured, Captain?'

Quickly the Captain outlined to her the events which had led to his injury, how, when he was in charge of a small armed troop engaged on a sortie into an area where there were still small pockets of Royalist resistance, they had underestimated the number and the fighting had been fierce.

'After being pierced through the shoulder, Lord Talbot was knocked from his horse and rendered unconscious. When he did not recover, the surgeon thought it advisable to send for you, Lady Talbot.'

'Thank you. I'm glad you did—even though he is now recovering. And don't worry, Captain,' she smiled. 'I am well acquainted with my husband's temper. Is his wound healing?'

'The sword cut to his shoulder is ugly and his arm will be incapacitated for some time, but a man as strong as Lord Talbot should be able to withstand worse wounds.'

'I see. Now, will you take me to him? I am impatient to see him.'

The Captain seemed to hesitate. 'There is something you should know before I do so, Lady Talbot.' He frowned, looking extremely uneasy suddenly, unsure how to tell her that after the arrival of a woman—a dark-haired, beautiful woman—and despite his weakness, her husband had ordered his horse to be saddled, then he had left the castle in a fierce and angry mood.

Waiting patiently for him to continue, Jane came to his rescue, believing she knew the reason for his hesitancy. She smiled. 'There is another person with him—is that it?

'Yes—there was—but—'

'Then rest easy, Captain,' she said with a lightness of voice which belied her true feelings. 'That will be his cousin, Mistress Marchington. I was not at home when the messenger arrived and so she came on ahead of me.'

Relieved that she already knew about the woman, some of the awkwardness passed out of the situation, but the Captain still had to tell her that Lord Talbot was not at the castle. He coughed nervously.

'I think you should know, Lady Talbot, that your husband left the castle over an hour ago.'

Jane gave him a puzzled look. 'Left? But I don't understand, Captain. My husband is injured—how is it possible for him to have gone anywhere?'

'Forgive me—but shortly after the lady arrived, he suddenly appeared in a thunderous mood and ordered his horse to be saddled immediately. The lady was quite beside herself and tried pleading with him not to go, and several of his fellow officers tried reasoning with him also, but he was deaf to any of their pleas and left the castle as if all the King's army had given chase.'

Jane's blood seemed to freeze in her veins as she dared to ask the question that sprang to her lips. 'And his destination, Captain? Do you know that?'

He nodded. 'Dover, I believe, Lady Talbot. That was what he said.'

Jane couldn't believe what she was hearing. Dover! So—what she had feared had happened. Somehow Isabel must have found out about Anne, and, giving no thought to the seriousness of Edward's condition, she had told him and he had gone in pursuit. Rage rose hot and fierce inside her when she realised what Isabel had done, but the expression she wore betrayed none of her inner turmoil to the Captain as she steeled herself to ask the question uppermost on her lips. 'In your opinion, will he make it, Captain? Is he in any condition to undertake such a ride?'

The doubt that fill the Captain's eyes and the dejected shake of his head told Jane all she needed to know. 'I see,' she whispered. 'And the lady?'

'Went back inside the house—and as far as I am aware she is still there.'

'Then be so kind as to take me to her, will you, Captain?'

Arriving at the small, half-timbered house where she had spent a wonderful night of love with Edward on her previous visit to Windsor Castle, Jane thanked him for his assistance, then the Captain left her— but he did not hurry away. No matter how unconcerned Lady Talbot had appeared to be on learning that her husband had been entertaining another woman in his rooms—cousin or not—he would wager there was trouble brewing and it wouldn't be many minutes before Mistress Marchington came out for air.

When he had taken her to Lord Talbot earlier, he

recollected how she had paused and looked at him when she became aware that he was staring at her with undisguised interest. Locking her gaze on his, her red lips had smiled invitingly, provocative and impressive. She was as sultry and dangerous as a tropical storm. What he wouldn't give for one night with her in his arms, making love to her, for he suspected there would be no pretences, no inhibitions, with a woman such as she. The thought was tempting and sent his blood pulsating hot through his veins. He grinned—perhaps he would wait around for a while in case she needed company.

Jane entered the house and, pausing on the threshold of the small, low-ceilinged room, saw Isabel was sitting alone before a burnt-out fire. In a split second she took in every detail of her features. She looked sultry and alluring in green velvet, but her face was red and her eyes swollen from crying—which was completely out of character for the usually composed and self-assured Isabel she knew.

'Why—what's this?' retorted Jane with scorn. 'Tears, Isabel? Forgive me if I appear surprised—but I always thought you to be incapable of such weakness.'

Isabel started and spun round, standing up quickly as all the colour drained out of her face. She was visibly shaken and stared at Jane as if she had seen a ghost, shaking her head slowly in confusion. 'Jane!' she managed to utter, her voice taut and strangled in her throat. 'What are you doing here? I—I thought you had gone to—oh, my God.'

'You thought what?' All of a sudden Jane seemed to freeze as a thought she did not want to analyse began shaping itself in her mind as black as a dark night. 'Isabel, what have you done?' she asked, her voice hardly above a whisper, knowing what the words would be before they were spoken.'

'Done? Why—what do you mean, Jane?' Isabel spoke nervously, as if she was guilty of some terrible misdeed she did not wish to be uncovered.

Jane moved to stand before her, her features like a hard mask, her voice as cold as ice. 'What have you told Edward? For it must be something terrible to send him hurrying to Dover in his condition.'

'Forgive me, Jane, but I could not help overhearing what you said to my aunt as you left the house. It is evident now that I misunderstood.'

'What? What did you misunderstand?'

'That—that you were to go to the Tower to be with Simon Butteridge—and after that to Dover. I thought it could mean only one thing,' she cried brokenly, 'that you were running away with him.'

'And this is what you told Edward?'

She nodded dumbly. Jane's face turned white. Appalled, she stared at Isabel in repugnant horror as she tried to put her shattered wits into some coherent order. For a moment she was silent, and then very quietly she said, 'Then you were mistaken, Isabel. It was Anne I went after—Anne who is in love with Simon, not I. She has gone with him to France. I went to try and stop her—but I failed. When I returned to Marchington House I was told that Edward had been seriously injured—and that out of concern for his well being,' she said with heavy sarcasm, 'you hastened to be with him.'

'Naturally I was concerned about him, Jane.

Because you were not at home—and knowing you could be gone for hours, if not for good—I considered it right that someone should come to Windsor.'

'And when you arrived you lost no time in maligning me to Edward—despite his weakness caused by his injury. How dare you, Isabel? In your jealous hatred you seized the first opportunity you could to drive a wedge between Edward and I. Well—I hope you're satisfied. Because of your malicious thirst for revenge, you have probably killed him. It would seem he was in no fit condition to leave the castle, let alone attempt to ride ninety miles or more to Dover.'

Fresh tears sprang to Isabel's eyes and she had the humility to lower her head, for she was ashamed of her actions. When she had arrived at Windsor she had been unable to stop herself from flinging what she believed to be the searing truth at Edward—that he had a faithless wife. His reaction had been swift and violent. The hurt and angry man who had looked at her hard was an Edward she didn't know, making her alarmed and regreting ever having told him about Jane.

When he had rushed outside she had followed and pleaded with him not to go after her, but like a man demented he had violently flung her away. Only then did she realise how much Jane meant to him. Until that moment she had refused to accept their relationship had ended—although if she had troubled to consider what the relationship had been between them, she would have realised long ago that it was a one-sided affair, which had ended in her wretched humiliation.

'You think you can go through life taking whatever you want, don't you, Isabel—including Edward?'

Isabel raised her head and faced her. 'It's a question I hoped you wouldn't ask—but I'll answer it. Yes—I admit it. I have made a play for him over the years—and if it makes you feel any better, like the gentleman he is, he has always spurned me. But don't misunderstand me, Jane. I'm very fond of him—but I don't love him.'

'Then why do you force yourself on him every hour you are with him—if, as you say, he spurns you?'

She shrugged, speaking airily. 'Because I saw in him everything I ever wanted in a man—in a potential husband. There's no denying he's handsome. He is also amusing and charming—and he knows how to make a woman feel attractive.'

'And he just happens to be rich,' scorned Jane. 'For I know you put wealth before such matters.'

'Of course,' she admitted unashamedly. 'I would never marry a poor man, Jane—and nor would I marry the richest man on earth if I did not find him charming and amusing.'

'I love Edward very much, Isabel—and he loves me. Nothing you can do will ever change that.'

'Yes—I know that now. I knew by his reaction when I told him you had gone to Simon that he loved you. The fact that he was prepared to ride to Dover in such a wretched state of health was confirmation of that—and you are right,' she admitted reluctantly.

'My monstrous vanity led me to believe I could have anything I wanted—even Edward. I could not endure knowing he loved you instead of me. I have behaved abominably—and for what it's worth, I'm sorry, Jane. I deserve your ridicule and contempt.'

Faced with Isabel's remorse, Jane was still too angry and concerned about Edward to relent. Nor was she certain that, after what Isabel had done, she was prepared to forgive so easily and develop a cordial acquaintance with the woman who had been so keen to come between herself and her husband. She turned from her, going towards the door.

'I must go. Forgive me if I don't ask you to share my carriage back to Marchington House—but I feel the need to be by myself. Goodbye, Isabel.'

Isabel watched her go, wiping the tears she was unaccustomed to shedding as the image of the handsome Captain swam before her. In need of someone to cheer her up, she had a mind to remain for a little while longer at Windsor.

Her whole being concentrated on her husband, it took all Jane's self-control to withstand the journey back to London. At the thought of his condition her heart filled with tenderness and concern; but when she realised what he must be thinking, what his feelings must have been like to have driven him to pursue her to Dover immediately, she felt wretched.

Her heart was breaking at the hopelessness of the situation, for she was unable to do anything but wait for him to return—should his health not fail him *en route* to Dover. To have been so happy and suddenly to see her whole world crumbling to pieces was almost too much for her to bear and she was unable any longer to keep back the tears that spilled down her cheeks. Oh—what must he think of her? Why hadn't she told him about Anne being in love with Simon? If she had not kept it from him, none of this would have happened.

Feeling cheated and betrayed, as Edward rode his horse hard towards Dover he was in the grip of such a dark and murderous fury that left him insensible to the pain in his injured shoulder. He kept telling himself that Isabel had lied, that in her viciousness and spite to get back at Jane for marrying him she had set out to cause as much damage to their relation-ship as she possibly could. But he had to be certain—for how else had Isabel come to know of Butteridge's release from the Tower if not from Jane?

As he rode his poor horse almost into the ground he tried to shut the memory of her beauty from his mind, but he could not. She was too much a part of him—the sweet smell of her, the warmth and soft-ness of her allure. She was lovely—perfect—and he would not let her go easily. His love for her was absolute—and that love was beyond price.

But if what Isabel said was true, then after declar-ing her love for him and promising there would be honesty and truth between them always, her act of betrayal was a profanation in itself. If he found when he reached Dover that he was too late, that she had taken ship for France with Butteridge, then each time he thought of her lying in his arms would be like dying a thousand deaths.

But the most bitter twist of all was all the more

terrible because he himself had been the instrument of Butteridge's release from the Tower.

Fortunately he knew the country towards London and through the county of Kent well. Bent over his horse's neck and with the fire of impatience burning inside him, he rode throughout the night, stopping for only the briefest respite to quench his thirst and rest his horse before going on his way to Dover. When at last he rode into the town and headed towards the quay he was nearing exhaustion.

Under a sky heavy with rain the quay was thronging with people. There were boats of every description and the rank odour of fish was strong. A cold, fresh breeze blew off the choppy sea as Edward began to make enquiries concerning Butteridge and his companion. Despite his apparent exhausted state and wild appearance as he led his horse—which looked as if he'd ridden the poor beast almost to death—his tall impressive figure drew the attention of an elderly fisherman mending his nets beside his boat. When Edward stopped to speak to him, he confirmed what Edward already feared.

He was too late. The ship taking the couple to France had sailed hours ago. Filled with desolation, Edward stared at the sea spread out before him towards the distant horizon. In his moment of weakness the pain was back in his head and his shoulder—but the most terrible pain of all that twisted and went screaming through his veins was in his heart.

The fisherman came to stand beside him as he was about to turn away, sensing his despair and suspecting the couple must have been a pair of runaway lovers whom he had come to Dover in the hope of intercepting. 'I remember them because the lady was such a pretty young thing—and clearly in love with the fellow, too, from the way she clung to his arm. Made a handsome couple they did—she as dark as he was fair.'

Shaking his head, the fisherman was about to go back to his nets when his remark caught all Edward's attention. 'Wait,' he commanded, his heart beginning to pound fearfully. 'What did you say? Was her hair not pale—blonde in colour?'

'Nay. Not the lady I saw. Dark, she was.'

Feeling life beginning to course anew through his veins, Edward looked again at the sea, the truth of the matter hitting him like a thunderbolt. Anne! It was Anne, not Jane, who had gone to France with Butteridge. Anne who was in love with him—not dear, sweet Jane who had tried to keep it from him. What a fool he had been, a stupid blind fool.

'Sir,' said the fisherman, interrupting his thoughts, having observed the lightening of his countenance and wondering what he had said to bring about this transformation, 'if you don't mind my saying so, you look quite worn out.'

Edward threw him a look of gratitude. 'Yes—yes, you're right,' he answered with a jaunty grin, for no matter how eager he was to return to London to see Jane, he realised he was in no fit condition to go anywhere until he had rested. 'Perhaps you would be so kind as to recommend a decent inn where I can rest.'

Daybreak found him back on his horse—both rested, but with Edward still suffering great discomfort from

his injured shoulder. He was extremely angered by
Anne's decision to go to France with Simon
Butteridge, which had come as a shock, but it was
tempered by his profound relief that Jane had
remained true to her word and to him. He returned to
London much weakened and in considerable pain—
though with a lightness of heart—and made straight
for Marchington House.

Without moving or speaking Jane stood on the stairs,
her hand on the banister, frozen in that very gesture
as, with a feverish joy, she watched Edward enter
the house. His head was bare, his dark hair tousled
and his clothes and face streaked with dust from his
hard ride from Dover. His features were lined with
weakness and fatigue.

Edward saw the anguish on her face, her lovely
amber eyes misting over with tears. Her cheeks had
no colour in them, but he perceived something about
her that was desperate and hurting. It was as if she
had come into contact with a power too strong for
her to fight or understand.

'Edward!' she said, her voice a sigh of relief, and
with a quick onrush of breath she hurled herself
across the space that divided them and became
locked against his chest, where he held her with the
last of his fading strength, unable to believe she was
in his arms at last.

All the pent-up misery and anguish Jane had suffered since her return from Windsor poured out of
her as she kissed his face, his mouth, with soft sweet
lips, clinging to him, trembling and crying. Looking
down at her, he thought she had the face of an angel

with tears lighting up her eyes.

'Oh, you fool—you fool,' she admonished gently through her tears. 'How could you go rushing off to Dover like that? You have put me through every kind of torture imaginable. Knowing how seriously injured you were, I feared for you so much. If you should leave me now, I shall die.'

Overcome with emotion, Edward tightened his arms around her and kissed her very slowly and tenderly until she became quiet.

There was no time to say more because Lady Marchington chose that moment to appear. She took charge of her nephew immediately, seeing to it that he was given nourishment before being bathed and that the doctor who was summoned attended to his wound.

It was only later, when they were alone and lay entwined at last, that Edward, his dark eyes burning with all the love and passion he was capable of feeling, placed his lips against Jane's sweet-smelling hair. 'My love—forgive me for doubting you. What a fool I've been.'

'You—you know about Anne?' Jane asked timidly, looking up at him, her eyes glowing with happiness.

'I know Anne has gone with Simon Butteridge to France. My God, I should have known. I should have seen for myself how things were between them.'

'How could you have known? Please forgive me, Edward. I should have told you before we left Derbyshire. But Anne was so afraid of your anger and that you would forbid her to see Simon that she begged me not to—and I hoped she would get over him when we came to London. But I was wrong— so very wrong. But look at you,' she said, stroking his lined cheek with concern. 'You look quite worn out. Oh, my dear, I have been so worried about you. When I was told of your injury I went directly to Windsor—and that was when I discovered from Isabel what she had told you. What must you have thought of me?' she said wretchedly.

The mention of Isabel's name brought a frown of disapproval to Edward's forehead, and he didn't have to be told that going to Windsor and finding Isabel in her place had been almost too much to be borne. 'Yes—Isabel has much to answer for. Where is she?'

'As yet she has not returned from Windsor. No doubt there is some attraction to keep her there— and I would probably not be far wrong if I said it had something to do with the handsome Captain I saw on both occasions I went to the castle. But don't be too harsh on her, Edward. She really did think it was I who had gone to Simon when he was released from the Tower.'

'And now I discover it is Anne—and that he has the sheer effrontery to take her with him to France,' he said, his voice quivering with scarcely suppressed anger, knowing that, short of taking a ship for France himself, there was not a thing he could do about it. 'Not in my worst nightmare could I have imagined Anne, my lovely, untouched sister, would do this. Was it not enough that he wormed his way into your affections without stealing my sister's?'

'Simon did not steal her affections, Edward, they were freely given. And as for my own, they were

nothing but the fancies of a young girl—and not
reciprocated by Simon, which, I must tell you, for a
short while left me feeling humiliated and extremely
foolish. But,' she murmured with her lips against
his, tantalising and soft, pressing her body against
his, 'had I not been left alone for so long to my
own devices by my betrothed—who had other, much
more important matters on his mind than to dance
attendance on the woman he was to marry—then
perhaps I would not have fallen prey to my emotions.
Can you wonder I was bewildered and confused?
Why—I even began to think I must displease you.'

He sighed and smiled, feeling warm and relaxed
beside her. 'No. Never that. But I must tell you that
I am beginning to regret playing any part in having
Butteridge released from the Tower.'

'Anne went with him willingly enough, that I
know. I did everything I could to try and stop her,
but she would not listen. She was determined,
Edward. She has made up her mind to marry him,
and because she has your temperament and your
same wilful, stubborn pride, she will do just that.
They promised to write to you when they reach
France. You will give your consent to their marriage,
won't you?'

'I suppose I must—though it will be against my
better judgement. Her thoughtless behaviour leaves
me with little choice if her reputation is to be pre-
served.'

'And what of you, Edward? The doctor has made
it plain that your injured shoulder will prevent you
from carrying out your military duties for quite some
time. Does that mean I shall have you all to myself

at last? That, like the swan maiden in the story you told me of, I can carry you away to Deighton Hall where we can spend the winter months together in glorious solitude?'

He laughed softly as she recalled the time they had spent together by the lake at Deighton Hall. 'Of course. But do not forget that one of the stories had a sad ending—for the couple were forced to part when she found her feather mantle and flew away to join her own kind, as I shall when my wound has healed and winter is over.'

'No—there was no sad ending, Edward. When I recounted the story to your mother, she informed me that the story you told me was not complete—for the swan maiden returned to her husband with a feather mantle, and when she helped him put it on he, too, turned into a swan and they flew away together and were happy ever after—as we shall be, my darling, when we return to Deighton Hall. Forever, I hope.'

'I, also—where a lifetime together awaits us,' he murmured, kissing her upturned face and tightening his arms about her. 'And, God willing, very soon the War will be over. I am happy everything is reconciled between us, Jane. Never will I doubt you again.'

She smiled, deliriously happy. 'I may have thought I loved Simon once, but then you came back into my life and I fell in love with you. You are the only man I have loved—the only man I shall ever love—despite your outward authoritarian manner you display to your troops—and to myself on occasion, which I shall do my best to ignore,' she teased him gently. But then a serious note came into her voice and a deep and abiding love filled her eyes. 'You are the kindest, the most compassionate man I have ever met. How could I help loving you? Now come, my love,' she breathed, drawing his head down to her, 'and kiss me. We have so much lost time to make up for.'

MILLS & BOON®

Historical Romance™

Coming next month

A REBELLIOUS LADY
by Gail Mallin

Spain 1809

Rafael de Velasco was dangerous, attractive and an enemy of her country. He was the last person that Désirée should be falling in love with, so why was she?

THE DESERTED BRIDE
by Paula Marshall

Elizabeth I

After ten years apart Drew finally returned to his wife, the only recollection he had of her as a child being that she resembled a monkey! But when a beautiful woman greets him on his return he can't help but wish he'd come home sooner.

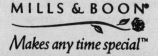

MILLS & BOON®

Makes any time special™

On sale from 6th April 1998

Available from WH Smith, John Menzies and Volume One

MILLS & BOON®

Relive the romance with

Bestselling themed romances brought back to you by popular demand

Each month By Request brings you three full-length novels in one beautiful volume featuring the best of the best.

So if you missed a favourite Romance the first time around, here is your chance to relive the magic from some of our most popular authors.

Look out for
Having His Baby **in March 1998 featuring Charlotte Lamb, Lynne Graham and Emma Goldrick**

Available from most branches of WH Smith, John Menzies, Martins, Tesco and Volume One

MILLS & BOON®

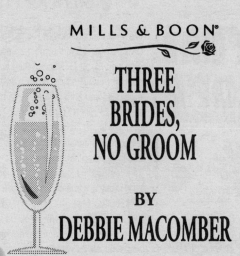

THREE BRIDES, NO GROOM

BY

DEBBIE MACOMBER

We are delighted to bring you three brand-new stories
about love and marriage from one of our
most popular authors.

Even though the caterers were booked, the bouquets
bought and the bridal dresses were ready to wear...the
grooms suddenly got cold feet. And that's when three
women decided they weren't going to get mad...they
were going to get even!

On sale from 6th April 1998
Price £5.25

*Available at most branches of WH Smith, John Menzies,
Martins, Tesco, Asda, Volume One, Sainsbury and Safeway*

MILLS & BOON®

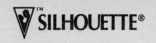
SILHOUETTE®

SPECIAL OFFER
£5 OFF

FLYING FLOWERS

Beautiful fresh flowers, sent by 1st class post to any UK and Eire address.

We have teamed up with Flying Flowers, the UK's premier 'flowers by post' company, to offer you £5 off a choice of their two most popular bouquets the 18 mix (CAS) of 10 multihead and 8 luxury bloom Carnations and the 25 mix (CFG) of 15 luxury bloom Carnations, 10 Freesias and Gypsophila. All bouquets contain fresh flowers 'in bud', added greenery, bouquet wrap, flower food, care instructions, and personal message card. They are boxed, gift wrapped and sent by 1st class post.

To redeem £5 off a Flying Flowers bouquet, simply complete the application form below and send it with your cheque or postal order to; **HMB Flying Flowers Offer,**
The Jersey Flower Centre, Jersey JE1 5FF.

ORDER FORM (Block capitals please) Valid for delivery anytime until 30th November 1998 MAB/0298/A

Title ....Initials ....Surname ....

Address...

....

....Postcode ....

Signature...Are you a Reader Service Subscriber **YES/NO**

Bouquet(s)**18 CAS** (Usual Price £14.99) **£9.99** ☐   **25 CFG** (Usual Price £19.99) **£14.99** ☐

I enclose a cheque/postal order payable to Flying Flowers for £.......................................or payment by

VISA/MASTERCARD ☐☐☐☐☐☐☐☐☐☐☐☐☐☐☐☐ Expiry Date............/............/

PLEASE SEND MY BOUQUET TO ARRIVE BY........./........../........

TO Title ....Initials ....Surname ....

Address...

....

....Postcode ....

Message (Max 10 Words) ....

Please allow a minimum of four working days between receipt of order and 'required by date' for delivery

You may be mailed with offers from other reputable companies as a result of this application.
Please tick box if you would prefer not to receive such offers. ☐

Terms and Conditions Although dispatched by 1st class post to arrive by the required date the exact day of delivery cannot be guaranteed. Valid for delivery anytime until 30th November 1998. Maximum of 5 redemptions per household, photocopies of the voucher will be accepted.